Zinnias Grow

on

Either Side

of the

River

 Al Allen

m & m
PRESS
FAYETTEVILLE ARKANSAS

Zinnias Grow on Either Side of the River

m & m Press
P.O. Box 338
Fayetteville, AR 72702

Printed on recycled paper

This book is dedicated to Nita
for her life of courage

It is through the idealism of youth that man catches
sight of truth, and in that idealism he possesses a
wealth which he must never exchange for anything
else.

ALBERT SCHWEITZER

...and on either side of the river was there the tree of
life.

REVELATION 22:2

Acknowledgments

Very few books are the work of one person alone, and this book is no exception. In 1985, Jeannie Flake Frauenthal encouraged me to write out my stories and worked with me on my first book, *Roads That Seldom Curve*. I thank her for getting me started and for her continued support.

I would like to thank Marcia Wilkinson for transcribing and editing my original stories. I would also like to thank Suzann Barr for her excellent editing and structural advice. I owe a great deal to Shannon Mitchell, William Poe, Eric Mantle, Connie Meginnes, and Warren Law for helping in ways that are too numerous to list.

I am especially indebted to my wife, Nita Allen, for all her hours of assistance as a listener, reader and editor, and for her patience and understanding as I mentally went back in time with my particular method of writing.

❧ CONTENTS ☙

Prologue

Zinnias and the Beggarmen

I WAS BORN on a cold, rainy night in late November of 1925 in the small farm town of Steele located in the flat, somewhat barren Bootheel section of Missouri. My father was a car dealer, and when I was young he would take me riding in his car down dirt and gravel roads that were very straight and seldom curved to visit our many relatives throughout the county. Sometimes he would take me over the levee to see the large river boats on the Mississippi or to watch the river flow. Once we crossed the river on the Cottonwood Point Ferry and visited relatives on the Tennessee side. Other times we watched field hands singing as they picked cotton under the autumn sun. One day we drove a long distance to a farm down near Arkansas to see three mules that had been struck dead by lightning. Another time my father showed me a man hanging from a tree.

We lived on Highway 61, the main route from St. Louis to Memphis. Our house was on the outskirts of town, the last house on the left going south. It was painted a bright yellow and had a front porch with white turned posts and a swing. We had a large backyard where I often played alone, because there were no other children in the area.

By the time I was five years old, I had learned to sit on the front porch and watch the highway for beggarmen who walked by every day, some going north, some going south. A beggarman would walk down our driveway to the screened back porch, knock on the door, tell my mother he was hungry and ask if she had any food to spare. The beggarmen were always alone, they always walked with a slow gait, they always seemed to wear old brown clothing and they usually carried a sack. My mother had a small table and one chair set up on the back porch for these beggarmen; when she cooked our meals each day she would leave the beggarmen's portion in every pot and pan. She would serve the beggarmen exactly what we had to eat, and along with the food she would give each of them a clean, white napkin. My mother would not always allow me stay out on the porch as the beggarmen ate, but when she did, she asked that I never bother them in any way or stare at them. Beggarmen always ate their food in a hurry. We seldom talked; they seldom smiled. If there was any food left in the kitchen from our family meal, my mother would wrap it up in a paper package, tie it neatly with a string and give it to the men to carry with them on their way. They were very grateful as they left. In those times, the visits by beggarmen from the highway occurred almost daily, throughout all seasons.

During those early years, life seemed best in the summer because the backyard would become my play kingdom. My mother had planted all kinds of flower beds, including rows and rows of zinnias. By midsummer there were red, yellow, orange and purple zinnias, and several other colors that were not in my Crayola box. Sometimes my mother would ask me to cut with scissors my favorite-colored zinnias for a special vase in the living room. Of course, I had to watch out for snakes and bees.

One summer day about midmorning, a loud noise occurred while I was playing out back. It was a loud blasting noise, and the earth trembled and the windows rattled. I ran into the house very alarmed, asking about that horrible noise. My mother was calm and comforting and said, "Don't be frightened, Alvin Junior, things are just blowing up." So I went back outside. I heard the blasting sound several more times. That night, as I lay thinking before I fell asleep, I concluded that "blowing up" meant everything was getting bigger, because when one blows up a balloon it gets bigger and bigger. I decided that sometimes there must be a loud noise when things get bigger.

The next day when there was a loud blasting noise, and the earth trembled and the windows rattled, I watched the zinnias carefully, hoping to observe them blowing up bigger. I did this for several days and I was a little disappointed when I didn't actually see the flowers blowing up. However, I knew the flowers had been much smaller earlier in the spring and they had gotten a lot bigger during the summer, so they had to get bigger sometime.

When my father got home from work one day, he saw me lying in a zinnia bed with my face just inches from the flowers.

"What are you doing down there?" he asked.

"Watching the flowers blow up," I responded. He didn't say anything at that time, but at supper he questioned me more. I told him Mother had explained that when the loud noise came and the earth trembled and the windows rattled, it meant things were blowing up and getting bigger. When he looked at me in a quizzical way, I said, "When you blow up a balloon, Daddy, it gets bigger and bigger, and sometimes the balloon pops and it makes a big noise. Mother said when there is a big noise, things are blowing up." I was satisfied that the loud explosions came from things getting bigger. My father talked to me for a long time about the difference between balloons blowing up bigger and flowers growing up bigger, but it still wasn't clear to me.

The next day my father and I rode in his car through town, over a drainage ditch bridge and down some dirt roads to a large field that had many felled trees. There were several piles of burning logs and numerous tree stumps throughout the area. We walked towards some men in the middle of the field; Daddy had me wait a good distance back while he went in closer to talk with them. When he returned he told me to get ready to hold my hands over my ears, because in about three minutes there was going to be a large blasting noise. I did as he said and there was a big explosion that almost knocked me down; the earth shook and smoke and dust was everywhere. I was a little scared. When things settled down a bit, we walked back to the car.

"Now, Alvin Junior, that's things blowing up. They're clearing this land of trees, and they're blowing up some of the stumps and burning some of the others." He pointed toward a man who had a team of mules hitched to a big stump being pulled out of the ground.

All the way home he explained carefully, again and again, the difference between blowing up and growing up. Nevertheless, I still thought things got bigger when they were blown up. At supper he told my mother that he believed matters were now clearer to me about the loud noise and the flowers, since we had gone over and observed the stump blasting. In the following days, word got around to my relatives in the Bootheel that Alvin Junior had thought things were getting bigger when there was an explosion.

Some time later, at a large family gathering at my Uncle Louis's house over near the river, this issue came up again. My father explained to everyone that I had come to an unusual conclusion about nature from balloons getting bigger when they were blown up and from tree stumps being blown up by dynamite. My Aunt Annie pulled me up in her lap and asked me what I had learned from all these experiences and explanations.

"Well," I said, "I know that balloons get bigger as you blow them up, and I know that tree stumps blow up real loud." I hesitated for a bit and said, "And I know that flowers don't make much noise as they blow up." My father appeared to be a little disappointed in my comprehensive but rather abstract answer. I'm certain that from that day on, my extended family knew that I was going to perceive the world a bit differently than others.

The following summer, when I was six years old, my mother took me with her on a Greyhound bus, down Highway 61 to Memphis on the other side of the river. We stayed with Aunt Estelle, who lived not too far from the tall buildings downtown. My mother got a job as a furrier at a department store, and she decided we would stay in Memphis. In September she enrolled me in the first grade at a local school. In the beginning I missed my father and all my relatives in the Bootheel, but I learned soon that the distance separating us wasn't that far. Sometimes relatives came to Memphis to visit, and we made many trips back to the Bootheel.

When Mother and I rode the streetcar downtown in Memphis, I often saw beggarmen in old brown clothes, walking slowly down the streets; some were standing on the street corners, begging. We didn't have a large backyard in Memphis, but the following spring my mother planted lots of flowers; by summer they were all blown up and blooming in splendid colors. It was good to know that zinnias grow on either side of the river.

Miss Pirtle, the Moon and the Big Bell

IN MEMPHIS when the time came in 1932 for me to start school it was decided that my Aunt Estelle would take me to register since my mother had to work. One morning she held me by the hand and we walked north six blocks to a big, three-story, dark red brick building that looked to me like an old castle that I had once seen in a picture book. It had a steep roof with lots of angles; a bell tower in the middle of the roof and a tall chimney off to one side. We walked along in silence and I wondered more than once if Aunt Estelle knew how afraid I was. As we approached the front of the building we walked up several white stone steps and when we reached the top level Aunt Estelle said, "This is going to be your school Alvin Junior; see the name above the door, it reads MERRILL SCHOOL."

We entered and Aunt Estelle informed a tall man just inside the doors that she was there to register me for the first grade. "Proceed straight ahead, lady," he said, "to the last door on the right; there you will find Miss Mattie Pirtle, she's the new first grade teacher."

So we walked down that long, dark corridor as other grown folks with children were walking around looking for the right rooms to get them registered. All the hallways were dark and dreary. When we entered the room, a lady and a small girl were just leaving the teacher's desk. We walked slowly across the room and Aunt Estelle, speaking softly, said to the teacher, "I would like to register Alvin Junior here for the first grade. I'm his Aunt. His mother is at work."

At that moment, being at the edge of her desk, I noticed that the teacher had only one arm. She was writing things down with her left hand but there was absolutely nothing on her right side, not even a stub. I had once seen a colored man without a hand at Uncle Will's farm in the Bootheel of Missouri, and also saw there a man with a stub arm down to his elbow, but I had never seen anything like that. It completely numbed my mind and body. I knew Aunt Estelle was giving her information about me but I was not listening good.

"What is his date-of-birth?" Miss Pirtle gruffly asked. She just slightly glanced at me.

Aunt Estelle looked down at me. "You do know don't you, Alvin Junior?"

I just stood there frozen and couldn't say a thing. There were moments of silence.

"We cannot register a child without a date-of-birth," Miss Pirtle barked. "I advise you to get this boy's date-of-birth and return later." The teacher was talking real loud.

So Aunt Estelle took me by the hand and we left the room, down the dark corridor, down the white stone steps and started home. "Alvin Junior, I'm really surprised that you don't know your birthday," she said as we walked. You've always been so good with your letters and numbers."

"Oh, I know my birthday," I said. "It's November the 29th." We stopped walking and she just stood there looking puzzled at me.

"But you didn't know a few minutes ago at the school."

"Yes ma'am; I knew." I was about to cry. "I just wasn't sure if my birthday was the same thing as my date-of-birth." I didn't tell her that the one-armed teacher had scared me numb.

So we turned around and went back to the school, up the white stone steps, down the dark corridor, back into the room and up to the teacher at her desk.

Aunt Estelle, speaking this time almost in a whisper, said to the teacher, "Alvin Junior now knows his birthday; it's November the 29th."

The teacher glared at me hard through real thick glasses. Her eyes were big and round like an owl's. "Why didn't he know before?" she loudly asked, looking up at Aunt Estelle and back down at me.

"He wasn't sure about what date-of-birth meant," she answered.

The teacher looked at me with disgust. I watched her hand from her one and only arm complete the remaining registration forms. Then Aunt Estelle took me by the hand and we went back down the dark corridor, down the white stone steps and turned toward home.

Three days later Aunt Estelle walked me the six blocks for the first full day of school. As we walked along she told me twice to be observant because I would be walking by myself from that day on. I would also have to find my way home at the end of school that day.

About fifteen minutes earlier we had heard the Merrill School big bell ringing at 8 o'clock as it did thirty minutes before the start of school on school days. It would ring again at 3 o'clock when school let out. The Merrill School big bell was a well-known thing in Memphis, being the last of its kind from the old schools built close to downtown at the turn of the century. The sound of the bell was so great it could be heard for miles around and all the way to the Mississippi River.

As we approached the first grade room from the dark corridor, there were several children crying, reluctant to enter the room with the mysterious one-armed teacher. Their comforting parents were assuring them everything would be all right. I didn't feel all that good about it myself but I went on in and didn't cry.

The one-armed teacher stood stiffly by her desk with some kind of stick about two feet long in her one and only hand. All the children were terrified; and as they entered she announced in a craggy voice, "Names are on the desks, children; each of you will find your own desk." She repeated this twice. So most of the first graders went from desk to desk searching for their names. I found mine right up front, the first seat in row one over on the window side.

Several children were just standing around so the teacher placed her stick on the desk and asked each of them their names and with her one arm and hand, grabbed them by their shirt or blouse and guided them to their desks.

When all the crying stopped and everything finally settled down, the one-armed teacher said harshly, "I am your teacher. My name is Miss Pirtle," and with her stick she pointed to it spelled out in big letters on the black board. She then talked to us for a long time about all the things we were not permitted to do. "These classroom rules will make you into good children," she said.

I listened as well as I could but it all began to muddle my mind. From that very first day when we learned of the things we were forbidden to do, the most difficult were: to always sit up straight, to never look out the window, and to never talk.

So life in the first grade became a dreadful time of waiting for the big bell to ring at 3 o'clock so we could go outside to be with the wind, the sun and the sky. It didn't matter to us about the weather; the outside was freedom and it was always wonderful.

Day in and day out I sat doing my pages of numbers and letters, forbidden to look out the window at the trees and clouds. Thus, if I got my work done early, I had to sit up straight and look at the blackboard or look at Miss Pirtle's right shoulder with no arm.

Sometimes, I would drift into a daydream with my eyes fixed on Miss Pirtle's armless shoulder, and she would suddenly look over at me with those owly eyes and I would turn to stone. I just knew she would be forever mad at me since I had given her so much trouble at registration by not knowing my date-of-birth.

It seemed to me in those early fall days that she spoke more harshly to me than she did to the other first graders. Sometimes I would complete my pages of numbers and letters and would look over and see Miss Pirtle glaring at me like she was angry. It was not a happy time.

One afternoon in October, Miss Pirtle whacked her stick hard against her desk to get our attention. She got up from her chair and stood there rigidly and said, "I recently read in the newspaper that the moon is made of green cheese." There was a long pause and then she said, "Those of you who believe this to be true raise your hands."

Immediately, half the class raised their hands and everyone looked around at each other. I had heard my Uncle Charlie say several times that the moon was made of green cheese, so I too put my hand up.

Miss Pirtle with her owly eyes looked over the class carefully and then said, "All of you with your hands raised, remain seated when the big bell rings." It became very quiet. Almost everyone had raised their hands.

At 3 o'clock the big bell sounded and a few children left. The rest of us remained in our seats. Miss Pirtle sat and stared at us in absolute silence. Then, in a blaring voice, she scolded us for believing in something as ridiculous as the moon being made of green cheese. Then she went on and said other things that I did not at all understand.

"Now, all of you sit at your desks perfectly still for ten minutes and think about it." You could hear all the children outside playing and having fun. Time passed slowly.

As I sat there I looked over at Miss Pirtle and thought that she looked much older than my grandmother in the Bootheel of Missouri. I also thought she was certainly meaner than my mean old Aunt Jessie who also lived there. I looked over at her armless right shoulder and wondered what the skin looked like under her sleeveless dress. I also wondered why she didn't tell us what the moon was really made out of. After a long while, she dismissed us.

One day she asked for those who believed that cats had nine lives to raise their hands. I'd heard that, too, but I didn't raise my hand. Some first graders were getting wiser because that day only ten children had to stay after school. Later on she asked if we believed there was a man in the moon. In early December she asked who believed that the reason reindeer can fly is that they have wings that no one can see. That day a large number of children had to stay after school. I always listened carefully, but seldom raised my hand so I could leave with the sound of the big bell and play outside.

On the last day of school before the Christmas holidays most of the children brought presents to Miss Pirtle and placed them on her desk. My mother wrapped a handkerchief that she had personally embroidered as my present for her. Miss Pirtle received two paper sacks of presents and asked me and Billy Brewer to help her by carrying a sack each to her house just two blocks from the school.

After the 3 o'clock bell rang we followed her through the dark corridor, down the white stone steps and down the street. As we walked it seemed to me that everyone stopped and watched us. She carried a small satchel in her one hand and a purse under her only arm.

It was the Christmas season and during that day we had been hearing Christmas songs being sung by the upper grade classes in the rooms above us. Grown folks for several days had been wishing each other Merry Christmas. I wondered how old you had to be to wish someone Merry Christmas.

When we got to Miss Pirtle's house, she told us to place the sacks of presents on her front porch. It was a very small, old gray house with no Christmas decorations. As we left she managed to say, "Thank you, boys," without any warmth. I wanted to say something to her, but I couldn't.

For a few days Billy and I were teased by the older boys and declared teacher's pets. Some fifth and sixth grade boys started calling Miss Pirtle "one-armed Mattie." I couldn't understand that.

During the winter months life became even more difficult. On several occasions Miss Pirtle whacked children's hands with her stick for misbehaving. She walked the aisles constantly and we became more fearful of getting whacked for something. One day she struck a boy across his back for falling asleep. He cried for a long time.

Once it snowed all day, and since it was forbidden to look out the window, we could not watch the snowflakes fall. Several times, however, I took quick, sneaky looks and risked getting whacked with the stick. More and more I wondered why Miss Pirtle had only one arm. At recess and in our neighborhood, older boys mocked and jeered at us for having one-armed Mattie for a teacher. It seemed to me she was becoming grumpier and meaner.

One Friday during Spring a school monitor brought a note to Miss Pirtle from the principal. I sneak-peeked several looks at her as Miss Pirtle read it. She then looked around at all of us in serious thought. Ten minutes before the big bell sounded she whacked her desk hard to get our attention. She then announced, "Alvin, Elizabeth and Judy Ann will remain in their seats when the big bell rings."

Fear rushed through me for I knew she had caught me and others sneak-peeking as she read the note. My heart was pounding and I wondered what she would do to us.

At 3 o'clock we three remained in our seats after the big bell rang. After about five minutes Miss Pirtle said, "You three pupils come up to my desk." I noticed that Judy Ann was already crying a little. Miss Pirtle said, "As you may or may not know, traditionally, the big bell at 3 o'clock has been rung by outstanding pupils who are doing well in their studies. They always begin in September with the sixth grade class and work down to lower grades." Her voice was softer for some reason. She continued, "Now the second and third graders have been unruly at recess and cannot participate next week, so for three days, first grade children will get to ring the big bell."

She seemed very proud. Then she said, "I have selected you three to ring the big bell on Monday, Tuesday and Wednesday. We will do this alphabetically; so, Alvin, you will ring the bell Monday, Elizabeth on Tuesday and Judy Ann on Wednesday." There was a lull. "That is all I have to say to you," she said. Then we were dismissed.

I was excited. I was going to ring the big bell that could be heard for miles around and all the way to the Mississippi River. On the way home I saw a few older boys playing softball in the street and I said to one of them I knew, "Henry, I'm gonna' ring the big bell Monday at school."

"You are not, you lie; first graders never ring the big bell," he said with arrogance.

"Yes, I am," I said.

"No you're not," he shouted. "You lie."

So I walked on toward home. Along the way, I saw some other children playing and told them the same thing about me ringing the big bell, but no one believed me.

On Saturday while playing cowboys and Indians in a vacant lot down the street from our house, a big boy from the fifth grade asked me, "Say, Alvin, my sister says you and her are gonna' ring the big bell next week. Is that true?"

"Yep, it's true," I answered. I felt bigger and better than I ever had. Someone knew I was gonna' ring the big bell.

Monday, the word was out about the three first graders ringing the big bell. I got a lot of attention at recess. I could hardly do any numbers and letters in class for thinking about it. At 2:45 on Monday, Miss Pirtle tapped me on the shoulder with her stick and said, "You go to the principal's office right now, he'll be expecting you."

I walked down the dark corridor and up some winding steps to the principal's office; a place I had never been before. The principal greeted me at the door and I followed him across the office to another door that he opened, and hanging down from the big bell in the tower was a thick rope. He pulled a stool from off to the side and placed it directly under the rope.

"Alvin," he said (I was surprised that he knew my name), "you will have to stand on this stool and reach high on the rope and pull with all your might." Then he picked me up and placed me on the stool. "Now," he continued, "see that clock across the office? It says three minutes to three. When that long hand jumps straight up to twelve you will pull the rope and ring the big bell.

"Yes, sir," I responded.

"Now," he said, "you'll ring the bell six times. I'll be here to help you pull." He really was a nice principal. We watched the clock together and when the long hand jumped up to twelve, he said, "It's three o'clock; ring the big bell."

I reached up as high as I could and pulled hard, with the principal helping me, and the big bell rang out loud. I pulled it five more times and the sound went out across the city. It was a glorious experience.

"Good job, young man," he said, as he helped me off the stool.

As I walked home from school, several children said they had heard the bell that I had rung. My mother said she was proud of me. The next day, at recess, some of the third and fourth graders even said nice things to me for having rung the big bell.

On Tuesday, Elizabeth rang the big bell. On Wednesday, just after lunch, Judy Ann got sick at her stomach and had to be sent home. At 2:30 Miss Pirtle tapped me on the shoulder and said, "Alvin, you go to the principal's office at ten minutes to 3 o'clock and again, ring the big bell since Judy Ann is not here." So, for a second time, I got to ring the 3 o'clock bell. It was even more exciting than the first time.

The next day I again got lots of attention and it lasted for several days. Later on, while playing kick-the-can in the vacant lot, I had a conversation with my cousin T.W. who was in the third grade. He had never rung the big bell. He wasn't so enthralled about my achievements at school. Then he told me about a boy who was in the sixth grade who had attended Merrill School ever since the first grade, and he had rung the big bell fourteen times.

"He really is smart," T.W. said. "He can recite 'by heart' fifty poems and knows the names of all the presidents since George Washington." That did dampen my spirit a little, but not for long; for I had at least rung the big bell.

In April the school windows were opened wide and we began to feel the spring air and hear the birds sing. I would occasionally sneak-peek at the green trees and rolling clouds. Miss Pirtle was steadfast with her rules and continued to consistently walk the aisles with her stick in hand. The grand sound of the big bell at 3 o'-clock became more welcomed each day.

One day three ladies and a man, all dressed in Sunday-like clothing, entered our room and stood on the side of the room opposite the windows. The class behaved perfectly as we worked quietly with our letters and numbers. Miss Pirtle walked the aisles with her stick in hand as if they were not there. After a while the four grown folks left.

When I got to school Monday, the children were lined up outside in the dark corridor and were slowly entering one at a time. A lady was sitting just inside the door greeting each student with a hug and short conversation. That took about an hour. Later, she told us she was our new teacher. That afternoon we sang a lot of songs, listened as she read stories and did a lot of coloring. Long before the 3 o'clock big bell rang, we all lined up and she hugged us goodbye for the day. This daily routine went on until school let out in May.

Nothing was ever said about Miss Pirtle and we never saw her again. That was a time when children just accepted unexpected changes. We were taught not to ask questions.

On the last day of school we got our report cards. On the back of mine it read: PASSED TO THE SECOND GRADE. We heard the big bell toll at 3 o'clock for the last time until the new school year started in September.

In June plans were being made for me to spend the summer with my relatives in the Bootheel of Missouri. One night my mother took me over to a drug store on Poplar Avenue. We got two ice cream cones and went and sat in the park. Suddenly, the big yellow moon appeared over the tops of some trees. We sat and looked at it for a while. I got brave and asked, "Mamma, where do you think Miss Pirtle is?"

"Oh, Miss Pirtle probably just went to some other place to teach," she answered. We didn't talk about Miss Pirtle anymore.

Then I asked, "Mamma, if the moon isn't made of green cheese, what is it made out of?"

She thought for a moment and said, "Well Alvin Junior, I don't really know." I'm sure she saw in my face a need for a better answer so she then said, "I think the moon is a question we don't have an answer to yet." I thought that was a good answer.

Then we finished our ice cream cones and walked home in the magical moonlight.

The Invisible Man

THE MOVE MY mother and I made to Memphis from the Bootheel of Missouri in the early thirties was permanent. She continued her job as a furrier in one of the large downtown department stores. Her hours were long and hard, from eight till five Monday through Saturday, but she never complained because many people had no work at all. I was in the second grade, and she had me well-trained to come straight home from school at three o'clock on weekdays and to stay near the house if I went out to play. Saturdays were of greater concern for her since she didn't like my being alone all day, so sometimes she had me walk the eight blocks downtown to meet her for lunch at Britling's Cafeteria.

One of those Saturdays was in early November of 1933; I was still seven years old but very much looking forward to my birthday on November 29. I played games that day with several of the neighborhood boys before leaving to meet my mother. I arrived downtown about an hour early, so I decided to walk to Riverside Park where I could look for river boats and watch all the action on the river front. It was always exciting to see the river and to look at the Harahan Bridge from a distance. After a while I left the park to meet my mother; I walked down a wide alley-like passageway between buildings from Front Street to Main Street.

23

There were some small shops on both sides of the passageway; a very thin but friendly-looking man wearing glasses was standing in the doorway of one of the shops. He said, "Hello, little man. Would you like to earn some money?"

"Yes, sir," I replied.

"Well, you just come in my new watch repair shop and we'll talk." It was a very small, freshly-painted shop that had a few chairs for customers and a long glass counter, displaying several watches. He asked me who I was; I told him and explained about meeting my mother for lunch almost every Saturday.

"I have a small job to be done," he said in a friendly way. "I'm having some small handbills made up this week and I need someone to stand at the end of this passageway on Main Street and hand them out to people as they pass by. I'm having about three hundred of them printed, and I'm hoping they will help in letting people know I'm back here in business."

His hand gripped his chin as he was thinking, and then he said, "So, little man, I tell you what. I'll pay you twenty five cents if you will give out my handbills for me next Saturday." With great enthusiasm I told him I would be glad to hand them out, and we agreed that I would do it after I had lunch with my mother on the following Saturday.

During lunch at the cafeteria, I told my mother about the watch repairman and my opportunity to earn twenty-five cents. She seemed to be as excited as I was and said she was very proud of me. All week long I looked forward to my first job and the prospect of earning some money.

Around one o'clock the following Saturday, I went to the watch repair shop, and the thin man had the handbills waiting for me on the counter. They were yellow with black lettering. He gave me some instructions that included not handing any handbills to children or to grown people who looked really poor. He handed me half of the stack and walked with me down to the corner to watch me get started. It was a cold, cloudy, windy day. I started handing them out and realized right away that some people were in such a hurry they would not take one; other people would accept one and thank me. In about an hour I was out of handbills, so I ran down to the shop to get the other half. I hurried back to the corner and gave them to people until I had no more. I returned to the watch repair shop and told the owner I was completely out of handbills; by then it was almost four o'clock. He told me what a fine job I had done. He had already had three customers because of the handbills, so he paid me the twenty-five cents and gave me an extra dime.

At lunch I had asked my mother if, provided I finished in time, I might spend a dime of my money and go to a picture show.

"Yes, you can," she had said, "but you come straight home afterwards, and remember, it gets dark real early these days."

I had seen people entering a theater about a block away when I was giving out handbills; I walked down to that theater, gave the lady in the booth a dime and went inside. I bought a candy bar, then walked all the way down close to the front to sit. There were coming attractions, a good Looney Tunes cartoon and a Fox Newsreel before the main picture show, *The Invisible Man*, began. From the moment a man in a dark heavy overcoat and a felt hat pulled down over his head staggered through a snowstorm on the screen, I knew I was going to see my first real scary picture show. A close-up showed the man's head completely wrapped with gauze, and he was wearing a strange-looking pair of dark glasses.

A few minutes into the movie the man became very angry at some people for not leaving him alone, so to scare them he took off his glasses and, starting at the top of his head, unwrapped the gauze, revealing that he had no head. The man removed his gloves and there were no hands. In a minute he took off all of his clothes and he was invisible. The invisible man was furious and, since he could not be seen, he began choking people and doing all kinds of terrible things. Doors were opened and windows were raised by the invisible man, who said, "I will rule! I will rant! No one will see me come; no one will see me go."

I had seen only about five picture shows in my entire life, and they were about horses, cowboys and Indians, and dogs and things. To me, picture shows were not stories acted out; they were pictures of real life. Once during *The Invisible Man*, I glanced behind me and saw a grown woman holding onto a man's arm like she was scared. Several times ladies in the theater made little screaming noises as the invisible man opened doors and entered rooms, unseen, to do his horror.

The destruction went on and on until one cold winter night. The authorities surrounded the invisible man in a burning barn; he ran from the barn, but his footprints in the snow gave him away and he was shot. At the hospital the invisible man began to die slowly; as he died, he gradually turned into a visible person. That was the end of the picture show.

I noticed that as people left the theater they appeared happy to be getting out of there; I knew I was. I needed to go to the bathroom, but just as I neared the men's room I saw a man in a black coat and felt hat go in, so I decided to wait until I was home. When I left the theater I turned north down Main Street. It was already dusky dark, and I knew immediately that it would be totally dark before I got home. For several blocks, at least, I had the bright lights of Main Street to give me a sense of security and some time to think about how to deal with invisible men in the world.

Earlier that summer I had spent my vacation time in the Bootheel of Missouri with many relatives, but I had stayed mostly with my grandmother and Aunt Annie. At my grandmother's, young Aunt Mary and Aunt Virginia were always talking about ghosts and haints. Aunt Virginia said she had once seen a kerosene lamp move from a dining room table, across the room to another table, with no one carrying it.

"The lamp just picked up and moved across the room and settled down on that other table," she said. "It had to be a ghost or something." Aunt Mary told me she had spent the night with some friends over in Tyler who had two rooms upstairs that they never used. One night they had heard someone walking upstairs, but when they went upstairs, no one was there.

"Had to be a haint or a ghost of some kind," Aunt Mary said.

Later in the summer I stayed at Aunt Annie's house; she read the Bible every afternoon and every night before bed. One afternoon she was reading a passage from the Bible about people being filled with the Holy Ghost. I asked her to explain the Holy Ghost, because I'd become interested in ghosts. Aunt Annie's explanation wasn't very clear, but she did say that the Holy Ghost wasn't a spooky kind of ghost; rather, it was something that couldn't be seen that got inside of you some way. I heard a lot about haints and ghosts that summer.

When I reached Adams Street and turned east, it was very dark; I was leaving the wonderful bright lights of Main Street. I walked as fast as I could with great caution. After two blocks I came upon a long stretch of old homes with iron fences, high hedges, large magnolia trees and practically no light. I decided to walk out in the street for that stretch. After a couple of blocks, I got back on the sidewalk. In the darkness, I could see the faint image of a man, about a block ahead and walking toward me, so I crossed to the other side of the street. As the man passed by, I looked over and saw that he wore an overcoat and a hat; it was too dark to see his face.

By this time I was about to die to go to the bathroom. I had thought of getting over in some hedges, but decided quickly I wasn't that brave. There were few cars coming by, so I chose to walk the remaining blocks out on the edge of the street. When I was a block from home, I started to run but decided I'd better not, since I had to go to the bathroom so bad I was almost going in my pants. I sort of shuffled along, walking as fast as I could, bent over with small knock-kneed steps, hoping I would make it. I did make it home and to the bathroom. It was a double victory.

During supper I did not tell my mother about the invisible man. I felt that being scared of the invisible man would diminish in some way the thrill of earning my first wages ever. I decided to deal with the fear on my own. The following days I didn't stay outside and play after dark. It seemed to me that every day in my neighborhood I would see a man in an overcoat with a pulled-down felt hat. At night the minutes before I fell asleep were the hardest, lying there thinking about whether an invisible man might be in the neighborhood. One day as I was crossing Washington Avenue at Manassas Street, I was certain a car passed by without a driver; when I looked a second time, I still didn't see anyone driving that car.

A few weeks later, in late November, four boys were at my birthday party. My mother lit the eight candles atop the cake and we were waiting for her to return from the kitchen with refreshments when, suddenly, something blew out three of the candles. My mother walked in about that time and asked me if I was all right.

"You look a little peaked," she said.

"I'm all right," I replied. She relit the three candles, and it was time for me to try to blow all of them out. I blew them out with almost no effort. It seemed they went out too easily, almost as if something had helped me. I had trouble falling asleep that night.

On New Year's Eve, as guns were firing and noise was being made in celebration of the new year, I was still wondering how many invisible men might be walking the streets of Memphis.

One day during school recess I talked to another boy who had seen *The Invisible Man* picture show. His father had explained to him that no such thing could happen or had happened in real life.

"But I saw him take off the gauze, and he had no head," I said.

"My father says its trick photography of some kind, and there ain't no such thing as an invisible man," he replied. I felt a little relieved, but was not convinced fully. I still had not figured out Aunt Annie's Holy Ghost that couldn't be seen and would get into you some way; I knew Aunt Annie wouldn't lie. I did, however, feel a little better about it all.

One night in January as my mother was going to bed, she came into the kitchen where I was trying to complete my spelling homework.

"I have a surprise for you, Alvin Junior," she said.

"What is it?" I asked with excitement. I always loved surprises.

"Look out the window," she replied.

I hurried to the window, pushed back the curtain and shouted, "It's snowing! It's snowing!" I watched the big flakes fall.

"Now finish your homework, and get to bed. You can have your fun tomorrow," my mother said as she left the kitchen. I returned to my homework but stopped twice and quietly walked over to the window to see the falling snow. I could tell it was sticking; the ground was already covered.

Just before I finished my homework I heard three firm knocks on the front door. I couldn't imagine who would be visiting us at that hour of the night; I hoped the sounds were from something the cat had knocked over outside or from a fallen tree limb. Besides, I was in my pajamas and wasn't at all interested in answering the door or doing any investigating.

Again, there were three distinct knocks on our front door. I eased through the small living room in my bare feet, unlocked and opened the door, but no one was there. I looked about and saw a single set of footprints in the snow on the doorsteps, on the sidewalk and across the street. I closed and locked the door quickly and ran as fast as I could to my bedroom. My mother heard the knocking and asked,

"Who was it, Alvin Junior?"

"No one was there, Mama," I answered. I was trembling as I lay there in bed thinking; I couldn't remember if the footprints in the snow were coming to, or away from, the house. Then I realized that if those footprints were coming from across the street, over the sidewalk and up the steps to the porch, there could have been an invisible man at the door. I thought for a minute about going to the living room window to look out at those footprints again. Instead, I quickly buried my head under the covers.

June Bug Lake

ONE PARTICULAR Saturday morning in 1934, about two weeks after school had started, I could not decide how to spend my day, so I went over and sat on some wide concrete steps at the house next door. Living in this neighborhood had been a problem for me because there was no one my age to play with. I was eight years old, just entering the third grade, and the other kids were either two or three years older or two or three years younger. I usually had to choose between playing Cowboys and Indians with the little kids or Cops and Robbers—or sometimes tougher—games with the older and bigger boys. While I sat there that morning, trying to come up with a plan for the day, I saw T. W. and two other older boys out on the sidewalk. They appeared to be excited about something, so I meandered over closer and listened.

T. W. was only in the fifth grade, but he was already twelve years old and a lot bigger than I was. My mother had told me he was a distant cousin. He lived across the street with his parents and grandmother; his father worked on a river boat and was seldom home. Sometimes T. W. would play games with me, but he would drop me fast if older boys came around to play.

The two boys with T. W. were about his size and age but seemed tougher and were dirtier. The tougher looking one of the two, Jake, had a new hatchet; the other one, Bob, had a hunting knife and some kind of hunting bag. I eased in close enough to hear them say they were going to hike somewhere and explore June Bug Lake. I had never heard of June Bug Lake, but nothing got me more excited than exploring, so I decided immediately to spend my day with them. I heard T. W. say he had to be home before dark, and the other two said that they did too.

"Before dark" was the standard time for all kids to be home, because "dark" was when most parents got home from work. It seemed like parents were always away working or looking for work.

The boys agreed they would go to their separate houses, each get a sack of food and return in about ten minutes. As T. W. crossed the street to his house, I ran up to him and asked if I could go exploring with them. He answered loudly, his voice full of authority, "No, you're too small and you couldn't keep up."

"I wanna go, T. W. Please let me go," I begged.

"No!" he shouted, and he ran across the yard and into his house. I ran to my house, made a jelly sandwich, wrapped it in a piece of newspaper and stuffed it into the front pocket of my short pants. Then I made half of a jelly sandwich, ate it quickly and ran back outside before the three boys got back. In a few minutes they returned and were ready to go. As they started down the street, I called out to T. W. one more time, "Can I go?"

"I told you NO!" he shouted. "You couldn't keep up."

I followed them as they went west down Adams Street toward downtown. We had walked perhaps a half-mile before one of the boys spotted me following them a block behind, and they stopped. I could tell they were discussing what to do with me. T. W. hollered down the block, "You go back home. You cant come with us" I didn't respond. They stood there a while longer before walking on. Then they broke into a run and tried to lose me by hiding in an alley, but I was swift for my age. I continued to follow. Suddenly, they turned and came charging after me, and I knew they would beat me up if they caught me. I ran as fast as I could until they stopped chasing me. They continued downtown, and I followed.

We crossed Main Street and Front Street and started down to Riverside Drive; I was a good distance behind. T. W. didn't holler at me anymore. They started walking fast down Riverside Drive, south toward the Harahan Bridge that crossed the Mississippi River into Arkansas. About a mile from the bridge, they spotted some other kids having great fun sliding down a steep river bluff on sheets of cardboard so they stopped and joined in. I sneaked in closer to watch. In time, I climbed the high bluff myself, got a piece of cardboard and zoomed down the steep grassy slope. It was a breathtaking ride that seemed to go almost straight down; it was more thrilling than any roller coaster I had ridden. When I reached the bottom, I ended up flat on my back at the feet of T. W. and the boys. T. W. had his right fist drawn back ready to hit me as soon as I stood up. I stayed on the ground, coiled up like a cowering dog.

"You're not coming with us!" T. W. shouted.

I just laid there pitifully until Jake said, "Aw, leave him alone, T. W. He'll never be able to keep up, anyway."

T. W. said, "All right. But if you do come, Alvin, try and keep up, and don't whine if you get tired."

I promised.

We walked on toward the big bridge that crossed the river. As we got close enough to see it fairly well, I began to wonder whether or not I really wanted to go on this exploring adventure. We started across from the Tennessee side, and I realized immediately that there wasn't a place to walk; there was barely room enough for a car. Crossing the river on the Harahan Bridge was one of the exciting things I always looked forward to when we made trips back to the Bootheel of Missouri. I had never noticed how narrow the traffic lanes were. The surface of the lanes was merely tar poured over large wooden planks. Along the edge of the lanes, where normally there would be a shoulder or pedestrian walkway, there was just open space for about nine inches and then there was a single width of wooden planks running parallel to the lanes. A metal railing ran about three feet above the single width of boards. I could look down between the edge of the traffic lane and those planks and see the mighty river far below. The gap didn't appear to be big enough to fall through, just big enough to get stuck in.

Luckily, there weren't a lot of cars going across the bridge at that time of day; only about twenty or thirty passed while we were crossing. When the coast was clear, T. W. and the boys walked smack-dab in the middle of the lane so fast that I sometimes had to run to catch up. When we heard a car we'd all step over onto the side and hold on to the railing until the car passed. I tried not to look down; I was afraid my spinning head would pull me over.

When we got halfway across, we stopped and took turns spitting into the river. We waited a while for a steamboat pushing barges to go under us. People passing in cars seemed to be looking at us as if we shouldn't be there.

When we got to the other side of the river, Jake jumped over a railing, slid down a steep bank to a cotton field, and headed north. T. W., Bob and I followed; soon we came to a dirt road between two cotton fields, at which point we turned right and walked about a mile. I could see a large thicket of willow trees at the end of the road.

I was tired, hungry and not as excited about this exploring trip as I had been earlier, but I didn't dare complain. Bob got a bottle of water out of his hunting bag, and they all had a drink. He gave me a drink last. Then we walked into the willow trees and there I saw June Bug Lake. Jake led us to a certain place where he uncovered someone else's old flatboat hidden under a pile of brush and limbs. It was unpainted, not more than a foot deep and maybe eight feet long. Jake, who was evidently an old June Bug Lake veteran, said there was also a bucket of tar hidden somewhere. The others found it and proceeded to patch up the cracks and seams in the old weathered wood of the flatboat while I took out my smashed-up sandwich and ate it. Jake took his hatchet and cut down two small willow trees to use as poles to push the boat. He said the lake was only about three or four feet deep. In fact, June Bug Lake was the Mississippi River backwater, about a quarter mile from the river on one side and a little more than a mile from the Arkansas levee on the other. It was perhaps a thirty acre lake, surrounded by willow trees.

The position of the sun indicated that it was already after three o'clock, and for the first time I became concerned about getting home before dark. Jake had finished hacking out the poles, and he and Bob took the boat out into the lake for the first test. The willow trees grew out into the water for almost thirty feet; then the water got pretty clear. I couldn't always see the boys, but I could hear them out there having fun. I asked T. W. if we shouldn't start back home. He glared at me and said, "We'll go home when we get ready." I didn't say any more.

Jake and Bob returned rather quickly because the boat was taking water. They pulled it ashore and poked more tar into the cracks. Then T. W. and Bob took the poles and pushed out through the willows into the middle of the lake. In a while they returned; T. W. was bailing out water while Bob pushed them back ashore. They emptied the water from the boat, pushed more tar into the cracks and seams and made several more trips.

Finally, as T. W. and Jake were coming in for the final trip out, T. W. called me over and said I could go with them. Without hesitation, I climbed into the middle of the boat and they pushed out. I reminded T. W. that I didn't swim all that well, and he replied that the lake wasn't deep anyway.

Fairly soon almost two inches of water had accumulated in the bottom of the boat, and T. W. and Jake instructed me to take one of the two small cans in the boat and start bailing out the water. I obeyed; they continued to pole and shortly we were way out in the middle of June Bug Lake. I could see the top of the Harahan Bridge and the city buildings across the river. I never let up on bailing, but it seemed like the water was getting higher in the boat. Jake noticed this as well and he began helping me remove water with the other can. We were still taking in water faster than we could bail it out, and T. W. and Jake began to show some concern. T. W. spied an island of dirt, not much bigger than my Aunt Annie's dining room table top, so he poled over beside it and ordered me to jump out; I did.

"We won't make it back with three in the boat," T. W. said. "This will lighten the load." Soon they were heading away from the little island. T. W. hollered as he bailed, "We'll patch up the boat better and come back for you."

"How long will it be?" I asked.

"Not long," he yelled back. "We'll be back for you."

The small island of red dirt was out in the middle of the lake, several hundred yards east of the landing place. I saw T. W. and Jake disappear into the willows, and I could hear faintly their voices. I sat there for a while and looked in all directions. This was the only island in the lake; there were two or three little weeds growing in the dirt. Suddenly, I realized that the sun was nearly down and it was going to be dark soon. I became afraid, and I yelled as loudly as I could across the water, "T. W.!"

Way back in the willows I heard him faintly answer.

"It's gonna get dark soon," I yelled. "Hurry!"

I listened for an answer but heard no response. "T. W.!" I yelled as loudly as I could in desperation, "Are you there?"

I heard him at a distance, farther away than I thought he should be. "Yes." There was a pause. "We'll be back."

I sat there frightened and forlorn. My tennis shoes were soaked from the water in the boat, and I was wet all over from splashing. I began to shake and quiver because it was growing cooler.

"T. W., I'm cold!" I hollered out across the lake. He didn't answer. I tried not to be scared. The water was very clear and I could see all kinds of little bugs swimming around; I saw some spider-looking things walking across the water, and way out in the lake I saw something that looked like a snake wiggling across the water.

The sun was setting with an eerie orange glow; I wanted to cry because I knew the sun wouldn't last long. I prayed for it to stay light, but the sky turned purple and then dusky blue. I looked east across the river and saw a few windows on top of the Memphis buildings reflecting the setting sun. To the south I could see the Harahan Bridge, black against the darkening sky.

"T. W., are you there?" I yelled. I listened; there was no reply. "T.W.!" I yelled. No reply.

During the next twenty minutes, I probably yelled for T. W. a hundred times. Then I just sat there and trembled in the deepening darkness and wondered what was going to happen to me. I wanted to cry but I couldn't. I remembered a picture I had seen once hanging on the living room wall of my Aunt Minnie's house back in the Bootheel. It was a picture of a little girl walking near a steep cliff with huge storm-tossed waves leaping up from the water below. Above her was a beautiful angel with a kind face. Aunt Minnie had told me it was a guardian angel and that good little children all have guardian angels to protect them from dangerous things. I wondered if I was too old to have a guardian angel, or if I was too bad. However, I was still alive after several years of living in Memphis. But I had never been abandoned on a tiny dirt island in the darkness in the middle of June Bug Lake, which was full of snakes and spiders and who knows what else.

It was out of the question for me to try to wade back to shore in that murky unknown; the water would have come up to my neck at least. Besides, I couldn't see much of anything by that time and I wouldn't have been able to tell where I was going. So I sat in quiet desperation, the most frightened I had ever been in my young life, for what seemed like a long, long time.

Then, from out of the darkness, I thought I heard T. W. calling. Soon I heard his voice again, more clearly.

"Alvin, I'll be there," he called. I had never been so glad to hear a human voice.

"T. W., where are you?" I yelled.

"I'll be there. I'll be there," he repeated, almost like a slightly irritated mother.

I peered through the darkness but couldn't see him. Finally, I heard his pole hitting the side of the boat.

"Here I am," I yelled.

"I see you," he said, and it wasn't till then that I saw him in the darkness not far from the island. In about a minute he was nearer and yelled,

"You watch out! I've got to run the boat up on the island a little bit."

I saw him coming and stood over to the side of the island as he pushed the boat's front ashore.

"Where have you been?" I asked, and then I started to cry.

"Come here, Alvin. Let's get the water out of this boat," he said, concentrating on the here and now and playing down the bad, just like a mother. We dumped the water out, and then he showed me a big yellow bucket that was much larger than the cans we had used for bailing.

"Where'd you get that?" I asked as I continued to cry.

"Tell you about it later," he said. "Now, once we get started back, I'll pole and you bail out water as fast as you can, and be real careful not to rock the boat." I said I would.

He pushed us off the little island and almost immediately I could feel water coming into the boat. I started bailing and he pushed us along. It didn't seem like we would ever get to shore again, but T. W. was encouraging.

"You're doing good, Alvin," he said. "Keep bailing out that water."

In the darkness we pushed across the water, then through the weeds and willows, and eventually we skidded up onto the muddy bank. T. W. pulled the boat farther up on the bank, and very soon we were on the dirt road, heading for the Harahan Bridge. T. W. walked very fast, and I had to run every so often to catch up. We climbed the steep bank that led to the bridge and started across the river.

"Stay close to the railing, Alvin, and watch the cars," he instructed. There was much more traffic on this trip, and the lights from the cars blinded us as we tried to hurry across. I was even more frightened than I had been on the island because every oncoming car looked as if it would hit us. I clung to the railing, scared to death that I would fall into the gap and hang there with my feet dangling underneath the bridge until my body would start to waste away and slip through, falling into the dark river far below.

It seemed like forever before we got to the other side. I had no idea what time it was because everything seemed to take so long. I started to feel good again when we were walking and running down the dark streets toward home. T. W. knew how we could save time up some alleys and down a railroad track or two. Pretty soon we were on Third Street, heading across town.

"T. W., I've got to rest a while," I begged.

"We'll rest in a little while after we go a few more blocks," he said. He was always in control.

A few minutes later we came to an Italian store. T. W. had a nickel in his pocket, so he went inside to get us something to eat; he told me to stay outside because I was so dirty and muddy. He came out with five penny-a-piece ginger cookies that were at least six inches across. He handed me two of them, and we sat on the store steps and ate them like hungry dogs. As we rested a little longer, I asked T. W. what had happened to Jake and Bob. He didn't seem to want to talk about it very much, but he said enough that I figured it out. Jake and Bob were too scared to go back out in that leaky boat after they had left me on the island, so they all decided to go for help. Just before they got to the bridge, T. W. spotted the yellow bucket on the side

of the road, probably left there by some cotton choppers. He figured he could bail out more water with it
than with the cans and the boat would make it without sinking. Neither Jake nor Bob would return with
him, so he came back for me alone. I couldn't imagine
how he poled and bailed at the same time without losing either the pole or the bucket.

We stood up and continued across town on Third
Street, running a while and walking a while. T. W.
saw a clock on a building and said, "It's almost nine o'-
clock, Alvin. We're gonna be in real trouble."

When we got about a block from home, we saw a
crowd of grown folks waiting out in front of T. W.'s
house. We were greeted with mixed joy and anger.
Bob's mother had called T. W.'s mother, and they
were planning to get a car and some men to go over
and try to find us.

Since my father wasn't there to punish me, my
mother gave me a hard whipping with a belt. I cried
really loud while she whipped me; later on she went up
to the front room of our house and cried herself. Two
days later T. W.'s daddy came home from his river job
and whipped him.

The following Saturday T. W. and the other older
boys gathered in front of his house with plans to go
exploring down on Nonconnah Creek. I walked up
the street to the vacant lot and played Cowboys and
Indians with the little kids.

The Kite

IN MEMPHIS during the Depression years, there were always seasonal activities that kept children's dreams alive. In the autumn of 1934, when I was nine years old, flying a kite at the park was the height of ecstasy. One could buy a regular kite for fifteen cents and a small ball of string for a nickel. That much money was not easy to come by; it often meant giving up picture shows and candy, so many boys tried making their own kites. Homemade kites were nearly always heartbreaking failures; kites would come unglued or the sticks would break, or they would not stay aloft.

I made three kites one week, but I never got any of them to fly very well. I found myself down at the park, sitting on a bench, watching the lucky boys fly their kites and hoping that sooner or later someone who had one way up high would let me hold the string just for a little while. That didn't happen very often.

After a while, my need for a high flying kite became almost unbearable. One afternoon while walking home from school, I saw a big orange King Kite displayed in the window of Kirby's Drugstore. I had two pennies and I'd planned to take two candy chances at the drugstore, so I went on inside. Candy chances were wafer like chocolate mints about the size of a quarter and not much thicker; they came in square boxes of five layers, about twenty mints per layer. For a penny I got a mint; after biting into the mint, if it was white inside, I lost but still had a little bite of chocolate and mint taste. If by chance the mint was pink inside, I would win a huge, thick all-day Hollowell chocolate sucker. I had never gotten a pink center, but I had seen boys get pink centers on two occasions, so I knew there was always a possibility.

That day I gave Mr. Kirby my two pennies and carefully selected two mints, but they both had white centers. I let the little mints dissolve slowly in my mouth, attempting to make them last as long as possible. I asked Mr. Kirby about the King Kite in his window, and he explained that there wasn't a better kite made and that it cost thirty cents—double the price of a regular kite—but was made of good material and would fly really high. I saw the kite in the window on the way to school the next morning and also on the way home after school; I decided that afternoon that I was going to find the money to buy me a King Kite and fly it high.

I knew that Marshall Gibbons, a boy in my fourth grade class, had made some money delivering hand circulars for Pollock's Grocery down on Poplar Street. The next day I went straight from school to Pollock's to inquire about a job. When I entered the small store, I noticed it was dimly lit for a grocery store, but I walked on back to the rear anyway where a big round man stood wearing a dirty white apron with a sun visor over his eyes.

"Well?" he growled.

"Sir, I was wondering if you need any circulars delivered?" I asked politely, trying to cover up the fact that he scared me.

"What makes you think you'd be any better than any of the other brats I pay good money to and then find my good circulars thrown in gutters and garbage cans and not even delivered to houses at all?" he demanded, almost yelling. He was very scary.

"Well, I don't know," I said.

"If you don't know, boy," he was really yelling now, "then the answer is no!"

"Thank you," I said, and I turned and walked toward the front of the store; I was almost out the door when he hollered, "Hey, boy, you wait up there." I waited; I was scared not to.

He came up front. "You be here at eight o'clock Saturday morning, not a minute later, understand?" His voice was strong but a little calmer.

"Yes, sir," I replied.

"What's' your name?" he asked.

"Alvin," I answered.

"Eight o'clock sharp Saturday, and we'll see then."

"Yes, sir."

I walked home thinking that he was about the meanest and scariest man I had ever met, and I wondered if I should show up on Saturday morning. I told my mother about it and she said he was probably just unhappy. I decided for a King Kite I'd give it a try.

On Saturday morning I was at the store by seven-fifty, and it was already open. The man ignored me at first, but after taking care of a couple of customers he called to me, still growling,

"Alvin, come over here." He pulled two large bundles from underneath the counter and slammed them heavily on top.

"There are three-hundred good circulars in each of these bundles." He gave me lengthy instructions, stopping once to ring up a small sale, about how to put each circular either in a mailbox or behind a screen door, or to fold them and put them in door handles and doorknobs, and never just to throw them casually on the porches.

"Deliver these three-hundred circulars to all houses and apartments east of the store, but don't go more than three blocks south or north of Poplar Avenue. When you run out of circulars, come back and then we'll let you deliver this bundle west the same way," he said, still shouting. He continued, "Now, don't you ditch any of these circulars, or you wont get paid a dime. Deliver them right, and you make twenty-five cents."

I delivered circulars all day just as he had instructed, and I finished, exhausted, about three in the afternoon. When I returned to the store, he snarled, "Now, did you ditch any of those circulars?"

"No, sir. Not a one," I replied.

He paid me twenty-five cents toward my King Kite and as I left, he said, "Come back in about two months and I might use you again."

On Sunday some lady friends of my mother's were visiting and they made the mistake of asking me how I was doing. I explained my endeavor to make forty-five cents for a King Kite and three balls of string. Hanging around the park, I had learned that it took at least that much string to get a kite really high. One of the ladies said I could rake the leaves from her yard on Monday afternoon and she would give me twenty cents.

That Monday I raked leaves after school until dark. I had the money for my King Kite and the three balls of string. Tuesday after school I went straight to Kirby's Drugstore, running most of the way, and purchased the orange King Kite and three balls of string. That night I assembled it very carefully. I held it up on its end, and it stood three or four inches taller than I was. It was a magnificent kite. I wound the three balls of string onto a stick I had saved just for that purpose, and I was careful to tie the string ends together doubly good. I had also saved an old pillow case to use as strips of cloth for my kite tail. I tied the pieces together and made a tail about sixteen feet long. I had learned to make kite tails from watching the boys down at the park. My kite was ready to fly.

Wednesday was a long school day; I noticed at recess that it was also a very still day, the wind rustling the tree leaves only slightly. After school I raced home and then straight to the park with my kite, but there was no wind. I ran with the kite for a time and got it up about thirty feet, but when I stopped running, it dropped to the ground. I wore out doing this, so I sat on a park bench and waited for the wind to blow; it never did. That night I asked my mother why the wind was strong one day and would hardly blow the next.

"That's nature," she said. "The wind is like the rain: it blows when it gets ready."

I wanted a better answer, but I accepted it and didn't ask what made nature work. Thursday the air was more still than Wednesday, but I went down to the park anyway and waited till almost dark for the wind to blow; it never did. On the way to school Friday I noticed the trees swaying back and forth and a few white clouds moving across the sky. It was another slow school day, but I watched the trees outside the windows, and the wind seemed to blow harder and harder as the day progressed. After school I raced home, got my kite, and ran to the park. In a short while, my kite was up and flying with a slight right-to-left movement, and it never nose-dived because I had known the proper length for the tail. There were other boys flying kites, but several people made comments about how smooth my kite was flying. Little by little, I gave the kite more string, and it was higher than I had ever imagined. My orange King Kite looked great against that blue sky, and it was higher than any other kite that day. A boy named Henry, who was in my fourth grade class, asked if he could send up a message to my kite. He took a piece of paper from his school tablet and punched a small hole in the middle; then he tore the paper carefully on one side to the hole, slipped the paper over the string, and we watched the wind take the message slowly but surely up the string to the kite. In a little while he sent up another message. I noticed that the kite was tugging hard from a strong wind, and I began to worry whether or not the wind could get so strong that I might not be able to hold the kite.

As it turned out, I flew the kite all afternoon with no problems. It was getting close to dark, and I knew it was about time for me to wind my kite down when two big sixth-grade boys walked over to me. One of them asked if he could send up a message and I said, "Sure." The other boy was playing with a knife, and as the first boy was placing a piece of paper on the string, I saw in a flash the second boy's knife slash my string; there flew my kite, off with the wind into the dark sky. All I remembered about that instant was that the boy had a smile on his face and he laughed. I could see my kite tumbling wildly and finally disappearing beyond some trees a few blocks away. I ran across the park, across Poplar Avenue, and out across the neighborhood where I thought it might land, but to no avail. I searched and searched several blocks away. I spotted some string stretched across the tops of trees and across a street, but the kite wasn't there.

It was very dark by then, so I gave up and went home. At supper my mother could tell I was upset and asked me what was wrong. For some reason I could not tell her about the older boy cutting my string, so I just said, "I lost my kite in a very strong wind."

"I'm sorry," she said.

I did not cry.

On Saturday morning I got up early and searched again for my kite but didn't find it. Midmorning I went to the park and watched the other boys fly kites, since the wind was still blowing strong. At noon I walked down to the corner of Washington Avenue and Manassas Street and sat on a short concrete wall watching the cars go by. I sat there often, thinking and watching. In about fifteen minutes a car on Manassas Street drove up slowly and stopped to turn right on Washngton Avenue. The lady who was driving called and motioned for me to come over to the car window opposite the driver's side.

"Yes, ma'am?" I asked through the open window.

"This is for you." That's all she said. She reached over and held out a five-dollar bill. I took it, and before I could even thank her, the car turned right and continued down Washington Avenue and soon disappeared. All I could remember was that the lady had a happy-looking face and very bright eyes. I looked at the five-dollar bill, then put it in my pocket hurriedly. I could hardly believe it. There were many possibilities now. I could get another kite, go to the picture show, buy some candy. I walked home, fixed a jelly sandwich and decided I'd think about it more.

By midafternoon I had decided I'd just play games in the neighborhood and not tell anyone about what had happened, and then show the five-dollar bill to my mother when she got home from work. That night, when I told her about the lady handing me the five-dollar bill, she seemed as startled as I had been. "How wonderful," she said. "You can now get another kite."

I thought about it a lot that night. The next day I decided to give my mother one of the dollars, use one dollar for picture shows and candy and a new tablet I needed for school, and put away three dollars for Christmas. I decided not to get another kite.

During the winter, when I didn't have anything to do, I often would wrap up warmly and go down to the corner of Washington Avenue and Manassas Street and sit on the short concrete wall to think and to watch the cars go by. The lady who gave me the five-dollar bill never drove by again. I had learned a lot that autumn: things can go good and things can go bad. But the main thing I learned was that the wind blows when it gets ready.

That's nature.

The Grapefruit Train

EVERYONE TALKED about it being a time of hard times. I was ten years old and in the fourth grade at Merrill School, about a mile from downtown Memphis. Things began to happen that year that contributed to my understanding of the difficulties people were having. If a pupil didn't have a sack lunch or any money for lunch, he or she could go to the principal's office and sign up for the free soup line at the school cafeteria. When the lunch bell rang, two lines formed in the basement leading into the cafeteria; one line was for those paying for their soup, and the other was the free soup line. Pupils with nickels began to poke fun and say all kinds of humiliating things to those in the free soup line. I could never understand this very well, because I knew some of the pupils in the nickel line, and they wore ragged clothes with patches and socks and shoes with holes. In fact, in my room at school there was only one pupil, a girl named Marcia Morganthall, who was considered well-off, and that was because she had two overcoats and several pairs of shoes. Almost everyone I knew had only one pair of shoes. More and more in those days, grown folks' conversations were about the shortage of jobs, the need for money, and how they looked forward to good times. One thing I had figured out: I never wanted to be in that free soup line at school.

One night in early January, just before school was to resume from Christmas holidays, my mother said she wanted us to have a little talk about something she needed me to do. Since she worked all day every day but Sunday, I often did chores and other things to help out. That night she handed me a small printed card and said, "I would like for you to carry this card downtown for me tomorrow and pick up whatever they give you and bring it home. Will you do that for Mother?" she asked.

"What do I do?" I responded.

She pointed carefully to the address on Front Street and a time of one o'clock on the card. "Go to that place at one o'clock and pick up whatever they give you," she instructed kindly. "Yesterday my supervisor at work gave me this card, since I had never before received one. I think on some days they give out free packages of food, and other days they have nothing to give out. But whether or not they give out anything, you have to be there at the designated time. I would go but they would dock my pay, and it may not be worth anything anyway," she said. I didn't feel all that good about her request, but I agreed to do it. The weather had been misty and foggy for several days, and I hadn't been able to play outside much anyway.

The next morning about eleven o'clock, after I had eaten a big peanut butter and jelly sandwich for lunch, I left for downtown. I had put on an extra shirt, my one and only coat, and my snow cap. I arrived early at the building on Front Street, so I walked down to see the river. It was so foggy I couldn't see the bank on the Arkansas side and I couldn't see the Harahan Bridge either, but I sat on a bench and watched a while anyway. When I walked back to the building and went in, I saw a lot of people—mostly grown folks—standing in a line that didn't seem to be moving. Some people were holding cards similar to the one I had, so I got in line. There didn't seem to be any happy people in that big room at all; there were just a lot of solemn-looking faces and a large number of older people.

In a minute or so there were maybe thirty people in line behind me. The man directly behind me asked gruffly, "You are in this here line, ain't you boy?"

"Yes, sir," I replied.

"Where are your mamma and papa?" he asked. He talked very country like.

"My mother is at work, and my father is in Missouri," I answered

He just grunted, "Huh."

The line began to move ever so slowly, and we twisted all about the big room; finally, I came to a counter that was slightly higher than my head. The man behind the counter leaned over the top and asked, "Are you here with your parents?"

"No, sir," I replied. "I'm here by myself. My mother asked that I bring this to you." I handed him the white card.

The man behind the counter, who sounded pretty nice, glanced at the card and said to the gruff man behind me, "Hold that boy up so I can see him and ask him some questions." He picked me up and sat me on the counter. The man behind the counter asked, "Where are your mother and father, young man?"

"My mother is at work, and my father lives in Missouri," I answered. "I live with my mother on Adams Street."

He fumbled with some papers and looked in some very large gray books for a minute or two before saying, Young man, I have to ask you this question: "Do you know if your mother earns more than forty dollars a week in salary?"

"I don't think so, sir," I answered. "I heard her say one time that she only earns thirteen dollars a week, but I'm not real sure."

"Can you write your name?" he asked.

"Yes, sir," I replied.

He had me sign a paper and then he handed me a yellow card and instructed me to go straight down from where we were toward the river to the railroad tracks parallel to Riverside Drive. "You'll see all the folks down there," he said. "The train should be there in about thirty minutes or so."

As I walked down the street on the river bluff, I could not see the river for the heavy fog that came all the way up to the railroad tracks. I noticed that the crowd of people gathered there were like dark, motionless forms, almost like a forest of dead trees. The fog moved quietly about them. I stood at the edge of the gathering. An older man wearing a heavy overcoat and brown cap was also waiting at the edge of the crowd.

He said, "No need of pushing in there, boy. If the train has anything on it you'll get just as much by waiting. Lots of people always want to push up front for some reason. Your yellow card will get you what they have." He must have seen the yellow card in my hand.

"What will be on the train today?" I asked.

"You never know that, boy," he replied. I'm sure he could tell I didn't know much about what was going on so he talked to me about the people gathering there for the train's delivery. He told me that people without jobs or with very low-paying jobs could get whatever free food arrived daily on two trains. He said that sometimes the food was pretty good and other times it was almost nothing, but it was helping keep people alive. I noticed that the man looked like he hadn't shaved in several days, but he was pleasant to talk with. He told me that about two weeks back there had been three trains straight of rice delivered; everybody got one large sack of rice from each train trip, and that was a very good thing for families with lots of children. The man told me that the early-morning train this morning had given out large sacks of prunes. Everybody with a yellow card got two five-pound sacks of prunes.

I could hear the train coming, and the people who had stood waiting so motionless began moving about. I couldn't see the train, but I could hear it getting closer and closer. When the train did come into view, it pulled to a stop and a boxcar door opened; people began lining up according to some official-looking man's instructions.

"No need getting in a hurry, boy," the older man repeated. "Your yellow card will get you what they've got whether you're first or last." I waited on the edge of the crowd with him.

It was hard to see much. The locomotive engine was still making a hissing noise and drowned out what people were saying. We started hearing, "Grapefruit . . . grapefruit," like people were passing the word around. A man came out of the crowd and fog with a large sack across his shoulder; as he passed us he said, "Boxcar of grapefruit, Coleman. Nothing there but grapefruit."

From that comment I judged that the elder man's name was Coleman and the train had grapefruit on it. "Well, it looks like we'll get a big sack of grapefruit, boy," Coleman said. "Let's go get ours."

I walked on down with him; in about fifteen minutes I handed my yellow card to a man, and a huge sack of grapefruit was taken from the train and placed on the ground for me. Coleman got his, put it on his shoulder, and knew immediately I'd have a problem carrying mine, so he said, "I'll be right back and help you." That sack of grapefruit was almost as big as I was, and it took all of my strength just to pull it along. Coleman came back and picked up my sack of grapefruit; he put it on his shoulder and we walked toward the top of the river bluff on Front Street. As we walked he said, "If you want to, boy, you can sell this bag of grapefruit for a quarter to a man on top of the bluff."

"Oh, I have to take mine home to my mother," I replied.

He took my sack of grapefruit off his shoulder and put it down on the sidewalk. "How you gonna manage it, boy?" he asked. "These things are heavy."

"I'll drag it home some way," I replied.

"How far you gotta go?" he asked.

"Over a mile," I answered.

At the top of the bluff on Front Street was the man in a truck giving people quarters for their grapefruit; he had already bought about fifteen bags and had them loaded. "Quarter for your grapefruit, boy," he blurted out.

"No, sir; I have to get mine home to my mother."

I managed to drag the sack across the street and then rested. Coleman walked up with a man who had a sack under his arm.

"This man will help you out, boy. He'll take some of your grapefruit and give you a sack of prunes." I never said anything; together they opened my sack and took out about a dozen or more grapefruit and placed that sack of prunes in on top.

"You might manage this sack better now, boy," Coleman said. He was right; I could drag it better, but it was still very heavy. I thanked them for lightening my load and started dragging my bag of grapefruit and prunes down Front Street.

I decided that I would stay on Front Street, thereby avoiding the busy sidewalks of Main Street where I might be seen by someone from school. I had concluded that being in that grapefruit line might be ten times worse than being in the free soup line at school, so I dragged and rested and dragged and rested until finally I reached Adams Street. Once there it took about another twenty minutes to reach Third Street with several blocks to go still.

While resting at Third Street I noticed the sacks tough material was so worn from dragging on the concrete that I was about to lose the bottom of the sack. After thinking about it for a while, I decided I would hide my sack of grapefruit and prune down an alley and go borrow my neighbor Clyde Hooker's wagon. I hid my sack, walked all the way to Clyde's, borrowed the wagon, and returned. I found two empty cardboard boxes in the alley, so I emptied all the grapefruit into the two boxes, placed the sack of prunes on top of one box of grapefruit and proceeded toward home pulling the wagon.

Everything was going well until I was about three blocks from home. That's when I spotted Blake Bishop and two of his buddies coming down the other side of the street. Blake was a big, tough sixth-grade bully who specialized in beating up everybody. If it had not been for my wagon of grapefruit and prunes, I'd have disappeared like a rabbit in high weeds, but I could only continue down the street. They spotted me, crossed the street and stood waiting in the middle of the block. My cousin T. W. had warned me never to respond to their comments and slurs, if at all possible, and they might leave me alone.

"Hey, Bloomers, what ya got in your wagon?" Blake asked as I passed by. I didn't answer. He called me Bloomers because my mother had bought me a pair of knickers in the third grade that lost their elasticity at the bottom and fell down to my ankles as I walked. Blake and the older boys kept calling me by that name even after I stopped wearing the knickers.

They followed me as I pulled my wagon. "Hey, Bloomers, where'd you get these yellow balls?" Blake asked. He picked up one grapefruit and pitched it to one of his buddies, and then he pitched another grapefruit to his other buddy. They started playing catch with several of my grapefruit and began rolling some of them down the sidewalk. I yelled for the three boys to stop; I started picking up the grapefruit and putting them back in my boxes, but Blake and his buddies kept taking them out faster. For some reason they never bothered my sack of prunes. The grapefruit were all over the sidewalk; I hauled off and kicked the smallest boy in the shin as hard as I could and he yelled out in pain. They cursed me really bad and grabbed me. Blake said, "Hold him and we'll give him the Indian Torture."

As they held me by each arm, Blake opened up my coat and two shirts and began rhythmically hitting my chest with his knuckles. I'd heard about the Indian Torture; the bullies would hit a boy over and over until he cried and begged for mercy. The blows were not all that hard, but in time one right after the other would become painful. My cousin T. W. had said if I ever got caught to let them do it as long as I could stand it and then start crying. T. W. said if I cried too early, they wouldn't have their satisfaction, and they'd just keep on doing it longer.

Blake had hit me in the chest about thirty times and it was beginning to be really painful; I was just on the verge of crying and begging for mercy when one of the boys spotted a police car coming up the street. They dropped me fast and were gone down an alley and out of sight in seconds. The police car drove on by; the police probably had not seen what was going on, but they had served a purpose by saving me from a lot of Indian Torture.

As I gathered up all of my scattered grapefruit from off the sidewalk, I couldn't help but start crying; the experience had been so humiliating. However, I didn't cry very long. I pulled the wagon the remaining blocks, carried the grapefruit and prunes into our kitchen, and returned the wagon to Clyde's house. My mother wasn't due home for another hour, so I washed the grapefruit.

When she got home she could hardly believe the things I told her about my ordeal with the grapefruit and prunes. I didn't tell her anything about Blake and the Indian Torture; she had too many things to worry about already. That night we decided to give half of the grapefruit to Mrs. Brown, a friend of Mother's down the street who had three children to feed. We carried the grapefruit to her, and she was delighted to get them.

Back in school one day, a very pretty girl named Dori came up to me and asked, "Alvin, did I see you dragging a big sack downtown the other day?"

"What day?" I responded.

"I don't remember what day, but it sure did look like you," she said.

"Well, lately, I've been doing a lot of chores for my mother. It might have been me." I sort of hemmed and hawed and never did say whether it was or wasn't me. The next day at lunch, while standing in the nickel line for soup, I looked over and saw Dori standing in the free soup line. She smiled at me sweetly and didn't seem at all to be humiliated. Some things are hard to figure, I thought.

That night Mrs. Brown knocked on our door just after supper; she had brought us a small warm chocolate cake. She only stayed a minute and thanked us again for all the grapefruit. I sat at the kitchen table, cut me a piece of cake and thought about it being a time of hard times. I wondered if the cake would be any better if it happened to be a time of good times. Then I cut and ate another piece.

The Plowman and the Water Boy

AFTER MOVING TO Memphis from the Bootheel of Missouri when I was six years old, I took advantage of any chance I could get to go back to visit my relatives. My favorite place to spend those adventurous summers was Aunt Annie and Uncle Will's house, only a few miles from Cooter. It was located on a flat, spacious cotton farm about six miles from Steele, where I was born. My Aunt Annie, who was really my father's sister, was more like a grandmother than an aunt, since she had raised my father after their mother died giving birth to him in 1900. Since Aunt Annie had lost a baby at birth a few days earlier, the family carried my father down the road to Aunt Annie's house, and she raised and nurtured him as her own. Uncle Will was a wise and wonderful man of the earth; he was the principal overseer of several hundred acres of farm land owned by John Barnes Thompson.

During my earliest summer vacations in the Bootheel, when I was seven and eight years of age, I played in the nearby woods lot and around the flower garden, and I romped barefooted up and down the dusty roads. Sometimes I chased butterflies and climbed young trees with my friend Martha Sue, who was two years older than I and lived down the road a piece. Other times in those early years, I sat and stared out across the spacious fields where it seemed I could see forever, and I listened for the whistle of a train I could never see.

I often followed my Uncle Will as he fed the farm animals and did his different chores. By the time I was nine, I was given chores of my own, things like helping pump water for three teams of mules, slopping the hogs, feeding the chickens and gathering eggs. Late during my summer vacation when I was nine, I grew big enough—and my arms became strong enough—to carry water to the field hands chopping cotton. For carrying water, John Barnes Thompson paid fifty cents a day; I got such a late start that year, I only earned seven dollars. All through my fourth-grade school year in Memphis, I anticipated the coming summer when I would be a lot bigger and stronger: I would return to the Bootheel and be a full-time water boy all summer, earning more money.

The summer of 1936 finally arrived. The crops were doing well in the Bootheel, and I was ecstatic about having a job and being able to work almost every day. I was to carry cool drinking water in two three-gallon buckets all the way from the home place hand pump to twenty-five or thirty field hands working out in the cotton fields.

Uncle Will was up early, feeding the stock long before breakfast every morning. Breakfast was generally country ham and eggs, fried potatoes, sweet onions and hot biscuits and sorghum. The field hands started gathering in front of the hoe shed, across the road and down a piece, long before sunup while the birds were welcoming the coming day and the morning mist hovered over the land.

Uncle Will checked and sharpened hoes in the blue-gray of the morning before slowly leading the men and women out to the fields where they would work that day. Uncle Will was as steady and accurate as the break of day itself, and by sunrise the field hands would be working. While all of this was going on, three colored plowmen harnessed their mules and drove their teams to the fields where they had left the plows the previous day; by sunrise they, too, would be at work turning the earth.

The cotton choppers worked in relative silence the first two hours of the morning, but when the sun got higher and the heat bore down on them, a colored man called Bug Eye would start the colored folks singing, and they would sing an hour or so. Sometimes I could hear them a mile away; other times they sang softly, like the wind. For some reason the white folks never joined in the singing.

I hand-pumped water for the huge mule trough for an hour after breakfast so the mules would have plenty of water at noon break. I would plan to get water to the field hands between eight and eight-thirty, about the time the singing began. This was not too difficult if the workers happened to be in the nearby cotton fields, but sometimes they were a mile or more away; that would require me to allow time for several rest stops along the way. I would pump each bucket almost full, place a dipper in each bucket, grab my straw hat and take off. When my arms ached really bad from the heavy weight of the buckets, I would stop for a short time and rest, but I couldn't rest long because the water would warm, and part of my job was to get the water to the field hands while it was cool enough to be re-freshing.

One of the buckets was marked with a red cloth string tied to the bucket handle; one of the dippers also had a red cloth string tied to it. The red-marked bucket and dipper were for the colored field hands. The un-marked bucket and dipper were for the white field hands. It was my job not to get the buckets and dippers mixed up in any way. I accepted this task but at times I questioned it, since the water and the buckets and the dippers were the same. No one had ever explained to me why it was done; I had learned it by observation when I was younger. I walked as fast as I could the long distance to the field hands, trying my best not to slosh too much water from the buckets. I carried the unmarked bucket of water to Uncle Will first, since he was the man in charge. He would spit out an old wad of chewing tobacco, take a half-dipper of water, slosh it around in his mouth and spit it out. He'd do this twice; then he'd drink two dippers of water and give his approval or disapproval. If the water was cool enough to be refreshing he would say simply, "Good water," after his second dipper and go back to work immediately hoeing cotton. If the water was not cool enough he would say, "The water is a little warm" I wanted to do anything to keep him from saying that.

If the field hands happened to be working in the far-back fields, I would take off in a half-running trot and rest as little as possible in order to keep the water cool. I got very few disapprovals through the years.

After Uncle Will drank his water I would take the unmarked bucket and dipper around to the white field hands. After all the white workers had their water, I would take the red-marked bucket and dipper to the colored field hands. I would begin with Old Jim, who was over eighty years old; he was the oldest and was considered to be their leader. Getting around to thirty field hands with the water often took a long time, and when the last person had drunk I would head back to the pump at the home place. The three plowmen somewhere out on the farm also had to have water. If I didn't get to them on the way out to the cotton choppers, I would have to find them on the way back, at which time I often would pour the water from the unmarked bucket into the red-marked bucket, because all of the plowmen on the farm were colored. By the time I found the plowmen and quenched their thirst, it was usually time to hurry back to the pump and draw water to carry to the fields for the late morning trip.

As a water boy, there was very little time to rest and no time to play, but I loved it. At dinner time, straight-up noon, Aunt Annie would ring the huge bell on top of the pole off of the back porch; that bell could be heard for miles around. If I happened to be back from my two morning rounds of carrying water, sometimes she would let me ring the bell.

Everyone got an hour and a half for dinner and rest. Dinner at Aunt Annie's was the big meal of the day, with cornbread, pork meat, fresh vegetables, green onions and pie or cake for dessert. After dinner Uncle Will took a long nap on his back on the rear porch; I took a nap too. After my nap I would pump water for the mules, since the trough was usually near-empty after they had returned to the lot from their work. At one-thirty the field hands gathered from their various resting places, and Uncle Will led them slowly back to the fields where they would chop weeds from the rows of cotton until the sun reached the horizon, marking the end of the work day. I carried them water about mid-afternoon and again later in the day. I was always pumping water for the mules between trips and looking for the plowmen. At mid-afternoon, when the sun was at its hottest, Bug Eye would start the colored folks singing again; it seemed that their afternoon singing was much louder and fuller of spirit.

At sundown the tired and weary workers with their hoes on their shoulders trudged slowly down the dusty roads to their respective living quarters, followed shortly by the plowmen with their mules. The cotton choppers had completed a full day's work for which they each would be paid seventy-five cents a day at the end of the week. The plowmen were paid a dollar a day.

There was lots to do before supper. Uncle Will fed the stock while I pumped more water for the mules. Aunt Annie would have covered the table with a large tablecloth after noon dinner, and supper was the same food as dinner but sometimes some of the food was warmed over.

It was nearly dark as we sat a while on the front porch before bed. Aunt Annie would be in her porch swing, swaying with the slightest motion. Uncle Will sat in a porch chair, looking straight ahead and offering very little conversation. I would either sit on the front porch steps or lie down between Aunt Annie and Uncle Will. We listened to the crickets gradually getting louder and louder, while the birds fussed in the trees before they settled in for the night. Aunt Annie sometimes would ask me to sing a song for them, and often I would. After a while we would go into the living room and by the light of a single kerosene lamp Aunt Annie would read aloud some scripture from the Bible. Then we would go to bed. I would go to the far back bedroom, where I listened to the night birds calling and other sounds out in the darkness. I thought about the happenings of the day and watched the stars before I fell asleep.

If it didn't rain, every day was pretty much the same as the day before. At Aunt Annie and Uncle Will's place, the sound of the mourning dove in the woods lot reminded me throughout the day of a sense of aloneness in the sparse Bootheel area. The stillness was so real I could hear the soft winds blowing. Up there I learned to love the enduring silence and became a friend to solitude.

As the summer went by, I got better as a water boy. I learned to climb up a young elm tree in the backyard and search out the exact location of the workers in the fields, so I could time my arrival with the water at the end of the cotton rows. That way if I had to walk out into the high cotton fields, I avoided getting grasshoppers and other bugs in the buckets. I timed my deliveries to the nearest spot from the pump house to save my energy. I learned that several times a day John Barnes Thompson would drive out in his car to survey the progress of the workers; if I timed it just right I could hitch a ride with my buckets of water. I took pride in carrying water to hard-working people who were always ready for a cool drink. Most of them would say, "Thank you, water boy," or show some other kind of appreciation.

I got to know some of the workers very well, but others didn't talk much. Besides Old Jim, there was Essie, a colored lady who had five children working with her in the fields. One child was a boy not much older than myself, and the oldest was a girl about sixteen. There were the Malcombs, a colored family of five that had a grown son called Spook who had fallen in an open fireplace as a child. His face was scarred and distorted; one eye looked bigger than the other, and his mouth had grown together on one side, causing him difficulty in getting water from the dipper into his mouth. Spook's appearance bothered me at first, but as the summer wore on I could tell that Spook was really a fine person. He couldn't smile and had no expression at all on his face, but I sensed that he was good.

By the middle of the summer in 1936, my favorite person working in the fields—besides my Uncle Will—was plowman Judd. I watched the three colored men harnessing their separate teams of mules from time to time at the mule barn, and I watched them drive the mules to and from the fields; Judd always seemed to have such good control of Sue and Sal, the black mules. Sue and Sal were the oldest mules of the three teams on the farm and were not considered the best. The red mules, Daisy and May, and the gray mules, Kate and Meg, were younger and stronger; they had been claimed by John Barnes Thompson's grandsons, Doolie and Toby. The old black mules were the only ones left, so I claimed them as mine.

Plowman Judd was strong, stout and friendly. When I brought the cool water to him he would take time to talk a little; once he said, "Alvin Junior, you about the best water boy I'ze ever knowed." One day I had walked a mile and a half to the farback forty before I realized that the red cloth string wasn't on the handle of the dipper in the colored bucket. There wasn't time to walk all the way back, and the plowmen really needed water, so all three drank from the white folks dipper and said nothing. As I turned to leave, Judd said, "Alvin Junior, that's about the best water I'ze ever had in my whole life," as a smile played across his face. I never said anything about it to anyone, not even Uncle Will.

I asked Uncle Will once who was the best plowman on the farm. "Judd's the best," he replied; Uncle
Will was not one to elaborate.

"Well, why does he have the old mules Sue and Sal
to work with? Why doesn't he have the better mules?"

"Well, Alvin Junior," he answered, "Judd has a way
with mules. He has worked with them so long, the
mules know him and he knows them, and he gets
them to work like young mules." I figured that I sort of
knew what he meant.

Late one afternoon, just as I had returned from my
last trip to the fields, John Barnes Thompson drove up
in his car and asked if I wanted to look over the crops
with him. I got in his car and we drove out and
watched the field hands chop for a while; then we
drove about two miles to the back side of the farm
where the plowmen were working. It was almost sundown; he stopped the car and we got out and walked
into the recently plowed field. Mr. Thompson examined some of the blooms on a few cotton stalks,
checking for signs of cotton worms. Judd was finishing
his last row for the day, since the sun had just dropped
below the horizon. He pulled his cultivator out of the
field, unhitched the team of mules, and had a short
conversation with Mr. Thompson. As Judd turned the
team of mules around to head back to the mule lot, he
turned to me and said, "Water boy, you wanna ride ol'
Sue back to the mule lot?"

"Sure!" I said.

Judd's big hands picked me up like I was no heavier than one of Aunt Annie's feather pillows; he straddled me on ol' Sue and we headed for the home place. Nothing yet in my life had been quite as wonderful as riding that mule down those straight dirt roads in the stillness of the blue-gray day. Mr. Thompson went on his way back to Steele, and I rode ol' Sue all the way to the gate of the mule lot at the home place where Judd helped me down to the ground. "You'll have to ride ol' Sue some more, water boy," he said.

"I sure will. I sure do thank you," I replied.

He took the mules into the mule lot, and I hurried to the pump house to make sure the mule trough was full of water. All six of the mules wallowed in the sand before they came to the mule trough to drink. After supper I had to pump extra water for about an hour for the mules, because the temperature had almost reached ninety degrees that day, and the mules drank more water on hot days.

In a lucky week I got to ride ol' Sue two or three times. I was careful to not neglect my work or chores in the process, but if I got the chance on any day, I'd ride that mule. One week the workers cut and baled hay for several days, and the hay-baler was such a loud machine that it made the home place almost as noisy as the downtown streets of Memphis. I carried water out to the men at the hay barn and watched Judd pick up those bales of hay and throw them up on the wagons. That night on the front porch I asked Uncle Will if he knew anybody stronger than Judd.

"Nobody's stronger than Judd," Uncle Will said; he answered in a way I knew meant that was all he wanted to say about Judd that night.

I replied, "Yep, he sure is strong." We sat in silence until we got up and went into the living room for Aunt Annie's scripture reading. Children in those days learned by listening; sometimes they learned by listening when they weren't supposed to. I had learned from listening both ways that Judd had no children, but he had a woman named Liddy Mae. She worked in the fields sometimes, but more often helped clean and cook at John Barnes Thompson's home over in Steele. Liddy Mae had helped Aunt Annie can fruit and vegetables on several occasions. She and all the other colored folks lived in a row of small gray shacks, a place they called Shaw Town, off the road behind some willow trees and over a ditch bank about three-quarters of a mile west of the home place. One day Aunt Annie sent me with two fruit jars of peaches to Shaw Town to place them on Liddy Mae and Judd's front porch. Aunt Annie told me it was the third house in a row of seven, the one with the blue curtains. Their weathered gray house was surrounded with beds of zinnias in all colors. The next time I saw Liddy Mae I told her I thought she had pretty zinnias in her yard and that seemed to please her.

Doolie, John Barnes Thompson's grandson, would come out from Steele sometimes to spend time on the farm, and we would talk about things. He told me that a few years back Judd had taken a team of mules and wagon to the river bottoms to cut wood for winter, and he had found a man trapped under several tree logs that had accidentally rolled over on him. The man was still alive under those logs, moaning and calling for help. All by himself Judd lifted those big logs off that man and carried him into Cottonwood Point to a doctor, saving the man's life. Later that day the injured man's people went to the river bottoms to get his mules and the wagon and logs, and it took four men to move every log that Judd had moved by himself.

"Judd's almost the strongest person alive," Doolie said.

"He sure is," I replied.

I learned a strange thing from talking with Doolie. The previous spring Uncle Will and John Barnes Thompson had planned to go across the river to Dyersburg to get some farm equipment; the trip was to take two days. Aunt Annie was deathly afraid to stay by herself, but all the relatives were too busy to visit and Uncle Will didn't have time to take her anywhere. Uncle Will and Mr. Thompson arranged for Liddy Mae to sneak down just after dark each night and sleep in the side room of the home place so Aunt Annie wouldn't be afraid. Liddy Mae would get up before daylight and go back to Shaw Town so no one in the county would know that Aunt Annie had let a colored woman sleep in her home. It was a secret, but everyone knew about it. As far as I knew no one had given Aunt Annie and Uncle Will any trouble about it. I know I never got brave enough even to ask about it.

One day a car drove up at the home place as I was pumping water in the pump house. A tough-looking man got out and walked into the yard. Aunt Annie came out on the porch, and I walked out to the end of the porch.

"Ma'am," the man said politely, "I'm trying to find a nigger named Clayton Biggs. Do you know if he works on this farm?"

"No one named Clayton Biggs works on this farm," Aunt Annie replied.

"Well, that nigger owes us four dollars for groceries over at Number 9 store, and I'm atryin' to catch up with him." He looked over at me but said nothing. "Well, I'll be on my way," he said. "I do thank you." The man drove away.

That night on the front porch I mentioned the man to Uncle Will and asked why some folks called colored folks "niggers" and other folks didn't. He didn't answer for a long time. "Well, Alvin Junior," he finally said, "colored folks will be colored folks to some and niggers to others. That's the way it is." I wondered if that was supposed to mean something to me.

After a while, I said, "My mother said I should never use the word 'nigger.'"

After about a minute of silence Uncle Will replied, "You'd better do what your mother says do." Aunt Annie's scripture that night was about Cain slaying his brother Abel, and afterwards she briefly discussed her version of how the Lord set a mark on Cain and that was why some folks were colored and some were not. I didn't at all understand.

Every Saturday morning we took turns taking a bath in the large wash tub in the side room. On Saturday afternoons the white and colored folks all went to town to get groceries and supplies. Most times the colored men would walk over to Cooter, and someone would take a team of mules and a wagon to carry the women and children and to bring back the food and staples. It was a well-known fact that many white and colored folks would do a lot of whiskey drinking and gambling over at Cooter on Saturdays. The white and colored folks had their separate sides of town where they would drink, revel and raise Cain.

John Barnes Thompson would drive Uncle Will to Cooter in his car every Saturday for a shave and a haircut and a few groceries. I would go along but was careful not to spend too much of my hard-earned money on candy and soda pops. I did a lot of walking around and one time I saw the area in the back of the downtown stores where the colored men were drinking and yelling and having a wild time. Then we would return to the home place early in the afternoon, but often late on Saturday nights I could hear the colored folks yelling and singing and sometimes fighting over at Shaw Town.

All summer I put my weekly wages of two dollars and fifty cents into a fruit jar that I kept in the back bedroom. I planned to return to Memphis with as much money as possible, so I could help buy my school supplies and have picture show and candy money during the school year. It rained a few days, but John Barnes Thompson gave me some special jobs so that I wouldn't miss my fifty cents a day.

Some days we would spend several hours in the storm house if a dark cloud appeared because Aunt Annie was deathly afraid of high winds and cyclones, but most days were peaceful and hot. There was no electricity at Uncle Will's nor anywhere else in the rural Bootheel area, but they did have a telephone with five other party-lines. Uncle Will told Aunt Annie that some day he might buy her a battery radio. She had wanted one for many years, but Uncle Will had little use for things like that.

As the summer wore on I got to know Judd better, and he continued to let me ride ol' Sue every chance he got. One Sunday afternoon John Barnes Thompson drove over from Steele, parked out front and asked Uncle Will to come to the car and talk with him. They must have talked thirty minutes while Aunt Annie and I sat under a shade tree; I was practicing a new game of Mumble Peg that Uncle Will had shown me. I knew that something must be wrong; they usually didn't talk that long unless something serious was going on. They got out of the car and walked over to the shade trees; we sat there and talked about the weather and everyday things for a while. I knew, though, that something was wrong. At supper Aunt Annie asked Uncle Will what Mr. Thompson wanted to talk about so long; Uncle Will just ignored her question and said nothing. Later, out on the front porch, Aunt Annie asked again about their long talk. Uncle Will said, "There's been a problem over at Cooter." She didn't ask for any more information, but I knew she would. After we went to bed I eased up in the darkness into the dining room near their bedroom, and I heard Uncle Will give Aunt Annie enough information so that she would let him get some sleep. He told her that a colored man who worked over on Bill Wagner's farm was found dead Sunday morning behind the stores in Cooter. Uncle Will had a deep voice, so I could hear him well. He said they were not sure if the man had just died of natural causes or if he had been killed. "They're examining the body over at Caruthersville tomorrow."

I tiptoed back into the back bedroom and thought for a long time about what Uncle Will had said before I fell asleep.

Monday morning things seemed to be normal enough; the cotton choppers were working in the north-eighty field, and the plowmen were working back in the south fields. This made it difficult for me because it meant special trips to the plowmen in a different direction. When I reached the south-eighty field at midmorning, I waited for Judd to finish a row out in the middle of the field to give him his water. When he got to the rows end, he called the mules to a stop with a "haw," and then took his dipper of water. I could tell he wasn't feeling well. Too, there was a big swollen knot on the side of his head.

"I thank you, water boy; I thank you for the water, he said." He turned the mules around and began plowing again. It wasn't like Judd to talk just a little. I carried the other plowmen some water and went about my trips to the other fields.

At dinner I asked Uncle Will if he had seen the big knot on Judd's head. "Hadn't seen Judd today," he replied, and I knew that was all I was going to get from him.

That afternoon as I returned from the fields, I saw John Barnes Thompson in his car headed out fast to the plowmen working in the south fields. He stayed out there talking with Judd for a long time. Then Mr. Thompson drove back to the main road and headed east toward his home in Steele. Judd brought his team of mules back early to the mule lot at the home place about an hour before sundown. He'd never done that before.

We didn't talk much at supper that night. When we did talk it was about Aunt Annie's plans to visit her sister in Blytheville. On the porch that night, before scripture reading and bed, we sat quietly and listened to the night sounds. We were all thinking to ourselves. Just after I went to bed, before I fell asleep, I heard the motor and saw the lights of a car pass in front of the home place and drive down towards Shaw Town. A little later the same car passed back by in front of the home place and went east.

The next morning, after all the cotton choppers had left with Uncle Will to the north-eighty field, I noticed that the mules Sue and Sal were still in the mule lot. They stood at the big gate as if they had been left behind; they looked as if they knew something was wrong. When I reached Uncle Will with the water that morning, I said, "Uncle Will, Judd's not plowing the fields this morning."

"Maybe he's sick," he replied. "I'll go down and check at dinner."

After dinner, instead of taking his nap, Uncle Will put on his hat, went out to the road, and started walking towards Shaw Town. I asked if I could go with him.

"You'd better stay here," he replied. When Uncle Will returned in about twenty-five minutes, he went to the back porch and took his nap. He didn't say anything, and I didn't ask anything. I took a nap, too.

That afternoon, as I carried my two buckets across the yard, I saw two cars coming from the east as fast as they could come, and dust was swirling behind them so thick it looked like the smoke from a forest fire. They zoomed on by, headed towards Shaw Town. In about five minutes they zoomed back by and turned and headed to the north-eighty field where the field hands were working. I climbed an elm tree and could see men get out of both cars and go out into the fields with shotguns. In a short time, they got in their cars, crossed the main road, and went to the south-eighty field. I couldn't get high enough in the tree to see them, since the plowmen that day were working on the back side of the south-eighty field. In about ten minutes the two cars came back to the main road and headed east, leaving the swirling dust behind them.

When I carried the water out to the field hands no one was talking much, at least not to me. Uncle Will was busy sharpening hoes, and I could tell he didn't want any questions. When I reached the south-eighty field I asked the younger of the two plowmen working that day, "What about the men in the two cars?"

"That was the sheriff looking for Judd," he said, and he was shaky in his talking. "Someone claims Judd kilt one of Mr. Wagner's field hands last Sa'day night over at Cooter." He paused for a little bit. "Judd wouldn't do that," he said.

I hurried back to the house and Aunt Annie confirmed what I had learned. "Lordy me," she said, "I just can't believe Judd would do that; he can't do bad."

At supper the three of us sat with little to say, and when I tried to bring up what had happened that day Uncle Will just ignored me. After chores and feeding the stock, we sat on the front porch and watched the blue-gray evening turn into darkness. There was a stillness that night that was different, and the birds seemed to fuss very little. After a while I couldn't stay quiet any longer. I asked, "Uncle Will, what happened to Mr. Wagner's farm hand at Cooter?"

A long time passed; Aunt Annie started humming a little church song, and after a while Uncle Will said, "Someone broke his neck. They found him dead with a broken neck." Uncle Will stood up and went to secure the farm buildings because it looked like a storm was coming. It blew over, however, and we didn't have to go to the storm house that night.

Things were solemn the rest of that week. For some reason John Barnes Thompson had not been on the farm since Monday, but he finally showed up on Friday. His grandson Doolie was with him and Doolie helped me by carrying one of my buckets of water to the field hands. Doolie said folks in Steele believed Judd had broken Mr. Wagner's field hand's neck in a drunken fight in Cooter on Saturday night.

"You know," Doolie said, "Judd can't be found anywhere, and they've searched all over the county." He went on, "Grandpa thinks Judd didn't do it, but lots of folks do. Do you think Judd broke that man's neck, Alvin Junior?" he asked me.

"No, I don't," I replied. "Where do you think Judd is?" I asked.

"Some folks think he's gone far away, he replied."

John Barnes Thompson decided to finish up the plowing that year with just two teams of mules, so Sue and Sal were given a well-deserved rest. Uncle Will said no one could get Sue and Sal to work but Judd. Of course, my rides on ol' Sue were over. Late in the summer they laid the crops by, and a water boy was not needed, so I made plans to visit some of my other relatives throughout Pemiscot County. After a short visit to my Uncle Virgil's over by the Mississippi River, I decided to visit my grandmother and various aunts and uncles and cousins who lived around Tyler and Cottonwood Point.

On the way to my grandmother's house near Tyler, it was getting late, so I stopped for a while at my cousin Luther's house on Jabo Nichols big farm, thinking I might spend the night there. Luther had a young wife who seldom talked and two small children. I had been there about ten minutes when cousin Luther asked me, "Alvin Junior, did you know that nigger on the Thompson place that broke that other nigger's neck over at Cooter?"

Somehow the way he asked the question made me feel really bad. "His name was Judd," I said tersely. "He was a good worker, a good plowman, and a good man, and I liked him a lot; I don't think he broke any body's neck."

Cousin Luther, who was a field worker in his mid-thirties, looked at me dumbfounded from hearing a reply like that from someone so young. I had been taught that older people were always right and should be respected even if they were wrong, but I lost control that day. He just stood there and stared at me. Finally, he said, "Well, they say he's one strong nigger anyway."

It was more than an hour away, but I decided to walk on to Grandmother's and not spend the night at cousin Luther's. I told them good-bye and left. I spent several days with Grandmother and other relatives in the area, and then in late August my summer vacation in the Bootheel was over for that year. I returned to Memphis with a total savings of twenty-eight dollars and fifty cents.

That winter Mother and I got several newsy letters from my grandparents, Aunt Annie and others about things in the Bootheel. In one letter my grandmother wrote that some folks thought harm might have come to Judd since he had completely disappeared.

"Some folks think he might be dead," she wrote. She also said that the Wagner family was mad about losing their best field hand. Aunt Annie's letter in November was a bit more cheerful; she wrote that Uncle Will was finally thinking about getting her a battery radio for her birthday to help keep her company. Her letter mentioned that Liddy Mae had disappeared sometime earlier, just like Judd had, but most folks thought that she had gone to meet Judd somewhere up north. Aunt Annie also wrote that the mule Sal had gotten sick and died in October. No one wanted ol' Sue by herself, and no one would buy her, so it was decided to destroy her.

Ol' Sue was no longer worth her feed, she wrote. At the end of the letter Aunt Annie said John Barnes Thompson had mentioned to Uncle Will that he wanted me to carry water to the field hands the coming summer. I knew that I would, but I also knew it would never be the same.

The Circle in the Field

IN LATE JULY or early August when the crops were laid by and I could no longer earn fifty-cents-a-day wages carrying water to field hands, I started my yearly adventures of walking out across the flat Bootheel land to see my many relatives. A walk of only four or five miles in any direction down straight and dusty roads would get me to another aunt's or cousin's house where there would be new things to talk about, to do and to see. I felt important telling them exciting things about Memphis, just seventy miles down the river. You could always count on something special being cooked for supper and after we ate we would all sit and talk late into the night.

I had already spent a short time at my Uncle Virgil's place that summer in 1936, riding a goat cart and attending a river revival. I had returned to my Aunt Annie's for a few days before deciding to take off and visit my Grandmother Bradie and other relatives between Tyler and Cottonwood Point, a distance of about seven miles. I always left early enough on any of these walking trips to arrive at my destination before dark, and I had little fear of anything with the exception of mad dogs and blue racer snakes. That particular day was hot and muggy, so I went by way of Cooter and bought me a Pepsi and a jelly-roll cake. I stopped and watched a ball game for a while at the Cooter school and lost a little time. I decided to walk to my cousin Luther's house about three miles from there. I had plans to spend the night, but things didn't work out; it was getting late, so I started east on the road to Cottonwood Point toward my grandmother's house.

I got lucky, because a man in a truck who was on his way to the Greenway Gin and Store gave me a ride, leaving me just a little over a mile to walk. When I was a quarter-mile away from Grandmother's house, I saw several women sitting around in straight chairs out under the shade tree in the front yard. My grandmother saw me coming down the road and came to the edge of the yard, greeting me with a strong hug; all three of their dogs ripped around and jumped on me with their greetings, too.

"Me and my women friends are talking over some matters, Alvin Junior. Now, you just make yourself at home, and I'll be inside in a little while to make you some tea cookies." Grandmother spoke warmly, but she sounded like she needed to continue her business with the women. She did take me over close to the group and said, "This here is Carrie's boy, Alvin Junior; they live in Memphis." She always said this as if she were proud to have a daughter and grandson living in a city. The women didn't seem to be that concerned with me one way or the other and continued to fan their serious faces; it had been another cloudless, no-breeze summer day. I went on inside the house with my little suitcase.

By that time my Aunt Virginia, who was back in the kitchen preparing supper, had discovered I was there. She hugged me good and helped me get some cool pump water out on the back porch. We sat and talked for a little while, and I finally asked Aunt Virginia about all those women outside.

"Well, Alvin Junior," she replied, "I don't rightly know how to tell you." She didn't say anymore, because she looked out the window and saw the women leaving in all directions. Aunt Virginia realized that Grandmother was coming back into the house, so she said quietly, "I'll tell you all about it later," and went about her kitchen duties.

Those were the times most grown folks believed young children should be told very little about anything. Good children were those who asked few questions and showed no curiosity at all. Aunt Virginia was about seventeen years of age and for some reason had never married. She had let me in on a lot of secrets in the past, and I knew she would bring me up to date on everything when she got the chance.

Grandpa Pete and the other men got home about dark from various farm jobs in the area. We all sat around the table at supper eating beans, biscuits, side meat, sliced tomatoes, sweet onions and corn on the cob. Meals were served on a blue-checkered oil cloth, placed over a long heavy eating table. Meals at my grandmothers house were not fancy, but always tasty. She believed in a hot meal three times a day, with fresh bread for each meal, but she did not believe in having desserts very often. Sorghum molasses was always on the table and, in season, she cooked dewberry cobbler.

The men started asking me questions about Memphis and the city life, and I had lots to tell them, but after supper the conversation changed. We were sitting out on the front porch in early darkness when, during a lull, Grandmother announced to Grandpa Pete, "Some of the women of the area came over here today, and in a few days we are a-plannin' to go over to see that place at the Bigelow farm."

There was dead silence. Grandpa Pete said, "Best you women forget about going over there. You won't know any more than you do before you go." More silence followed. "Best you women don't go," Grandpa Pete said again.

"We're a-goin'," Grandmother said.

I had no idea what they were talking about, but in the moonlight I had Aunt Virginia's eye and could tell that she would fill me in later. They talked a little more but didn't discuss the Bigelow farm anymore. Grandmother said, "It's a little late for making tea cookies, Alvin Junior, but I'll make you some tomorrow."

I went on to bed in the back room that faced south. I was awed by the utter stillness of the Bootheel nights, which was only slightly disturbed by strange night sounds and the occasional call of a night bird. There was not much of a breeze that moonlit night. I was always a little frightened by the dark, eerie silence of the nights there, but in a strange way I also loved it.

At breakfast everyone was quiet and slightly grumpy. Aunt Virginia had fixed a big wooden bowl of chocolate gravy to go with biscuits, side meat, and potatoes. I was pleased that she had not made me any baby biscuits, since I was going on eleven years of age and was also earning money. In the Bootheel it was a custom in several of my aunt's homes to use very small biscuit cutters to make baby biscuits for the children. It was a sign of a child's coming of age when they were no longer served the baby biscuits. Aunt Virginia's biscuits were wonderful and as big as saucers. I poured chocolate gravy over two big biscuits I'd broken apart and didn't eat much side meat and potatoes. The men talked about dreading their work that day. Then they finally got up, put on their hats and jumpers and left.

Grandmother went out to the small garden to pick string beans and left Aunt Virginia to clean the kitchen and wash the dishes; I helped Aunt Virginia. She told me about the work the men were doing. Grandpa Pete and Uncle Charlie were helping build a barn over on the Nichols place, and Uncle T. L. and Uncle Doss were doing some work on the roads for the county. Uncle Doss was really my cousin; he was the son of my Uncle Eli, and wasn't very old—maybe about twenty-five—but I still called him uncle. I called most of my male cousins uncle since I was taught to show respect with a "Yes, sir" and a "No, sir" to any male who was at least a few years older.

Aunt Virginia finally got around to telling me about the place at the Bigelow farm. "Well," she said, "back in June one night, people all over the county saw strange things in the sky, and then a day or two later they found a big circle in one of Mr. Bigelow's cotton fields."

"What kind of circle?" I asked.

"All I know is it's a big circle that's been burned right out in the middle of one of his cotton fields. They say the cotton was burned so bad that nothing was left but a few stalks. Everything was burned to a crisp," she said. Grandmother came in with a large dishpan of beans, so Aunt Virginia didn't say any more.

The three of us sat on the back porch and pulled strings and snapped beans. Afterwards, I went out and played with the dogs for a while. I noticed someone had planted two large zinnia beds in the backyard; they looked pretty. I wondered if my mother's zinnias in our backyard in Memphis were doing as well.

About mid-afternoon I saw a woman walking down the road toward the house and mentioned it to Grandmother. She went out and met the woman, and they stood under a shade tree in the yard and talked about thirty minutes. The woman left back down the road and grandmother came into the house. That night after supper, as usual, we all sat out on the front porch. The grownups talked about the happenings of the day and other things. Suddenly, several of us saw a falling star over in the east sky. Uncle T. L. said, "There goes one, by golly! By tomorrow they will be reporting that as a wagon of fire pulled by burning horses." Uncle Doss giggled a little.

"Best we don't make fun of things like that, Doss," my grandmother said firmly.

"Now, Aunt Bradie, everyone has made entirely too much about things going on in the sky lately; nobody has seen anything more than a shootin' star."

"Well, we can't be all that sure it ain't nothin'," Uncle Charlie asserted.

Uncle T. L. started talking and cursing bad, and Grandmother said, "That's enough of that, T. L., and he stopped." Grandpa Pete had said nothing. Aunt Virginia just smiled at me, as I seemed to be spellbound by the mystery of it all.

"Wha'd they see?" I asked Uncle Doss.

Before he could answer, my grandmother spoke up quickly with a touch of anger in her voice, "Now, look, you'll scare this young'un to death with all this talk. Best we not get into all this tonight."

Aunt Virginia was still smiling, and I knew I'd get more information later. We were quiet for a while; after a bit Grandmother said, "Pete, the women are still a-plannin' to go over to the Bigelow farm one of these days and see that place in the field."

He didn't respond; everyone looked at Grandpa. He sat there for a long time before saying, "Best you women forget about going over there; you won't know any more than you did before you go."

No one spoke, so we listened to the crickets for a while. Sometime later Grandmother said, "We're a-goin' over there, Pete." There was no response. We all got up and went to bed.

The next morning I could smell breakfast cooking, so I went up to the eating room early. "Well, young man, are you ready for biscuits and chocolate gravy this morning?" Grandmother asked cheerfully.

"Yes, ma'am," I answered.

"Well, we'll have it ready in just a little bit," she replied.

Aunt Virginia was tending to the side meat and potatoes on the big black stove.

"You know, Alvin Junior, I clean forgot to make you tea cookies yesterday," Grandmother said.

"Aw, that's all right," I replied.

"Well, my mind has been a little bumfuzzled lately. I won't forget today," she said with a smile. I spooned the chocolate gravy over the big biscuits and began eating before the men arrived. I went outside and played with the dogs as the men ate, and in a little while they were off to their work. As soon as they were out of sight, Grandmother put on her bonnet and told Aunt Virginia to clean the kitchen and wash the dishes.

"I'm going over to visit some folks for about an hour or so. I'll be back for dinner."

Dinner was not a big deal at that time, since all the men were carrying biscuits and side meat sandwiches in their dinner buckets for their noon meals at work. As I helped Aunt Virginia with cleaning and washing dishes, she started telling me more about things seen in the sky and the circle in the field.

"Well," she said, "a woman who lives over on the Cottonwood Point road claims she saw a wagon on fire goin' across the sky about ten o'clock one night.

Another woman all the way over at Red Town—on that same night—said she saw it too, but it had what looked like horses pulling it." She went on, "One of Mr. Howard's daughters said she saw a red devil in a rocking chair in the sky one night. There were about twenty or thirty reports of things in the sky according to the Caruthersville newspaper." She continued, "Then this field hand found that circle burned in the Bigelow cotton field shortly thereafter. It sure has got people riled up and scared. Some people have been praying a lot more lately."

"Have you seen anything, Aunt Virginia?" I asked.

"Nope, and I hope I don't," she replied.

Grandmother returned and she and Aunt Virginia did washing by boiling clothes in a big black kettle out in the backyard all afternoon. Grandmother kept the stove fire going from dinner, and about midafternoon she went into the kitchen and made me tea cookies. I ate so many I wasn't very hungry for supper.

That night as we sat on the front porch, I could tell that everyone was avoiding any talk about things in the sky or circles in the fields. We talked about the heat, and Uncle Charlie talked about walking over to Henry Bostick's house the next night to listen to a prize fight between Jack Sharkey and a new colored boxer named Joe Louis. The Bosticks had just bought a new battery radio. Henry Bostick had seen Uncle Charlie at the Greenway Gin and Store and invited him—and anyone else who wanted to—to come over. This was a big thing for Uncle Charlie, because at

Grandmother's house there was no electricity, no telephone, no running water or anything except a hand pump for water and a lot of sky and space.

Right out of the blue Uncle Doss asked me, "Alvin Junior, have you ever had a sugar tit?" He asked me that question so quickly I was stunned, and even though I was sitting in the dark on the porch, I was sure everyone knew that I was embarrassed. I tried to remember what some of Uncle Virgil's boys had told me about sugar tits when I had visited there earlier, but my mind wouldn't work.

"What's that?" I asked finally.

"You mean you are going on eleven years old and you ain't had a sugar tit yet?" Then I remembered that sometimes grown people in the Bootheel put a little sugar in a small rag and tied it up with string, so it was about the size of a sows tit, and they asked a child to suck on it like a baby pig until the sugar was all gone. It was supposed to be a custom in the Bootheel when a child got to be nine or ten years old. It was said to be part of growing up.

"I haven't had one and I don't want one," I answered.

Uncle Doss said, "T. L., go in the kitchen and make this boy a sugar tit."

I was sitting on the edge of the porch, so I got up to flee the situation, but Uncle Charlie grabbed me right quick and started laughing; then Uncle Doss helped hold me.

"Now, boys," Grandmother said, "I'm not so sure that Alvin Junior should be treated like a regular Bootheel boy; he lives in Memphis."

"He was born here in the Bootheel and that's enough," Uncle Charlie answered.

I struggled to get away, but they just kept laughing. Uncle Doss said, "The more you fight this, Alvin Junior, the worse it's gonna be. Take it like a little baby pig."

Uncle T. L. came out of the front door with it in his hand. Uncle Charlie had me by one arm; Uncle Doss had my other arm, and he had pushed me against the porch post. Uncle T. L. held the sugar tit about two inches from my mouth and said, "Now, Alvin Junior, open your mouth and suck this sugar tit."

"No!" I yelled.

He pushed it toward my mouth. I turned my head, kicked upward, and hit Uncle Doss hard in the stomach. He cursed loudly, and I started kicking with both feet as hard as I could. All three uncles started cursing bad, and Aunt Virginia said, "You all shouldn't be doin' this; this is ridiculous."

They held me down flat on the porch, but I turned my head from side to side so fast they couldn't get it in my mouth. One of them held my head, and eventually someone had to hold my nose, so that when I gasped for air they crushed that sugar tit in my mouth and held it there about a minute. My legs got loose again and I kicked T. L. hard in the chest. He cursed some more. Finally they let me go, satisfied that they got it in my mouth enough to say I had sucked a sugar tit. I never did suck it though.

"That's enough, boys," Grandmother said. "Leave him alone now."

"Well, now, Alvin Junior, you're on the way to bein' a man," Uncle T. L. announced.

I thought that was about the dumbest thing I had heard of. I wanted to cry, but I kept from it. The entire time Grandpa Pete just sat in his rocker, never said a word, and had a big grin on his face. Grandpa Pete had lost all of his teeth a few years earlier and refused to get false teeth, so his smile looked just like a big hole in his head. Aunt Virginia came over and put her arms around me and tried to comfort me.

Uncle Doss asked in a teasing way, "Was that a good sugar tit, Alvin Junior?"

"You pay him no mind," Aunt Virginia said.

"I have already said that's enough, boys," Grandmother said in a loud, firm way. "You've had your fun; now, leave him alone."

We went in the house and prepared for bed. My arms hurt where they had held me so tightly, and my mouth was sore from them forcing that thing in my mouth. I still felt bad, but I figured Id better not show how I felt or they might get the idea to do it again. I listened to the night sounds and heard the night birds calling, and finally fell asleep.

At breakfast most everyone was a little draggy and droopy. Aunt Virginia was the one who was always the most cheerful at breakfast.

Uncle Doss broke the silence with, "Was that sugar tit good last night, Alvin Junior?"

Grandmother responded quickly and in a loud voice, "Doss, that's enough of that; not one more word."

"All right, all right, Aunt Bradie," he replied, but I could tell from his face he didn't mean it. I decided right then that Uncle Doss had a little mean streak in him.

The men went to work and Aunt Virginia cleaned the kitchen. About ten o'clock that morning two women walked up into the front yard. Grandmother went outside; the three of them sat under a shade tree and talked. I moseyed up, pretending to be playing with one of the dogs, and heard them talking some more about going to see the circle in the field. When I lingered around and got too close, Grandmother would give me a certain stare, and I'd wander on off to the other side of the yard. I knew they were planning to go though, sooner or later.

At supper that night Uncle Charlie talked to the men about walking over to the Bostick place to hear the prize fight. They all planned to go, and Uncle Charlie said they had to leave in about thirty minutes to make it on time. Grandmother, realizing that there would be no porch talking that night, said, "Pete, some of us women are going over there to the Bigelow farm tomorrow to see if we can find that circle in the field. We might be a little late getting back, but Virginia will fix supper for you."

All of the men acted like they didn't like that idea. "I've said it before," Grandpa Pete said, "best you women don't go over there; you won't know any more than you did before you go."

"We're a-goin'," Grandmother said.

I sat out on the porch as the men prepared to leave for the Bostick place. Uncle T. L. and Uncle Doss shaved and washed up good and put on some smelling lotion. Uncle Charlie and Grandpa Pete planned to go just as they were, having worked all day, and they were awfully dirty and smelly. The men gathered in the front yard, then walked a short distance down the road where they stopped and talked for a while. Uncle Charlie hollered back, "Alvin Junior, you come on and go with us."

I asked Grandmother if I should go. "Go on with 'em, boy, and have some fun," she answered. "Go hear that prize fight with the men."

I ran and caught up with them but showed my respect by walking slightly behind them and staying out of their conversations. After about a quarter of a mile we came to a main dirt road and turned north; it was one of those straight roads that seldom curved and looked endless. Twilight was upon us, and the cricket sounds were getting louder. We walked at an easy pace, so it was not hard for me to keep up. We may have walked slowly because of Grandpa Pete. He was in his seventies and walked bent over like it hurt him to walk. No one talked much except Uncle T. L. and Uncle Doss, who were hoping there might be some young women at the Bostick place. Uncle T. L. and Uncle Doss were discussing prize fighting and both were referring to Joe Louis as a nigger fighter. I wasn't surprised about Uncle Doss, but I was a little surprised about Uncle T. L., because he was my mother's half-brother and she would not use that word.

I'd been walking all summer long, carrying water to field hands, and I didn't get tired, but there was something about straight roads that made me think I wasn't getting anywhere. This made me feel tired. When darkness came that night, the full moon turned the dusty road into a blue-silver color, and the road seemed to almost shine, with the dark cotton fields on both sides making it even more bright. Nothing broke up the sameness of long walks like this except an occasional bridge over a drainage ditch and a tree or two here and there. When no one talked there was just the soft sound of footsteps to break up the awesome stillness of the land. I had walked these roads alone before and sometimes felt that being far, far away from people like that made me feel good inside in a way I never felt with lots of people around. Even that night, when I was out there in that spacious place with my uncles and Grandpa, I started feeling good inside. I loved that feeling.

We walked and walked, and after a long while we saw a distant light on the right side of the road that Uncle Charlie said was the Bostick place. When we got closer we could hear the voices of the radio announcers talking about the two fighters. As we walked closer, we could see the radio set up on the front porch of their farm house. Uncle Charlie had timed our trip so we would get there fifteen minutes before the fight. About thirty grown folks, mainly men, stood around in the yard near the porch as quiet and as reverent as they would be in a church. I could see Uncle T. L. and Uncle Doss milling in and out of the crowd, looking for some young women. The sound of the radio wasn't very clear, and Grandpa Pete quietly kept asking me what they were saying.

We heard the introduction of the fighters, the clang of the bell and then the fight. Round one was over very fast, and it sounded to me like Joe Louis was the only one landing any blows. Round two was almost the same, but then in round three Joe Louis knocked out Jack Sharkey. After Joe Louis was announced the winner, everybody started talking, and then it was like being outside the church on Sunday morning. Uncle T. L. came up to us and said he and Uncle Doss would hang around there for a while, so we decided to go back home without them. In a short time Uncle Charlie and Grandpa Pete started back down the road with me about five yards behind. In another ten minutes we were out of hearing distance of anything from the Bostick place, and we walked in silence toward home. For a while as we walked, Uncle Charlie explained his theory about the prize fight and why Jack Sharkey didn't win. He was doing all of the talking. Eventually there was no conversation going on, so I eased up and walked even with them. Every minute or two Grandpa Pete would make a hurting sound like a dog whining. I asked him if he was all right.

"Jus' my bones, boy, jus' my bones," he said.

I thought about the fact that Grandpa Pete had never hugged me like my Uncle Will and some of my other uncles, and I wondered why. I knew he liked me, but he never seemed to want to do anything with me or talk to me much. My mother's real father had died when she was a little girl. Grandpa Pete was my step-grandpa, so I wasn't really his true-blood grandson, but it didn't matter to me. As we walked along in the warm silence of that night, down the blue-silver road, I reached up and took hold of Grandpa Pete's hand and walked with him that way for a while. He didn't make those hurting sounds quite as much. Uncle Charlie walked a little piece out ahead of us. After a while Grandpa Pete turned my hand loose and placed his hand on my left shoulder, shifting a little of his weight on me as we walked. He didn't make any hurting sounds anymore all the way home.

The next morning Uncle T. L. and Uncle Doss were late for breakfast. Grandmother spoke firmly to them about how bad it was to get to their jobs late like that. They paid her little attention. After dinner that day two women about sixty years of age came up to the house and waited outside on the porch as Grandmother gave instructions to Aunt Virginia about what to prepare for supper. The women sat in chairs on the porch and discussed their plans, which involved lots of complicated talk about the directions to the exact area of the Bigelow farm to find the circle in the field. I could tell they knew how to get to the Bigelow farm, but the two women had slightly different ideas about how to locate the right field on the farm and how to locate the exact area in the field once they found it. In that area of the Bootheel there was field after field after field of cotton, and I could tell the women were not overconfident with the directions they had received from their men folks. However, finally the women agreed that they had enough information and that they were going to go and find the circle in the field.

All along I had been fascinated with the mystery of it, and suddenly I became brave enough to ask Grandmother, "Let me go with you. I'm sure I can help in some way. I've carried water to the field hands all summer over on John Barnes Thompson's big farm, and I'm sure I could do something to help."

The other two women didn't appear to be at all agreeable with my request. Suddenly, I remembered climbing up high in the trees in Aunt Annie's backyard to see the location of cotton choppers in far-away fields. I knew that long ago when the Bootheel had been cleared often, a tree or two were left in each of those massive fields for shade and rest.

"You may need me to climb up a tree and help search out that circle in the field," I said. "I'm good at climbing trees, and I can get way up high and look out across the fields," I continued in a pleading manner.

"Please let me go, Grandmother, I'll not be any trouble."

One of the women who never smiled said, "It's all right with me, Bradie, let him go."

Nothing else was said, and within minutes we were heading north toward the Bigelow place. My grandmother and the two women were dressed in long dark dresses that reached almost to the ground. It was over ninety degrees that day, yet the women had long-sleeve blouses and each wore a bonnet. As I walked behind them I noticed they were small, thin women. They looked just like the women in one of Aunt Annie's pictures on her living room wall of three women working near haystacks in a field. Their bonnets were blue, white and orange, just like in the picture. My grandmother's bonnet was the blue one; I wondered if they had ever seen that picture. Before we had left the house, one of the women mentioned that the Bigelow place was about four miles away. We walked perhaps two miles north on a main dirt road before the women cut out across a narrow field road going east towards the river.

We came upon a gray shotgun house on this narrow road and stopped there; Grandmother asked a heavy woman standing on the porch if we could pump ourselves some cool water. The woman was friendly and replied, "Sure can." She seemed pleased to see people out there miles from nowhere. One of Grandmothers friends asked if she could use the woman's outhouse. "Sure can," she said, and in time everyone went to the outhouse. We sat on her porch and cooled off for a while. The women talked about the fact that back in June Mr. Bigelow had gotten tired of people tromping all over his cotton fields, looking for the circle in the field, so by July he quit telling folks where it was and asked people to stay away. The women had gotten this information from their husbands, and that was one reason the husbands were not giving many directions. The best information they had was that the circle was in one of Mr. Bigelow's fields about a quarter-mile north of a red barn on the old Tyler road.

The heavy woman walked out to a small orchard, brought back about six small apples in her apron, and offered us some. We each took one, washed it off at the pump and ate it as we went our way. We were taking a shortcut to the Bigelow place; this meant walking along a drainage ditch for about a half-mile. That part of the trip was weedy and I was ever so careful in watching out for blue-racer snakes. I mentioned my fear of blue-racers to my grandmother, and she said as hot as it was, they were all down in cool places near the ditch water. At last we were near what the women thought was the west side of the Bigelow farm. We stood in the middle of two roads that crossed, and one of the women said, "All that land on the right of this road goin' east is Bigelow land, and it goes all the way to the Mississippi River levee. He has about two-thousand acres of land, and it stretches south maybe a mile."

We could see the two barns far off, but one looked white and the other one was a dark-green color. Grandmother said, "Are you sure the barn is red, Gerta?" That's the first time I heard her call that woman by her name.

Gerta, who wore the orange bonnet, replied, "My Henry says it's a red barn, and that the circle is about a quarter of a mile north of that barn. It took a lot of doing for me to get that out of him."

We proceeded down the road toward the white barn. When we got fairly close we cut across the field toward it and tried to determine which field was north of the barn.

"Why are we doing this, Grandmother?" I asked. "This is a white barn."

"Well, Alvin Junior, her husband may have been wrong about the color." We scattered out and walked across the field that we thought was north of the barn. The cotton in all of the fields was as high as the top of my head, and in some fields it was even higher. We walked through that field and, after a long time, came out on a farm road on the other side; we did not find any circle. We turned back and walked another direction but found no circle. We decided to make our way to the next barn about three-quarters of a mile away. As we got closer we could see that it was definitely a dark green barn. I had been looking for a tree to climb, but there were none in that particular area. It was way past mid-afternoon when we reached the green barn. We walked north through a field out from the green barn but found nothing. Then we spread out in all directions from the barn but found nothing. We went back to the main road and Grandmother said, "We'd better give up and start home. It's gettin' late, and we want to get home before dark."

We saw a truck coming slowly down the road; it stopped, and the driver said, "Afternoon, ladies; you all looking for someone?"

Gerta said, "We thought we'd like to try and find the circle in the field that everybody's talked about so much."

"Well, ladies, that circle may be just a lot of talk." The man grinned, didn't say another word, and drove off. He acted like he didn't see me.

I had noticed that the green barn was a hay barn and was not fenced in, so I told Grandmother and the other women to rest on the side of the road and I'd see if I could get up in that barn, or up on something near the barn, and look out across the fields. I took off running through the cotton. Once inside the barn, I found a ladder that led up to the hay loft. I climbed up the ladder, walked over to an open end of the hay loft, and looked out as far as I could, but I saw nothing that looked like a circle. I went to the other end of the barn, looked out and saw no circle in the field. Perhaps a half-mile away, way off to the left, however, I spotted something like a thin pole sticking up out of the cotton. I decided I'd check out that pole. I climbed back down the ladder, ran out of the barn and down the cotton rows. I walked a while and then ran some more. The cotton there was slightly higher than my eye level, so every so often I would jump up to check my direction. Suddenly, I just ran out of the cotton into a black open space; I was there for maybe twenty seconds before I realized I was standing in the circle in the field. I looked down and the earth was all charred and black. I walked out into the middle toward the pole and saw that it was about eight feet tall, sticking right in the center of the circle.

"Grandmother!" I yelled as loud as I could; I yelled a second time.

I could hear her answer far away. I calculated that the road I left them on was only about four hundred yards to my left, so I ran like a deer through the cotton and found the road. I saw them way down the road, still resting. "Grandmother!" I hollered out, holding my hands up to the sides of my mouth in order to be heard, "I've found the circle, I've found the circle!" I watched them get up and come as fast as they could, which wasn't very fast.

When they got close to me, Grandmother said, "Have you really found it, Alvin Junior, have you really?"

"It's out there about four-hundred yards; if you just look out, you'll see a pole marking it," I answered.

They squinted and looked hard, but perhaps they all had bad eyes and couldn't see the pole. I led them across the rows of cotton. As we got close I said, "We're about there."

When we were on the edge of the circle, still standing in the cotton, the woman in the white bonnet said, "Bradie, listen to me! I'm a-not gonna go in that circle. You, Gerta and the boy can, but I'm not goin' in it. I'm gonna stay out here and watch."

Grandmother looked a little surprised and said, "Well, if that's your liking, Rose, you stay out here." That's the first time I heard Grandmother call that woman by name. Grandmother, Gerta, and I went out in the famous circle and left Rose watching back in the cotton. Grandmother said, "Lordy, me, its bigger 'round than I thought it would be, and look, Alvin Junior, how perfect the circle is." I had noticed that, too. It had been two months since it was first discovered and there was still not a blade of green grass growing anywhere in that black scorched earth.

Gerta spoke to us softly, "Rose thinks that this here circle is the work of the devil. She almost didn't come, you know."

We walked completely around the circle, and Grandmother asked me to count how many rows wide the circle was. Whatever had burned that circle had also flattened out the earth, but I could still tell where the rows of cotton had been. I walked across the circle twice and told Grandmother it was either twenty-four or twenty-five rows wide. Grandmother picked up two or three small charred sticks from the ground and put them in her dress pocket. We agreed it was about time to go, and Rose led the way back out of the cotton field, walking faster than she had before. Grandmother said, "Rose, you slow down; we got miles to go. We cant go at this pace." Rose didn't say anything and didn't slow down; she seemed relieved once we got to the main road and started home away from that circle in the field.

The long walk home was hot and humid, but the talk about having seen the circle made it seem shorter. Gerta was very proud that she had persisted with her men folks in getting information, and all of the women seemed most satisfied about having done what the men thought they should not do.

"Good thing you came along, Alvin Junior; we'd have never found it without you," Grandmother said. "You're gonna get a lot of tea cookies for helping us find that circle."

It was getting cloudy in the west, and as the sun went down the sky was again gray-blue up high, but it turned into a rich lilac color down near the earth. Gerta made a comment about the clouds bringing much-needed rain. It was dark when we walked into the yard, and the dogs romped and jumped like we'd been gone a month.

"We saw the circle!" I called out loudly with excitement as we crossed the yard. "We saw the circle in the field!"

I could tell the men were all dumbfounded, and Uncle T. L. said, "Aw, hell, you didn't."

"Yes, we did! It took all afternoon, but we finally found it," I said, "and the earth was black and scorched." The men were stunned and quiet.

Aunt Virginia said, "I've kept supper warm for you all; come on back and eat."

After supper we sat quietly on the front porch before I finally asked Uncle Charlie, "What do you think made that burned circle in the field?" He sort of mumbled something, and I didn't understand him.

"Uncle Charlie, was it as big around as you thought it would be or smaller than you thought it would be?" I asked.

Uncle Charlie didn't say anything. Uncle Doss said, "Truth is, Alvin Junior, no one here but Uncle Pete has been to see that circle."

"Well, I couldn't find the damn thing," Uncle T. L. blurted out.

Grandmother sat in silence and didn't say a word. Grandpa Pete stood up and said, "Think I'll go pump me some cool water."

When he returned, I asked, "What do you think that circle is all about, Grandpa?"

"I been a sayin' for two months now, Alvin Junior, you go and you don't know any more than you did before you go."

The next morning my father showed up in a new car he was trying to sell to a man over in Portageville. He wanted me to come stay with him for a few days. I got my small suitcase and we were gone in minutes; my daddy never lingered around my mother's people very long. As we drove down the gravel road that led to Highway 61, Daddy asked, "Well, boy, what have you been up to at your grandmothers house?"

"Well," I said, "I walked with the men a long distance one night to hear a prize fight on a battery radio. And everyone is talking about things that people have been seeing in the sky, real bright things."

My daddy laughed out loud, slapped me on my leg, and asked, "Did you see anything in the sky?"

"No, sir," but I went just yesterday with Grandmother and two of her women friends and we found a mysterious circle in a field that was all black and charred, and nothing at all is growing there now."

"You don't say," he replied. He didn't comment further. We just rode along.

I thought about it for a long while, but decided I wouldn't tell him anything about the sugar tit.

Rag Man a-Comin'

IN 1936 WE MOVED to a different area of Memphis and I became a new fifth-grade student at St. Paul Elementary School. A newcomer usually had to fight the tough guys in a school and neighborhood before they would accept him, and it was no different at St. Paul and that area. While walking home after my second day of classes, a big sixth-grader named Maxie Morgan was the clear winner in a fight that he insisted on having with me. It is possible I may have landed two or three of the fifteen or so blows thrown, but one of Maxie's many blows aimed at my head caught me on the throat, and I ended up flat on the sidewalk. I had taken a hard beating, so I exaggerated my agony by squirming and gasping for breath. This caused Maxie and his two friends to go on down the street, thinking I was whipped. I was picking up my books and tablets and regaining my composure when a fifth-grader from my room named Trey Brown rode up on his silver bicycle and asked me what had happened. I explained the whole encounter to him. He didn't say a word but just rode off in another direction.

I never fully understood it, but the next day at long recess, Trey Brown approached Maxie Morgan and beat him up all over the playground. When he had finished, after Maxie had begged Trey to quit hitting him, Trey pointed over to me standing in a crowd of students watching the fight and said, "Alvin over there is my friend, and if you're gonna fight him you're gonna answer to me." Trey wasn't all that big, but his fists were fast, he talked tough and everyone seemed to be afraid of him. From that day on the bigger and tougher sixth-grade boys didn't bother me.

In early November I was sent unexpectedly to the Bootheel in Missouri to live with my father. The flooding and high waters that winter led to my return to Memphis and St. Paul Elementary in February of the same school year. Shortly after I had returned, a group of sixth graders who had forgotten Trey's early September proclamation were shoving me around at recess and preparing to beat on me. Trey Brown suddenly popped up out of nowhere and reminded them that they would have to answer to him if they didn't leave me alone. Again, Trey had come to my rescue and saved me from a fist whipping by the tougher and bigger boys. It was a mystery to me why Trey had decided to be my protector. I was afraid to ask him why for fear that he might not know himself and stop protecting me. I went that entire spring without getting beaten up. I had several other close encounters with tough guys in the neighborhood and at school, but they always decided at the last minute to leave me alone.

After school let out in May, I left Memphis and spent another exciting summer with my relatives on the spacious cotton farms in the Bootheel of Missouri. Several times, there in the quiet of the evening, I would think of how Trey Brown had made my life so much easier by protecting me from the rough and tough boys, but the reason for his actions remained a mystery.

The following September I was two weeks late getting to Memphis, because I'd been trapped with my Uncle Otis and Aunt Mary on a company farm in Arkansas. My first day back at St. Paul Elementary, because I was late enrolling, the school principal made me sit on the punishment bench in the hallway outside his office. The bench was supposed to be a humiliating experience, but it wasn't all that bad since everyone knew I had been adventuring in the country. While I was sitting there that day, Trey Brown walked up and asked, "What's the punishment for, Alvin?"

"I was two weeks late getting back for the opening of school," I replied. He didn't say anything and walked on down the hall. Lots of times Trey didn't have anything to say.

That fall I began to assess my new neighborhood and school. There had been so much unsettledness during the fifth grade, I had never given much thought to the St. Paul area. I lived with my mother in a small duplex on Tate Street, four blocks from school. North of us on Vance Avenue and on several nearby streets running north and south, were large stone and brick mansions; most houses south of those fine homes were small, inexpensive older houses, and there were a couple of blocks of long shotgun-type houses for those with little money. Like most public schools in

Memphis, St. Paul had a mixture of children, from
families that had little or almost nothing to well-to-do
families. However, it seemed to me that wherever we
lived in Memphis people were having financial
difficulties. Many folks who had very little felt that
they were better off than a lot of others. No one ever
claimed to be poor, and I seldom heard the word used
unless it was directed at someone who had less. South
of the St. Paul area, there was a large, extremely
destitute section with many run-down houses. That
probably accounted for the somewhat different
atmosphere from our previous neighborhood on
Adams Street.

It was in the St. Paul area that I first experienced
the Rag Man and other late afternoon and night
buyers and sellers. A colored man walked up and down
the streets, singing out, "Rag Man a-comin'." He
pulled a rickshaw-like two-wheeled wagon that had a
large bell without a clapper. Every so often he would
strike the bell one time with an iron rod. The sound
would reverberate throughout the neighborhood, and
just as it ended he would sing out, "Rag Man a-comin'," in an eerie, haunting voice. He usually entered our
neighborhood at dusk or dark, and would hit the bell
and sing out every four or five minutes. Children and
grown folks would collect rags in big sacks, and the
Rag Man would give them two pennies or three pennies a sack depending on its size. I never knew what he
did with all those rags.

In this area at night I would also hear the Hot Tamale Man. "Hot tamales," he would sing out in a voice as clear as Nelson Eddy's that could be heard three or four blocks away. He, too, was a colored man. Hot tamales sold two for a nickel; there were no bargains in buying hot tamales.

The virtuoso of the night singers was the Snowball Man. He had a song that he would repeat about every twenty minutes. After his melodic, "Snowballs," echoed off the houses he would sing, "Talk about, tell about; tell ya what I'll do; I'll sell ya one for a nickel; two for a dime; that's the way I sell 'em, all the time." Then he repeated, "Snowbaaallllls," carrying out the end of the word for a long time. He, also, was a colored man. Snowballs were ice cones made from a special kind of gadget he shoved across a block of ice that he carried on his cart. He would place the ice shavings into a cone-shaped white paper cup and squirt on some flavoring from a bottle. Flavors to choose from were orange, grape and strawberry.

There were other street vendors who made their rounds during the daylight hours: the Vegetable Man, the Watermelon Man, the Cantaloupe Man, the Ice Man and a few others. But these vendors didn't sing. The Rag Man, Hot Tamale Man, and the Snowball Man were singers and in late summer, just after dark, when things were very still and people were resting on their front porches from a hard day's work, all three men might be heard singing at the same time somewhere out in the darkness of the neighborhood. My mother said they liked our neighborhood at night, because they could buy and sell to mothers and fathers who worked during the day. The three singing vendors were unique to the St. Paul area of Memphis and gave the nights a special mysterious aura.

When fall came and nights grew cooler, the Snowball Man would stop making the neighborhood rounds. The Hot Tamale Man and Rag Man came on through the winter. Come spring, all three would sell hot tamales and snowballs, and buy sacks of rags.

By November I had grown to love my new home and neighborhood. I had made a good friend named Craig Ball who lived two blocks away from me and about two houses down from Trey Brown. It was from Craig that I began to learn more about Trey and his family. One day while walking home from downtown, Craig asked me, "Why does Trey take up for you so much against all the tough guys?"

"I don't know," I answered. I told him about the day when Maxie Morgan beat me up and for some unknown reason Trey beat up Maxie Morgan the next day. Craig didn't say anything for a while; then he started talking.

"You know, they say Trey's daddy sure is a strange man," he said. "He has some kind of job that no one knows anything about, and he only gets home about once a month and then for only two or three days. When he's home there's all kinds of yelling and fighting going on down there, day and night. They say Mr. Brown gets drunk and then gets mean and starts beating on everybody in sight. My mother says that the older two sisters just leave home and wait until their daddy leaves before they come back."

"Golly, that sounds pretty terrible," I replied.

"Someone called the police last summer and they carried Mr. Brown away in a squad car, but he came back the next day," Craig added.

One day in November there was a big commotion on the playground at lunch; when I got there I saw Trey and one of the school tough guys fighting. I climbed up on a concrete ledge to get a better view. Right away I realized that Trey didn't seem to be fighting like I had seen him fight in the past. His opponent was landing direct blows to Trey's head, and Trey would just shake them off and wade in for more. This went on about three minutes. Finally, Trey exploded on him with a barrage of fast fist blows and hit him hard on the nose; blood started running down over the tough guy's mouth and he quit fighting. Trey had won again. However, as they walked back into the school building, other than the blood on his opponent's face and shirt, Trey looked more beaten up than his opponent because he had several knots on his head and a swollen eye. The next day at school Trey looked dreadful with a black eye and several bruises on his head and face. I thought it strange that he waited so long to fight back with his fast fists. It was almost like he wanted to be beaten up.

By January of my sixth-grade school year, I had become even better friends with Craig. He had been

named the school's best singer from his rendition of
"Swing Low, Sweet Chariot" at a school talent
contest, and he had to sing "America" for the school
PTA meeting. I was designated as the school's artist by
winning a poster contest. Every day I spent the last
hour of classes at an easel outside my homeroom,
making signs and posters for various school activities.
We both felt good about our honors.

After Christmas Trey started missing school a lot.
Craig told me what his mother had learned from
neighbors: she had heard that Trey's report card had
been really bad all year and that he might fail the sixth
grade. He was already one year behind. Craig also said
that his mother had heard from neighbors that the
Brown family had been having lots of problems ever
since a son who was two years younger than Trey had
died back in 1934. Neighbors said they thought he died
of diphtheria. Craig and I were concerned for Trey; we
believed he was smart but just didn't care much for
studying. On several occasions we had tried to get
friendly with him, and we once asked him to go to a
picture show with us, but he wouldn't go.

We all had our problems at St. Paul, and one of my
most aggravating was my shoes. It was the one problem on which my mother and I could seldom agree
and an area of great conflict. Like most other boys, I
could have only one pair of shoes at a time. That one
pair of shoes was for all occasions, rain or shine. I
would wear them to school, to church, to play football,
to play kick the can, to climb trees, to run the

Memphis river bluffs or to walk the five miles downtown and five miles back. In the summer I could take them off and go barefooted some, but in the winter my shoes wore out fast. My mother would get me another pair only when they literally fell off my feet. I had a box of shoe repair gear that I would use in gluing down floppy soles and patching large holes. I had a large needle and some tough thread and a cobblers thimble that I used to sew tops and sides back together. Once the shoes started coming apart, however, it was a mighty chore to get them back together for just one more day. It would get to the point where I would stand around and decline recess games for fear my shoes would fall off my feet. When my mother saw me wobbling along as I walked, or when the soles came completely off, I might buy another pair of shoes if there was money available. New shoes gave me a good feeling and I would walk in pride for a few weeks. Then the new shoes would begin to run over and come apart, and I would go through the holding-them-together routine for as long as I could.

In March I was at the very end of a pair of shoes and was somewhat embarrassed at school because I was down to holding my soles on with rubber bands. There was an ad in the *Memphis Commercial Appeal* about a great shoe sale down on South Main; one could get a pair of fine shoes for three dollars. My mother gave me the money on a Saturday morning to get a pair. I used seven cents of my own money to ride the Elmwood

streetcar downtown because I knew the rubber bands
would never hold up for a five-mile walk. It was a store
that had just opened, and they had new shoes on my
feet in a matter of minutes. I decided to walk the five
miles home to break in my new shoes. That night my
mother was elated that I got a nice pair of shoes for
such a good price.

"Try and take good care of them," she said. "Maybe
they will last you through the summer."

Tuesday morning, three days later, as I walked to
school it was raining so hard that water stood several
inches deep in the streets. In several places I had to
wade across water up to my ankles, and my feet got
soaking wet. As I sat in class that day I noticed that my
shoes felt loose. At noon recess I looked down and saw
two or three places on each shoe that had torn loose
from the seams; I walked around gently and didn't play
any running games. When school let out I had the
feeling I was going to have real shoe problems in getting home, so I stayed after school and worked on a
poster at an easel in the hallway. When it looked like
everyone was out of the building, I decided to give it a
try and walk home. As I headed down the street I
could tell my shoes were coming apart. After walking
another block my right shoe actually fell off my foot; I
sat down on the curb and examined the shoe. The day
was overcast and a little cool, but I decided I would
take off the other shoe and examine it also. I was
sitting on the curb in my socks. I looked up and there
stood Trey Brown looking down at me.

"You havin' shoe problems, Alvin?" he asked.

"Yep," I replied. "I got these new shoes downtown last Saturday and they got wet comin' to school this morning; they're comin' apart already."

He didn't say anything but took one of my shoes and pulled on it a little; it tore apart completely.

"These shoes are made of cardboard," he said.

"They sure looked like leather when I bought them," I replied.

He stood there a minute without saying anything; he looked like he was thinking hard. "What size shoe do you wear, Alvin?" he asked.

"Five," I answered.

He stood there thinking another minute or so without saying anything. Finally he said, "You come with me." I stood up and followed him in my sock feet with the cardboard shoes in one hand and my books in the other.

"Where are we goin'?" I asked.

He waited a few seconds before he said, "Don't ask questions; just follow me." We passed in front of Craig's house and on by Trey's house and cut back up the street to the alley that ran behind their houses. I followed him into the alley; it had lots of high fences and large storage houses and garages on both sides. We passed through the gate of a high wooden fence into his backyard.

"You wait here," Trey said. He returned from the side of the house, carrying an eight-foot stepladder. "Put your books and shoes down over there," he instructed, pointing to a bench, "and help me with this ladder." We went out in the alley and down about fifteen yards, then through some bushes that led to a space three yards wide between his garage and the storage building belonging to the house next door. There were big bushes at both ends of the space between garages and no one could see us there. We leaned the ladder up against a small opening no more than three feet square that led into a floored area up above the storage building. The clapboard building belonged to the house next door and it appeared unused. Trey told me to climb up and crawl into the opening and he would follow. It was still cloudy outside and I was surprised after crawling in there that we could see very well.

Trey reached over and got a long three-battery flashlight that gave us more light, and then he lit a small lantern that was hanging from a wire in the middle of the room. The angle of the roof allowed for only about four and a half feet headroom in the middle, so we couldn't stand up straight. Neither of us had said anything. I looked around and saw that the space was filled with lots of boxes and other things.

"You can't tell anyone about this place, Alvin. It's my secret place, and I don't want anyone to know that it's here," he said firmly.

"I won't tell a soul, Trey," I said. "I swear, I'll never say anything to anyone." We sat for a moment then he pointed to a box with the flashlight.

"Pull that box over here," he instructed, since it was closer to me. I pulled the medium-size box toward us. He started pulling out shoes until there were six pairs on the floor. "Find you a pair that fits you," he said. All kinds of things were racing through my mind. I wanted to ask him where the shoes came from and why he had so many pairs, but I didn't. All of the shoes looked good and some looked brand new as if they had never been worn. The pairs of shoes were neatly tied together by their shoestrings, and I had to untie the strings in order to try them on. The second pair I tried on fit good.

"Boy," I exclaimed, "these feel real good! They're nifty shoes."

"You can have 'em," he said.

"You mean I can have 'em for keeps?" I asked.

"They're yours."

"Are you sure it's all right, Trey? Your mother might get mad if you give away your shoes," I said with concern.

"These are my shoes; that pair is yours. No more talk," he said with authority. I started putting the other shoes neatly into the box and shoved it back over where I had found it. I looked around and saw several other boxes and wondered what was in them. There was a suitcase and a large coil of rope over to one side. He'd made a pallet bed to sleep on from lots of newspapers, with several blankets for cover. He saw me looking around, especially at the pallet, and said, "Sometimes I come out here to sleep at night. I like it here.

Mosquitoes bother you a lot in the summer, but it's a good place to sleep at other times. I discovered this space up here about two years ago. No one knows about my comin' up here."

We sat there for a minute; then he reached back, picked up a stack of magazines, counted down to the third one from the top, pulled it out, and pitched it over in front of me. I opened it and saw pictures of two naked women, one on each page. They were gorgeous. I turned the page and there were more pictures of women stripped naked. It was a magazine full of pictures of naked women, so I looked through the whole magazine.

"Where did you get this?" I asked.

"Louisville," he answered. "I visit my Uncle Vernon in Louisville whenever I get a chance, and he takes me places and buys me things you can't get here in Memphis." He went on, "My Uncle Vernon is a great guy. He used to live in Memphis but moved up there about three years ago. He has a good job and makes good money. He's twenty-two years old." I remember thinking that Trey was the oldest-acting fourteen-year-old boy I had ever known. He placed the magazine back third in the stack and shoved them way back, out of the way. I wondered what was in those other magazines. I didn't say anything, but I could tell that it was time to go. He blew out the lantern light and we climbed down the ladder, crawled through the bushes and carried the ladder around to his yard. I picked up my books and my shriveled cardboard shoes.

"I sure appreciate these shoes, Trey. Thanks a lot," I said.

He said nothing, but he nodded his head. After a while he did say, "Don't tell anyone about my secret place."

"I won't," I said.

My mother was very pleased that Trey had given me such a nice pair of shoes, but she was quite upset that my new shoes had fallen apart. I said nothing to her about his secret place.

The next few days were difficult for me when I was around Craig, not because I wanted to tell about Trey and his hideaway, but because I wanted to talk about all those pictures of beautiful naked women I had seen. I kept my word and said nothing to anyone. The pictures of those naked women stayed in my mind for days.

That spring the boys at St. Paul began to worry and talk about the coming fall. We would be entering the seventh grade at Bellevue Junior High School, where we would have to face the dreaded belt-line initiation and the possibility of getting Sophye Olive Fink for a teacher. In those days it seemed like there were always serious things in the future to worry about.

At long recess one Friday in late spring, Trey went around aggravating all the tough guys, trying to provoke a fight. No one would do battle with him no matter what he said or did. Finally, the bell rang to go inside and there had been no fighting. On Saturday morning I saw Craig down at the grocery and he said to me quietly, "Mr. Brown is home for the weekend and he's raising all kinds of hell. The lady next door to them called my mother and told her about it. They say he gets real mean when he gets drunk." I didn't say anything.

I had a secret business adventure that Saturday with a boy named Earlus Johnson; we checked out pigeon nests for baby squabs that we sold to the Hotel Peabody. We had finished about dark and after I left Earlus at his home, I decided I would walk down the alley that led behind Trey's house. When I was still pretty far away from where he lived, I could hear a lot of yelling and screaming. When I got to the fence behind his house, I could hear Mr. Brown cursing and Mrs. Brown screaming back at him. For a while I stood there and listened. It was awful. Daylight had turned to dusky dark, so I got up on a large oil barrel and looked over the fence and through some bushes at the commotion. Mr. Brown was on the back porch yelling and throwing things at Mrs. Brown; then I saw Trey on the porch with them. Mr. Brown walked over and started slapping his wife and Trey stepped in between them. Mr. Brown slapped Trey to get him out of the way, but Trey just jumped back in between them. Mr. Brown hit Trey again with his fists two or three times and cursed him. Then Mr. Brown went over and collapsed on the daybed on the back porch. Trey and his mother went back into the house.

The following Monday Trey didn't come to school, but he did on Tuesday, and he had bruises all over his face. Everyone said he had been out fighting in the neighborhood again, but I knew that his own daddy had beaten him up. I didn't say anything to anyone. I figured it was like Trey's secret hideaway and his secret books of naked women; it was something he probably wanted to keep a secret.

School let out at the end of May and I headed for the Bootheel of Missouri. I decided I would put all of the dreaded things about Bellevue Junior High School and all the unusual things I knew about Trey out of my mind until fall. Summers in the Bootheel were too much fun to be spoiled by city worries.

In late August I returned to Memphis and started junior high school. Not only did I get whipped hard in the Bellevue belt-line initiation, but I was the only St. Paul student to get the dreaded Sophye Olive Fink for homeroom teacher. I was feeling pretty low about it when I realized I had not seen Trey since I had returned.

Perhaps he can help me with all these tough guys at Bellevue, I thought. I went over to Craig's house for a talk about it all.

"No one knows where Trey is, Alvin," Craig said. "They say that for a few weeks this summer he went to stay with his Uncle Vernon in Louisville, Kentucky, but left there to come home and never got here. His family is hush-hush about it."

"No one knows where he is?" I asked.

"No one will talk about it," Craig replied.

Trey never did return to Memphis and, according to Craig's mother, the Brown family was planning to move.

One night, just after dark, I sat out on our front porch when things had become really quiet, and I tried to figure out how I was going to keep from getting beaten up without Trey protecting me. I was still wearing the shoes he had given me, but they were beginning to show signs of wear and I could tell they were not going to last much longer. I wondered if he had carried all those naked women magazines with him wherever he was. I could hear the Hot Tamale Man singing for sales as he came down our street. In a minute I heard the Snowball Man singing about three blocks away. I knew that in a little while there would be one heedful sound of a bell and just as it died away I would hear a haunting voice singing, "Rag Man a-comin'."

The Storm Splitter

I HAD ALWAYS wanted to visit my Uncle Estes and Aunt May, but in most summers I had spent in the Bootheel, I had never stayed at their place. The summer I was twelve Uncle Estes saw my father in Caruthersville, and he asked Daddy to bring me to his farm sometime to stay a few days. So late in July of that year, Daddy came in his car to Aunt Annie and Uncle Will's house and picked me up, and we headed out across the county. We drove east for a while and then turned south down a road that followed the Mississippi River levee. As we drove along we talked about Uncle Estes; I could tell from the things Daddy said that he had a special liking for Uncle Estes more than some other aunts and uncles on Mother's side of the family.

"Your Uncle Estes has done well for himself, and in spite of the fact that he drinks heavy at times, he's a good man," my daddy said. "Of course, some folks think he's not quite all there at times." He laughed at what he had said. "But that's Estes and he's his own man. He says exactly what he thinks and does things other folks would never do, but I'll tell you this: he would give you the shirt off of his back."

We were quiet for a while. Daddy said, "Your Uncle Estes is a might sight better man than most of your mother's people." My daddy's people and my mother's people never did get along well.

I remembered one cold winter day, when I was seven or eight years old, we drove up from Memphis to the Bootheel for the funeral of Uncle Estes' young son Eldon. They said Eldon just got sick one night with spinal meningitis and died a few days later. I sat right behind Uncle Estes at the church funeral that day, and he was wailing and making loud suffering sounds that I had never heard before. The service went on and on for a long time; when we finally left the church and arrived at the cemetery, for some reason they made me stay in the car. I could hear Uncle Estes moaning again all across the graveyard. I heard him holler out, "Why did God take my boy? Why did God take my boy?" After a while I didn't hear him anymore, but I saw some people leading him out of the cemetery. I felt really bad for several days. I knew Eldon had been about my age; I had played with him during large family gatherings, but I had not known him very well.

We kept driving down the levee road. "You know about your Uncle Estes swimming across the Mississippi River, don't you?" Daddy asked me.

"Yes, sir, Uncle Will told me about that. Did he really do it?" I asked.

"Sure," he answered and went on, "He always was a good swimmer, and one summer when he was nineteen years old someone bet him twenty dollars he couldn't swim across the Mississippi River. Well, a few days later a crowd gathered at Cottonwood Point to watch. He crossed the river on the ferry to the Tennessee side, walked up the river about four miles to where the river bends a little, jumped in the river in short pants, and started swimming. He ended up two or three miles down below the ferry on the Missouri side about thirty minutes later. He'd worked on some river boats about two years earlier, and he really understood those river currents. You know that's the secret of swimming the river, don't you?"

My daddy gave me a talk about the currents of the river. A person could take a corked bottle, he said, and throw it in the water about thirty feet in certain places from the Tennessee side, and that bottle would end up downstream very close to the shoreline on the other side .

"So you learn to swim the currents. But your Uncle Estes was also a good swimmer anyway." We rode on for a while. Then daddy laughed and said, "You know, your Uncle Estes is supposed to have lots of strange beliefs and a lot of folks think he has some special powers."

"What kind of powers?" I asked.

"Some say he can make headaches and backaches disappear," he replied. A little more time passed before he said, "And then some people say he has special powers with the weather and can actually break up thunderstorms and cyclones." I was about to question him more when we turned off the levee road onto a narrow road that led to Uncle Estes' dark red house. It sat back about a quarter of a mile, in a huge cotton field surrounded by six large shade trees. A barn and several other farm sheds could be seen farther back. There were all kinds of flower beds around the house.

Aunt May greeted me warmly and said that Uncle Estes and their second oldest son Edmund, who was about eighteen years old, were out on the back side of the farm working on some fences. My daddy never stayed long when he dropped me off to visit, so in a matter of minutes he was ready to go; just as he left he said he'd be back to get me in a few days. There were only three children left at Uncle Estes' house, since their oldest daughter had married and set up house-keeping over in Blytheville, Arkansas, and their oldest son had gone to work in St. Louis. Besides Edmund, they had two girls, Dora, who was sixteen, and Dena, who was six, still in the house.

Aunt May, Dora, and Dena quit what they were doing, got out some ice from their icebox and made lemonade. We went to the living room and talked about relatives and Memphis; people always wanted to know about Memphis things. In a while Uncle Estes and Edmund returned in a wagon, pulled by mules. We went outside, and Uncle Estes saw me and shouted, "Hey, there's Alvin Junior!" He jumped off the wagon, came over, picked me up, and hugged me like I'd never been hugged before. He made me feel good, and I wondered why he liked me so much.

Uncle Estes was tall, lean and strong. He was different from most of my uncles, because he would never wear overalls but always wore blue work shirts and what looked to me like cowboy pants with a big belt and buckle. He had a lot of gray and black wavy hair and didn't wear a hat as most farmers did.

"Soon as we unharness these mules we'll be in and talk," he said, and they continued back to the mule barn.

I went back into the kitchen with Aunt May and the girls, and they started getting supper ready. I noticed that not only did they have a new icebox, but they had put an inside hand pump and a sink around it for washing dishes. During supper they encouraged me to talk more about Memphis; they liked to hear about the different animals at the zoo and special rides at the Memphis Fair Grounds. Uncle Estes gave me more attention than I had received all summer. After supper we sat free from mosquitoes on the screened-in back porch and talked about an hour. Uncle Estes said, "Alvin Junior, me and Edmund are gonna take you over to the river tomorrow and catch you some fish for tomorrow nights supper."

"Great!" I replied, "Are the fish biting now?"

"They always bite when I go fishing," he said in a laughing way.

They let me sleep on a small daybed out on the screened-in back porch, near the kitchen. Aunt May and the girls were up early the next morning making all kinds of noise as they prepared breakfast. The food they fixed was the same as at my other aunt's breakfasts, except the biscuits were not as large as Aunt Annie's or Aunt Virginia's, and they didn't have any chocolate gravy.

The sun had been up for about two hours as Uncle Estes, Edmund and I walked straight down from the house, across the levee road and over a fence to the top of the levee itself. We walked north on the road on top of the levee three-quarters of a mile before we went down to the lush land between the levee and the river. We had brought cane poles and two big buckets with us. All along I had smelled something rank or rotten, but I didn't say anything. One bucket held our lunch and the other was full of hooks and corks and bait and stuff. The river was farther out from the levee than I had thought it would be, but we finally arrived at a point of land that jutted out into the water. As Edmund and Uncle Estes began baiting the hooks, I got another whiff of what ever was in that bucket and it smelled terrible.

"What is that bait," Uncle Estes?" I asked.

"Well, we got two baits, Alvin Junior: chicken entrails and dough balls."

"Chicken what?" I asked.

"Chicken guts," he said. "We saved 'em from the chickens we had for dinner the other day." Edmund took a large three-inch long hook on a big line of heavy cord and lead weight and pushed chicken entrails all onto it. He circled it about three times above his head and let it fly out into the river. He did the same with two other lines. He tossed me a hook and line and said, "Bait this one up, Alvin Junior."

Putting my hand down in those chicken guts and placing them on that hook was one of the hardest things I had ever done. When I finished baiting the hook, Edmund threw my line out into the water for me, and we washed the slimy chicken entrails off of our hands in the river. Uncle Estes was putting dough balls on the cane poles and setting them out. "Sooner or later the dough balls or the chicken entrails one will get us some fine fish," Uncle Estes commented.

They sat down and started rolling cigarettes from their tobacco sacks. They lit up their cigarettes and sat there on the bank, watching all the lines out in the water. Sometimes they just seemed to be watching the river flow. "Now this is the life, Alvin Junior," Uncle Estes said.

It was over an hour before a river boat came by pushing barges and then there were three river boats in about fifteen minutes. We waved at the deck hands; one boat blew its whistle. Around that time Edmund saw a line tugging, and he pulled in about a three-pound catfish. He put more chicken entrails on that hook, circled it over his head and threw the line back out into the water. I realized I was thirsty, so I asked, "Where can I get a drink of water, Uncle Estes?"

"Bring that bucket over here, he instructed." I grabbed the bait and hook bucket and carried it over; he began taking the lid off, got a whiff of those chicken guts, and said, "No, no, Alvin Junior; get me the lunch bucket." The lunch bucket and the bait bucket looked just alike. I brought over the lunch bucket; he pulled off the lid and said, "I'm pretty thirsty too, really." I looked in the lunch bucket and saw that

Aunt May had placed a small towel on top of some biscuit sandwiches; she had put several spiced pickles on top of the towel. The bucket was so full of sandwiches that the pickles had been right at the top of the bucket and had become smushed into the lid. Uncle Estes saw the squashed pickle and juice on the bucket lid, so he washed it off a little in the river water. Then he scooped up some of the river water in the lid, held it up to his mouth, slightly tilted it toward him, and drank. He did it again so I would see how to do it. After his second lid of water he said, "It's a little warm and it's a little murky, but its pretty good water. Now, you get you some water, Alvin Junior."

I carefully washed the lid four times, and then scooped a lid of water from the river. When I got it up to my mouth to drink, I saw all kinds of things swirling around in the lid. And the water wasn't murky at all; it was brown. The lid smelled so much like those spiced pickles that it made me gag. Too, I had visions of that bucket on previous fishing trips being used as the chicken-gut bucket. I got a little river water in my mouth and quickly sloshed it around and spit it out. I didn't say anything; I didn't drink any of that water either. Uncle Estes and Edmund didn't know that I hadn't, and I didn't want them to know.

Our lunch was biscuits filled with things, like side meat, chicken and different kinds of jelly. I ate three, and then I was very thirsty. I tried the bucket lid with the river water again, but every time I would get the lid up to my mouth I would smell the spiced pickles and imagined I got a whiff of chicken gut and I'd gag, so I gave up.

By three o'clock we had caught three pretty good size catfish, but Uncle Estes kept saying he wanted four, so we fished on. About three-thirty I said, "Uncle Estes, I haven't been able to get much of that river water down. Is there a hand pump anywhere around here where I could get a drink of water?"

He laughed loudly and replied, "No, there ain't, boy. What's your problem?"

"Well, I can't make myself drink that river water," I answered. "I really do need a drink of water bad; I'm really thirsty."

I think he saw my condition. "Well, don't feel too bad Alvin Junior," he said. "Your Aunt May can't drink from the river either. In fact, my oldest son Edward would never drink from the river. We'll be goin' in a little while, and we'll be back at the place and you can get you some real good, cool pump water."

Just after Uncle Estes spoke, Edmund caught one more fish, and we started back home after pitching all those leftover chicken guts and dough balls into the river. I couldn't help but think that someone downstream might be fishing and drinking that river water. I helped keep a fast pace going home. As we got near the house Uncle Estes said, "Now, Alvin Junior, when you get to the pump, take care to drink real slow; just three or four swallows of water maybe, and then wait a while before you drink a lot of water."

"Why, Uncle Estes?" I asked.

"Well, a stomach acts up after it hasn't had water in a long time. So just drink it slow." I guess I was so thirsty I only half-heard his advice, because I ran to the hand pump, and when I got there and saw the water coming out, I started gulping it down. After I had drunk quite a bit, I remembered what he had said and stopped. I was at the stock pump in the backyard, out close to the barn, and as I walked back toward the house I suddenly threw up all that water in one or two big heaves. Edmund came up to me and let me hold on to him, because I was really feeling bad.

"Go get on that daybed on the back porch," Edmund said. "You'll be all right in a minute."

I did, and he was right; in about an hour I felt pretty good. All along Uncle Estes was over near the storm house, cleaning the catfish for supper. Before we ate I scrubbed my hands five times with lye soap. I didn't have much food, but I had several extra glasses of iced tea. Uncle Estes told Aunt May about my difficulty with drinking the river water.

"People with good sense don't drink river water," she said with a smile on her face.

"Lots of good minerals in that river water," Uncle Estes replied with a grin. We talked a while on the back porch, then we went to bed.

The following days were full of fun. The crops were laid by, so Uncle Estes and Edmund were working on fences and repairing things around the farm, getting ready for cotton picking. Sometimes I went with them and helped, but more often I stayed at the house and kept out of the way. On two days they left their work early, and we pitched horseshoes and washers and played other outdoor games. Several afternoons we played card games on the back porch; one time we took Uncle Estes' twenty-two rifle and shot at bottles and tin cans set up on a fence. Uncle Estes was very good at hitting targets, and afterwards Edmund talked to me a long time about how good his father was at hunting squirrels in season.

About four o'clock one afternoon, while the men were off working, I was out by the side of the house practicing horseshoe pitching. I heard a distant rumble like thunder, so I went around back and found Aunt May standing on the back porch steps, looking seriously toward the southwest where a dark blue storm seemed to be brewing.

"There's a possibility we might get some bad weather in a little while," she said, still scanning the horizon.

"You think it's coming this way?" I asked.

"Can't quite tell yet," she answered, "but it looks like it's got wind in it wherever it goes."

There was one thing all Bootheel people had in common and that was taking storms and cyclones seriously. Almost all the farm families had storm houses built deep in the ground to help protect them from the high winds and cyclones that often ravaged that part of the country. Aunt May began securing things around the house and doing what she could to get ready in case it was a bad storm. Hurriedly I helped her take down the laundry from the clothes lines; we just threw it all on a bed in one of the side rooms. We let down three inside shutters hooked to the ceiling of the screened back porch in order to keep out the rain. There was a tremendous streak of lightning in the distance, and in a few seconds there was the sound of thunder. Aunt May said, "It's only about ten or fifteen minutes away, Alvin Junior, and I believe were gonna get a blower; I can tell."

I saw Uncle Estes and Edmund coming as fast as they could, the mules pulling their wagon through the fields; they were leaving a billowing dust trail behind them. I couldn't help but think that they looked like something I'd seen in a cowboy picture show in Memphis. I saw a woman racing across the cotton field with her three little children, one in her arms and two small ones barely able to keep up. I learned they were the wife and children of a sharecropper who lived about a mile and a quarter beyond the cornfield. They only had a two-room house and didn't have a storm house, so they always came to Uncle Estes' storm house for protection from high winds and storms.

Once Uncle Estes and Edmund got the mules in the barn lot, Edmund rushed to remove the harnesses and put the mules in the barn. Uncle Estes was walking around securing things, but he didn't look at all to me like he was disturbed or even in a hurry. Aunt May had already lifted the storm house door that was almost flat with the ground. She walked down five steps, where there were some benches and a few chairs, and lit a coal-oil lantern. The children and the sharecropper's wife were already in the storm house, sitting in the darkness. Aunt May went back and waited for Uncle Estes on the back porch. I stood out in the middle of the backyard, watching the action in all directions, and keeping my eye on the storm. Uncle Estes came across the yard and said, "Best you all get in the storm house now, Alvin Junior." He was yelling, and then he called for Aunt May to come on and get in too. The storm door was laid open for the rest of us to get in. I looked back and saw the wide blue black cloud almost on the ground, stretching wide across the land; it was now about a half mile away. Uncle Estes came from around one of the sheds with a big yellow-handled ax; we converged in the middle of the backyard.

Uncle Estes said firmly, "You three go on and get in the storm house right now."

I started over with Edmund, and Aunt May said, "Estes, please don't challenge this storm; it looks real bad. Come on in with us."

He didn't respond to her but kept looking at the storm. The wind was blowing strong now, and Edmund started pulling me and his mother toward the storm house. Uncle Estes, never taking his eye off the storm, said, "I'll have to stay here and split this storm; I'll have to stand up to it. You all go on and get in that storm house."

Edmund and I were the last two in, and as he pulled the door shut, Edmund yelled, "Come on, Papa!

Come on to the storm house!" but Uncle Estes paid him no mind.

We pulled the storm house door over to close it, but left about six inches of space so we could watch Uncle Estes. I made sure I got a good view and pushed myself right up beside Edmund as we watched Uncle Estes leaning into the hard-blowing wind.

"What's he gonna do?" I asked Edmund.

"He's gonna split that storm," he answered.

"How?" I asked.

"Keep watching; you'll see," he replied.

Then just like Uncle Estes received some kind of sign or signal, he did it. He swung the ax over his head and crushed it deep into the ground; he directed it straight at the middle of the storm that was coming across the fields toward the house. Aunt May hollered for us to close the door tight, so Edmund did. One little baby was squalling so that I couldn't hear much of anything. In the next few minutes, I did hear some drops of rain hit the storm house door along with a few small tree limbs. Edmund raised the door, peeked out, and said, "I think the storm has blown over or has gone around us. However, it still looks bad about a mile north of here."

I peeked out, too, and saw the ax still in the ground, but Uncle Estes wasn't there. Edmund pushed the door open; the two of us stood near the storm house door and saw Uncle Estes over on the back porch steps, cleaning mud off of his shoes with a small stick. It had rained only a little. I heard thunder in another direction and looked back south; it was storming over there, but both storms were swiftly moving east. I saw the sharecropper's wife and children walking out across the fields, back toward their house. I followed Edmund out front beyond the trees and could see the two storms about two miles apart, going east beyond the river.

"That storm just went on both sides of us, Edmund," I said.

"Yeah, Papa split one again, I guess," Edmund responded and shook his head in question.

We went around to the back; Uncle Estes was wiping the dirt off of the yellow-handled ax blade and getting ready to put it back in the wood shed. I went with him.

"Uncle Estes," I asked seriously, "did you split that storm so it would go on both sides of us as it did?"

I followed him into the wood shed, and he was slow to answer. "Nah," he replied, "the ax split the storm. I just put that ax down at the right place at the right time."

"How do you know when to do it?" I asked.

"Well, that's a little hard to explain, Alvin Junior, but I can say that you do have to stand up to those storms like a lot of other things, or else they'll blow you away. If you stand right up to 'em and swing that ax right up the middle of that cloud at the right time, it'll split."

"How do you know the right time?" I asked.

He hesitated a few moments and answered, "That, my boy, would be hard to explain." He walked toward the house.

In fifteen minutes the storms were gone, the air was cool, and the women were cooking supper. During supper everyone ate as if nothing had happened, so I didn't ask further questions. After supper Aunt May took me to the front living room and showed me her photograph album. She pointed to one: "Here's a picture of you and Eldon together when both of you were very small. You were both about six years old," she said. "It was taken over at your grandmother's house in 1931." I didn't say anything. "You all were born only a month apart, you know. He'd be about your size if he had lived." There was a long time when nothing was said. "You remind me a lot of Eldon, Alvin Junior," she said softly, her eyes a little moist. "I'm so glad you came to visit us."

"Oh, I've had a great time, Aunt May," I said as I fumbled with the pages of her album.

My daddy came to get me the next day. The hugging at leaving time took about fifteen minutes. As we drove down the river levee road, I told my daddy about many of the things I had done while I was there, especially the fishing with dough balls and chicken guts. We had a good laugh. For some reason I didn't tell him anything about Uncle Estes splitting the storm.

About four years later, back in Memphis, Mother and I got word that Uncle Estes was visiting some of

Aunt May's relatives up near Portageville and was challenged by some men to swim the Little River. They said he had been drinking heavily that day. He took the challenge, and halfway across the river—it was not a very wide river—he went under and never came up. His body was not found for several days. We did not get to go up to the funeral.

In 1944, just before I was drafted into World War II, I visited the Bootheel area for a couple of days. One day I spent a long time talking with Mr. Rushing at the Tyler Store. I asked about my scattered relatives in the Bootheel. Eventually, I asked about Uncle Estes.

"Well, after your Uncle Estes drowned, your Aunt May remarried and she now lives over near Kennett." He continued, "Edmund kept his daddy's farm but is in the army now; he's overseas in Europe somewhere." Mr. Rushing didn't say anything for a while; then he said, "You know, they tell me that Edmund had the power to split storms with an ax just like his daddy. Several folks saw him do it before he was drafted."

I didn't say anything, and we just sat there for a while.

"You know, I've always wondered how a man can split a storm like that," he said in a serious tone.

"A man doesn't split the storm," I said, "the ax splits the storm." He looked confused. I thanked him for all his good information and headed back to Memphis.

On the Road to Cottonwood Point

IT WAS A Sunday afternoon in late August, just before I was to return to Memphis after spending another wondrous summer in the Missouri Bootheel. A dozen of my aunts and uncles on my father's side of the family had gathered at Aunt Annie and Uncle Will's house for a big dinner and an afternoon of talking. It was a common practice for them to do this, especially in the summer. We sat out under the shade trees, and everything but their voices seemed to be smothered in the stillness and warmth of late summer. Shadows moved slowly across the ground, and the heat caused sparrows to fuss and hardly chirp. No other children or even young grown folks were there for the gathering. I sat with them for a while, but they began to talk so much about aches, ailments and dying that I went to Uncle Will's tool shed and did some hammering and nailing.

In a while I went over to the woods lot and walked around under the giant trees. It was a slow and thoughtful Sunday afternoon. Later, as everyone was preparing to leave, Uncle Winston approached me and said, "Alvin Junior, why don't you come on home with me and Myrna and spend a few days with us?" I looked at my daddy for approval and he said, "Sure, that's fine."

That afternoon, still an hour before sundown, my father drove me, Uncle Winston and Aunt Myrna to their house out from Tyler, about a mile from the road to Cottonwood Point. Their house sat back off the road under four large oak trees and, like most places in the Bootheel, was isolated a good quarter-mile from the nearest neighbor. I had been to their house to visit before, but never to spend the night. As Daddy left he said, "I'll come to get you in four or five days and we'll see about getting you back to Memphis."

We had supper and shortly after sundown prepared for bed; not long after dark I lay in their spare bedroom, listening to the night sounds and thinking. I always had to do a lot of listening and thinking after going to bed in the Bootheel because I was never sleepy that early, but my relatives went to bed with the chickens. It seemed to me I was hearing night sounds and calling birds that I had not heard before. Across the flat fields I could faintly hear the sound of human voices singing, and every so often there was a louder sound, like the voices were cheering. Over and over I heard the same rhythmical sounds and an occasional loud cheer late into the night.

Uncle Winston was up before daylight and had gone to do some carpenter work on a farm near Cottonwood Point. He and Aunt Myrna lived and worked on a cotton farm, but Uncle Winston did carpenter work on the side. Aunt Myrna let me sleep late and kept my breakfast warm. She was a small, kind lady with little eyes, and even though she seemed to be happy, she seldom smiled or laughed. I had heard Aunt Annie once say in a conversation with some other women that Aunt Myrna quietly grieved over not being able to have children. Aunt Myrna sat with me as I ate breakfast. I asked her, "What in the world was that singing and cheering I heard off in the distance last night?"

"Well," Alvin Junior, she said, "you were probably hearing the holy rollers over on the road to Cottonwood Point. They're having their summer jubilee over there in the old Sutton Store. They have it somewhere in the county every summer and they still have another week to go."

"What's a holy roller, Aunt Myrna?" I asked.

She didn't answer right away. "Well," she finally said, "they are folks that get carried away with their religion and they..." she hesitated, "they sing loud and speak strange words." She waited a long time before saying, "They scream and yell a lot and sometimes they even fall down and roll around on the ground. It's different from Baptist revivals. Ill get your Uncle Winston to tell you more about it tonight."

That morning we didn't talk anymore about the holy rollers. After breakfast Aunt Myrna walked me out to see her vegetable and flower gardens. She brought buckets and pans and I helped her gather tomatoes, string beans, radishes and other things. She cut some fresh flowers from her garden and took them into the house and put them in a vase in her sitting room. I noticed that like most of my relatives in the Bootheel, she had planted zinnias in the beds near the house and along the walkway up to the house. I asked her why everyone always had zinnias around their houses.

"Well, Alvin Junior," she spoke softly, almost with reverence, "you can count on zinnias to always grow well, even when the weather is bad and dry, 'cause they are a very hardy flower. Zinnias ask for so little and give you all their brilliant colors. They're like good dependable friends; when things go bad and crops burn up and people are sick of summer heat, zinnias are always there to cheer you up." She smiled a little, something I had never seen her do before. She didn't say anything else for a minute or two; then she said, "Iris, hollyhocks and petunias are beautiful flowers," she hesitated and looked out across her garden, "but I think zinnias are God's chosen flower."

I didn't know what she meant; I had never before heard Aunt Myrna talk like that. At family gatherings she would sometimes sit for hours and never have anything to say. Of course, with Aunt Annie and Aunt Lou and Aunt Minnie talking a mile a minute, she never had much of a chance.

That afternoon after dinner, Aunt Myrna asked if I would take a bucket of tomatoes and a sack of vegetables to Mrs. Moore who lived about a half-mile up the road. "They have a twelve-year-old son named Marvin," she told me, "and you might want to stay there and play a while. Marvin is a sweet boy."

I walked up the dusty road, knocked on the porch, and called out a hello. In a moment a plumpish lady wearing an apron came outside; I told her who I was and gave her the vegetables. She thanked me kindly. About that time a boy near my age came out on the porch. Mrs. Moore said, "This is my son Marvin," as she turned, went back into the house with the vegetables, and left us alone. I could tell right away he was shy; he just stood there and didn't say a word.

I started talking and spent about ten minutes explaining who I was and why I was spending a few days at Uncle Winston's place, and as usual I said I was from Memphis. Saying I was from Memphis to anyone in the Bootheel immediately made them pay more attention to me.

Finally, Marvin started talking; I noticed that he spoke so slowly there was almost a time lapse between each word he said, and every word had the same tone. At first he was difficult to understand, but I got used to it after a while.

"Let's go to the barn and see our new mules," he said. So we went back to the barn and looked at a new pair of brown mules his father had bought in Portageville. His daddy appeared from around the barn and said, "That's a fine lookin' pair of mules you boys are lookin' at there. Sure gonna help with the crops next year."

I realized right away that Marvin's daddy said one word at a time also; they talked just alike. I walked over and told Mr. Moore who I was and why I was there. He smiled and didn't say anything, but I assumed that everything was all right. He turned and walked into the barn. Marvin and I went over to a giant oak tree that had a swing hanging from a high limb. We took turns swinging and pushing each other; then—one at a time—we pumped-swung as high as we could standing up. It was one of the finest swings I had ever been on. Then we each got an old rubber automobile tire and hand-rolled them up the dirt road as fast as we could run beside them. We had taken our shoes off and were barefooted in the delightful thick summer dust. Our tires kicked the dust upward as we made sounds like automobiles. Suddenly, we were at the road that led to Cottonwood Point, and as we rolled our tires under some shade trees to rest, we heard the strange sound of a woman's voice coming from the old store where the jubilee was being held.

"What's that?" I asked Marvin.

"That's someone filled with the holy ghost and speaking the unknown tongue," Marvin answered in his slow, one-word-at-a-time tone. "Sometimes people get so filled with religion and the Lord, they stay here all day long from the night before and speak on and on. We've been hearing them all week, day and night, but mainly at night."

"Yeah, I heard them last night," I replied.

Marvin sounded like he knew a lot about the holy rollers. Out of that old store, on and on, we could still hear a woman's voice shrieking, "Oba da, ola de, uba da, oda de so egga wosa bo, inni gu, posa de boba."

"What do those words mean?" I asked.

"My daddy says it don't mean nothin', but my mamma says God is telling them what to say." We were on the side of the road across from the old store, so we left our tires under the tree and crossed over to the grassy area around the store. We were reluctant to get too close, but we wanted to get a glimpse inside. The store hadn't been painted for years and there were three large windows on each side without screens or window panes. We got close enough to see a few people inside; a middle-aged woman was up front, standing on a platform, speaking those strange words.

Marvin said, "Let's come up here tonight and watch 'em up close."

It was spooky to me, but I agreed. We crossed over the road to Cottonwood Point, got our tires, and rolled them back down the dirt road. When we got to Marvin's house I told him I would return as early as I could after supper; it was planned for about seven o'clock. He said he would be waiting.

At supper Aunt Myrna said, "Winston, Alvin Junior heard the holy rollers singing last night and had some questions about them. I told him you'd explain their religion to him tonight."

Uncle Winston looked at her with a puzzled expression. "Good glory, Myrna, nobody can explain the holy rollers." Then he looked at me and said, "Those people believe in strange things, Alvin Junior, and seem to get possessed with something that makes them go crazy."

I told Uncle Winston about being down at the Moore's house, and rolling the tires up to the old store, and hearing the woman inside speak the unknown tongue. Then I said, "Marvin says his daddy thinks the unknown tongue doesn't mean anything, but his mother believes its God telling them what to say."

"I've heard that Marvin's mother comes from a family of holy rollers," Uncle Winston replied. "I heard Mr. Moore comes from a Methodist family and belonged to a Methodist church before moving over here from Kentucky a few years back. I'm not sure where or if they even go to church now." No one said anything for a while; then I asked Uncle Winston, "Is it all right if I go up with Marvin tonight to the holy roller jubilee? We just want to watch through the windows."

Uncle Winston thought a while and finally said, "Well, Alvin Junior, you can go but don't stay long and whatever you do, don't go inside. I'll have a hard enough time explaining this to your Aunt Annie as it is, her believing the holy rollers are full of demons and things." I assured him that I'd just watch through the windows, and I started up the dirt road as the day was slowly turning into darkness.

Marvin was sitting out on the edge of the road, waiting for me. We walked on toward the jubilee. It was dark before we got there. We could hear the jubilant singing a quarter-mile away, and the closer we got, the louder it got. Out front of the building there was a large torch burning on a tall pole that was casting an eerie flickering light on everything. There were several teams of mules with wagons tied up along the dirt road and a few cars parked nearby. People were crowded around the old store, and at every window there were at least four or five people pushing to get a better look inside.

At first we stayed back on the grassy yard and just listened. But we were close enough to hear the words distinctly as the people inside sang at the top of their voices.

"One, two, three, the devils chasing me; four, five, six, he's always chunkin' bricks; seven, eight, nine, he misses every time; hallelujah, hallelujah for me!" Then they sang the same verse again, over and over, louder and louder. We saw two people leave the middle window, so we hurried over to squeeze in close so as to get a good view inside.

There were several coal-oil lanterns hanging around on the walls that cast a dim orange glow on everything. They were still singing "The Devil's Chasing Me" song with no musical instruments. There were people clapping their hands, some jumping to the rhythmic sounds, and others dancing around like Indians I'd once seen in a picture show. Finally a young man jumped on the platform and started preaching in a loud voice; he sounded serious and talked so fast I couldn't tell what he was saying. Much of the time he sounded like he was gasping for breath, and the only words I could understand occasionally were Hell, the devil, and Jesus. I glanced over at Marvin; his eyes were big and it looked like he understood what the man was preaching.

About a dozen grown folks got up and gathered over a lady who had been sitting quietly by herself. All of them began shrieking and placing their hands on her and saying over and over, "Devil, get out of this woman," and, "Jesus, fill her with the holy ghost." They crowded in so close that we couldn't see her. The congregation was again singing "The Devil's Chasing Me" song and some were stomping the floor and waving their arms side-to-side as they looked upward. Suddenly, the woman the group had hovered over so long screamed and started gibbering and jabbering; they helped her up to the platform like she was going to faint. On and on she started speaking the unknown tongue, "Ibba lu, ada gu, ugo imawa, so da bigo." A man fell backward onto the floor and looked like a dog having a fit. A woman fell on the floor and started jerking and rolling around right beside him.

I felt a big hand on my shoulder, and when I looked up I saw a huge man. He had his other hand on Marvin's shoulder. The man asked in a deep voice, "Are you boys right with God?" Neither of us answered. I was so scared I couldn't talk.

You boys come on inside and get right with God, he said, and he gently began pushing us toward the front of the building. We were out from the window a little on the grass, and I was just about ready to break away to run when someone called him away. We stood there a moment before I said I had better get back to Uncle Winston's house, and then began running down the dirt road. We could still hear the woman speaking the unknown tongue and the congregation singing "The Devil's Chasing Me" song as we stopped running and walked for a while. Marvin asked in his one-word-at-a-time voice, "Do you think we should have gone in, Alvin?"

"Uncle Winston said I couldn't," I replied.

We walked along in the darkness, a little stunned. "Do you think you're right with God, Alvin?" he asked suddenly.

I didn't know how to answer him. My Aunt Annie had talked for as long as I could remember about God and Jesus and salvation, but I still wasn't sure about how I would know if I was more right than wrong. I said, "My daddy is gonna pick me up in two or three days and take me to my Aunt Annie's house before I go home to Memphis, and I'm going to find out from her how you can be sure you're right with God." He didn't say anything.

"My Aunt Annie has read the complete Bible twenty-seven times in her lifetime." He still didn't say anything.

When we got to his house I said I'd come down and swing some the following afternoon. He said, "Swell."

When I got back Aunt Myrna was still up sewing by two coal-oil lamps. She told me that Uncle Winston had been in bed some time because he had to get up early for work. I went on to bed and could hear the holy rollers singing off in the distance mixed with the night birds calling.

At breakfast I told Aunt Myrna some of what had happened the night before. She said, "Perhaps you'd better not go down there anymore, Alvin Junior; it's not like regular church revivals." That morning I helped her with various things, including snapping a whole bushel of beans that she planned to can. I also chopped some weeds and grass from her vegetable garden. She went to a huge trunk and showed me, one by one by spreading them out, sixteen quilts she had made over the years.

That afternoon I went up to the Moore's house and played with Marvin. We rolled the tires around the house and did a lot of swinging. His mother brought us glasses of lemonade, and we sat and talked under the big oak tree.

"My mamma says me and my daddy ain't right with God, Alvin," he said. "She says when you're right with God, you know it, and you ain't got no doubt about it at all."

Again I was at a loss for words, so I grabbed a rubber tire and took off rolling it, challenging Marvin to catch me. After about fifteen minutes we became so hot and tired that we went back to swinging. Nothing else was said about God that afternoon. When I was getting ready to leave Marvin asked if I was going to the jubilee that night.

"Aunt Myrna thinks I'd better not go again," I replied. He looked disappointed.

That night at supper Uncle Winston, Aunt Myrna, and I talked about a lot of things but didn't discuss the holy rollers. It had been a hot day, close to a hundred degrees, and we sat out on the porch and watched the day fade into darkness. Long before we went to bed we could hear the jubilee singing and cheering, coming across the fields of cotton and corn.

"I'll be glad to get this jubilee week over," Uncle Winston said. "It's downright eerie to hear them going at it as they do, night after night."

We went to bed, and the holy rollers singing seemed louder than ever. I could tell from the rhythms of the sounds that they were singing "The Devil's Chasing Me" song, and I knew when they cheered that someone was getting right with God. Late in the night I fell asleep.

About midmorning the next day, I went up to the Moore's house but no one was at home, so I returned and helped Aunt Myrna with her canning. Bootheel people canned vegetables and fruit during the summer to get ready for winter. That afternoon Aunt Myrna asked if I would go to the Tyler General Store to get some things she needed. She wrote all of the items on a sheet from a writing tablet and gave me a clean tow sack for the groceries. She said to give the list to Mr. Rushing, the owner, and to tell him to put it on the books.

It was only a mile to the store, and I had been there several times in the past. I got a Pepsi Cola and a candy bar while Mr. Rushing sacked up the groceries. Three old men were sitting in the back, playing checkers and talking. They looked at me once, but then paid me no mind. I overheard them say one of the Moore boys had been filled with the holy spirit at the jubilee and had spoken the unknown tongue almost all night.

"They didn't take him home until around two o'-clock in the morning," one of them said. "And they carried him back this morning, and he's been speaking the tongue all day."

"Was that the older boy, David?" one asked.

"No, it's Marvin, his youngest boy," another answered.

When I heard that a strange, frightful feeling rushed through my body; I was shocked. As I walked back with the tow sack of groceries, all kinds of things ran through my mind. I couldn't imagine Marvin screaming, jumping, rolling on the floor and speaking the unknown tongue.

Later that day when Uncle Winston got home he said, "Young Marvin has been down there at the jubilee speaking the unknown tongue all day. And they say he may go into the night."

Aunt Myrna put her hand over her mouth and made a painful sigh. "Sweet little Marvin, speaking the unknown tongue," she said softly, "I can hardly believe it."

After supper we sat on the front porch as it got darker and listened to the sound of singing, again coming across the fields. We didn't talk, but I could tell everyone was thinking about Marvin. After things got quiet, and the night was fully dark, the holy roller sounds seemed to get louder.

"Uncle Winston," I said, "can I go down there and see what's happening?"

"Oh, no, Alvin Junior, you'd better not do that. That's funny business down there, and your Aunt Annie will never forgive me for letting you go down there the other night. No, no, you'd better not go." We sat and listened. Aunt Myrna acted like she was spooked by it all and faintly hummed a tune, like she wanted to drown out the jubilee singing.

"Uncle Winston, why don't you walk me down there, and let me just look in the window about five minutes? I'll never ever mention it to my daddy or Aunt Annie," I begged him.

He said no three times before he finally said, "I got to go to work tomorrow early, so you can only stay five minutes, and not a word of this to anyone in the family."

I promised.

We eased down the road and could see the flaming torch a half mile away. There were more cars and wagons than the previous night and there were also more people standing around. When we got to the road to Cottonwood Point, Uncle Winston said, "I'll wait for you over here, Alvin Junior; now, you hurry up."

I went across the road and through the crowd, up to the window with the fewest people. I knew I had to hurry so I got on my all-fours and crawled through people's legs, trying to get a look inside. One man cursed me before he remembered he was at a religious gathering, then he moved over and let me look in.

There standing on the platform with the orange light flickering on him was Marvin, saying all those meaningless words. It was the scariest thing I had ever seen. It was different from the other time, when the woman was speaking, because Marvin was saying his words more slowly and the congregation was quieter. There was no expression on his face and he looked tired. A woman was standing beside him, fanning him with a big straw fan. Everyone was looking at him in wonderment like he was speaking the tongue in some different way. Very slowly he said, "Iba oni wana, poda uppa, lopa," and on and on. No one was rolling on the floor; no one was screaming; no one was singing. I had seen enough, so I backed out through the crowd and ran across the road to where Uncle Winston was waiting.

"He's speaking the unknown tongue, Uncle Winston," I told him.

"Really, Alvin Junior?" he said like he hoped it wasn't true. We started back and hadn't gone more than a quarter of a mile when the singing began again; it was "The Devil's Chasing Me" song. We heard it all the way home and late into the night.

All morning the next day Aunt Myrna and I didn't have anything to say about Marvin or the holy roller meeting. I thought it strange that she acted like it had never happened. I knew it was about time for my daddy to come and get me so I didn't bring up the subject either. That afternoon I was overwhelmed with curiosity, so I walked up the road to Marvin's house to see what was going on. However, I was not quite sure how I would act if he should be home and I had to talk with him. Halfway there I noticed that the field on my right was a corn crop that was about two feet higher than my head, and it went all the way to the edge of the Moore's yard. I hopped over a ditch and went back about eight rows deep in the corn field, being very mindful of blue racer snakes. The rows ran parallel to the road, and I knew I could get up close to the yard and house and get a look at things. I was very careful not to make any noise, and I knew they didn't have any dogs that would give me away.

When I reached the corn field's edge, I saw Marvin sitting in his swing under the large oak tree. He was just staring out into space. There was a slight swaying of the swing, probably from the wind, because he wasn't making it move. I was close enough to see that his eye sockets were dark; he was so motionless that he looked like he was in a trance. I squatted down to make sure I would not be seen and watched him a while, but he never moved. I eased back through the corn field, and when I was far enough away, I got out on the road and ran back to the house.

A little later my daddy arrived in time for supper. We talked some about the holy roller jubilee but there was no mention of my visits there. It was beginning to get dark as I hugged Uncle Winston and Aunt Myrna good-bye and thanked them for letting me stay with them for a few days. As my daddy and I drove up the dirt road toward the road to Cottonwood Point, we passed the Moore's house, where I saw Marvin still sitting in his swing. I didn't say anything to my daddy. We went on up the road and we saw the people gathering at the old Sutton Store with the torch burning out front. Daddy said, "Guess the holy rollers are gonna go at it again tonight."

After we turned down the road to Cottonwood Point, we stopped at the Greenway Store so Daddy could see a man who was interested in buying a truck. I stayed in the car and waited; then we were on our way again. As we were riding along my daddy said, "I've decided to put you on a Greyhound bus tomorrow to get you back to Memphis that way. I was planning to drive you down, but I'm really busy now and can't take a day off." I told him that was fine with me. We drove through the darkness down the gravel road without talking much. The nights in that flat, barren part of the world were exceptionally black and empty. Every so often I thought about Marvin and wondered if he was at home or at the jubilee. Suddenly, I said to my daddy, "Don't hit that man in the road."

He kept on driving pretty fast and asked, "What?"

"Don't hit that man in the road," I repeated.

"What man?" he asked as he glanced over at me. I didn't say anything more. He seemed to slow down, and after driving another quarter of a mile, he slammed on the brakes and the car skidded to a stop about thirty feet from a man lying in the middle of the road. We just sat there a few moments with the engine idling. Daddy left the engine running, got out of the car, and cautiously looked around before going over to the man. He bent down over him, stood back up, and spotted a house a few yards down the road. He disappeared off the road into the darkness and I heard him calling out; a light came on in the house. In a matter of minutes a man and a woman appeared with daddy in the head-lights. They helped the man up on his feet and assisted him off the road toward the house. My daddy got back in the car, and we were on our way.

"That man was dead drunk," my daddy said. "He didn't quite make it home. That bootleg whiskey will sometimes knock you out cold." We rode along in si-lence; after a while he asked me,

"How'd you know that man was in that road?"

"I don't know," I answered.

We rode along. "You said there was a man in the road a mile back. How'd you know that?" he ques-tioned.

"I saw him in my mind," I replied. He didn't ask anything else, but I could tell he was looking over at me occasionally. I felt strange and was a little scared about what had happened, but I figured that the whole summer had been full of curiosities.

We spent the night at Aunt Annie and Uncle Will's place. The next day I got my small suitcase and box of clothing, hugged everybody good-bye and we drove to Steele, where I was placed on a bus destined for Memphis. On the way home I had some time to think. It had been an unusual summer full of mystery and wonder. About halfway home, at Luxora,

Arkansas, on Highway 61, we passed a schoolhouse already in session in August, so they could close school for cotton picking later on. I saw a boy swinging on the playground. I thought of Marvin and sure did hope he was all right. I wondered if he had gotten right with God.

The Comb

LIFE IN MEMPHIS during the late thirties was difficult for thirteen and fourteen-year-old boys. There were many problems: two major ones were finding jobs to make much-needed spending money and avoiding capture by young white gangs who roamed the neighborhoods. The need for my own spending money intensified when my mother became very ill and spent many months in and out of hospitals; the basic necessities of food, shelter and clothing took every penny she had, and often there were shortages in one or more of these areas. Money for picture shows, drugstore milk shakes and trips to the Memphis Fair Grounds had to come from my own ingenuity.

Every time I walked across town to check out a job lead or to go to a job to earn some money, I had to use secret passages down back streets, railroads and dark alleys to avoid getting caught by a gang. There was no question in my mind what would happen if I got caught. They would take my money if I had any, and then two or three of them would take turns beating on me.

These white gangs would usually have ten to twenty members. Most of the members were from thirteen to seventeen years of age, but the gang leaders were generally older, around eighteen or nineteen years of age. Everyone said that Charlie Bowman, leader of the largest and most feared gang of thirty or more members, was every bit of twenty-two years old. Two other well-known Memphis gangs were the Club Copeland Gang and the Rick Patterson Gang. A gang took the name of its leader and, as one would expect, gangs were often rivals. Every so often I would hear of a gang war.

No one knew Club Copeland's actual given name, because schoolmates had dubbed him Club ever since he had attended Guthrie Grammar School and learned to beat up the other kids. Someone said they thought his real name was Cedric, but I knew of no one who had ever been brave enough to ask or call him that. Stories went around that Club had knocked out a third-grade boy with one blow when he was ten years old and ever since had kept it up as a hobby. People said Club knew the exact number of single-blow knockouts he had accomplished and that the count was well over two-hundred. They said they called him Club, because when he hit someone it was like being hit with a big club. No one knew how true or how accurate these stories were, but I certainly could vouch for his ability to knock out someone with a single blow, because once I saw him do it.

Late one autumn day, when I was still thirteen, I went down to the corner of Vance and Linden to a *Press Scimitar* newspaper district meeting with a friend named Dale who was a little older than I and who had been throwing an afternoon paper route for several months. The meetings were held every Monday night, right out in the open, on a well-known street corner. The district manager would give a pep talk and encourage the paperboys to get new subscriptions. Dale had convinced me that if the manager saw me there a lot of times, I would have a better chance of getting a paper route—some steady money—when I turned fourteen. It had just turned dark and everyone was standing on the corner waiting for the district manager to arrive when I looked across the street and saw ten or twelve guys swaggering slowly down the other side; one of them left the group and started out across Linden Avenue toward us. I had spotted them early, so I backed up between some high hedges in a yard just off the sidewalk. It happened so fast I didn't have time to say anything to anyone; also, I wasn't sure it was one of the gangs. The muscular guy about six feet tall nonchalantly walked up to our group and asked politely, "Is there someone here named Grover?"

A skinny little fourteen-year-old boy with blond hair stepped forward and said, "My name is Grover."

Just like a lightning bolt, this fellow hit Grover square on the chin and he was out cold on the sidewalk. Everyone was stunned. I had backed even deeper into the hedges and kept my eyes on the gang across the street; I was ready to bolt if they started coming over. The paperboys just looked down at poor flattened Grover as the large, broad shouldered hoodlum stood over him; no one said or did anything.

"This fellow Grover has been messing around with my girlfriend," the tough guy announced as he stood with his hands on his hips, daring someone to move or say something. Everyone was frozen and speechless because they had seen the gang across the street. I edged up out of the hedges to get a better look at Grover's face; I thought he might be dead because he wasn't moving.

Someone said softly, "That's Club Copeland." I had heard of him for several years and had seen him at a distance, but this was my first close-up look at him. He didn't look all that mean, but he sure was broad and muscular and tough looking.

Club reached into his pocket, pulled out a handful of change, and gave a nickel to one of the pale-faced paperboys.

"Go over there," Club said, pointing to the drugstore across the street, "and get Grover here a Coke." The boy took off running without hesitation. Another boy got down on his knees and began shaking Grover's head gently; Grover started to move a little. I was still standing back far enough to take off if things suddenly changed for the worst. The guys across the street looked as if they were waiting for a signal to charge. The paperboy got back with the Coke, and the strangest thing happened. Club Copeland turned up the Coke and guzzled it down himself. Grover was helped up to a sitting position by two boys, but I could tell he was mostly out of it. Club looked down at Grover and asked, "What's your last name, Grover?"

Grover still couldn't talk, so another small tenor-voiced paperboy replied, "Henderson; his name is Grover Henderson."

Club looked at the boy and said, "You sound like a girl, boy." No one said anything; there was a long, tense period of silence. Club finally remarked, "Well, someone named Grover over in this neighborhood has been messing with my girl over at Tech High, so let this be a warning to everyone in this neighborhood: don't mess around with Club Copeland's girls." He turned slowly and swaggered across the street toward his gang; they moseyed on up the street and disappeared. Once the gang was out of sight, everyone started talking. A few boys were concerned that the gang might return. We got Grover on his feet and someone volunteered to help get him home. Grover was still in bad shape when he left. The district manager finally arrived and there was perhaps a twenty-minute meeting.

Afterwards, I walked along with Dale as he did some collecting on his nearby paper route. As we walked we shared our knowledge of and told stories about the Memphis gangs.

"That's the way Club Copeland operates," Dale said. "He will just walk up to someone and cold cock him with no warning at all. That whole thing tonight was a setup to try to give his gang some fighting fun with smaller, less tough boys. It also added to his knock-'em-out-with-one-blow reputation. I'll tell you this, Alvin, it's a good thing no one said anything or tried to take him on. That Club Copeland gang is one tough bunch, and our blood would have been all over the street corner if someone had made the wrong move."

"I know," I replied. "Last year I saw Charlie Bowman's gang take turns beating up poor old Terry Greenway from school, and as everyone knows he's still scared from it all." We walked along Dale's paper route, careful to keep our eyes peeled, looking in all directions.

It was common practice to be alert and cautious, especially at night. If a neighborhood street wasn't heavily traveled, I was always better off walking out in the middle, away from the hedge rows and heavily treed areas. I would never cross an alley walking on the sidewalk if I was on the dark side of a street; I would veer out into the street. I had to be aware of slow-moving cars coming from any direction, because Charlie Bowman's gang had access to two cars and they often combed the central area of Memphis, searching for someone to beat up.

"I've never understood why the cops haven't put a stop to all of these gangs," I said.

"My brother says it's three things," Dale replied in a serious voice. "One, most of the gang members have brothers—and some even have fathers—on the police force; two, on occasion, when the cops have arrested them and have taken them over to the juvenile court on Adams Street, in a matter of hours they're released and back on the streets. Three, the cops are really afraid of them."

"Afraid of them?" I responded with doubt. "That's hard to believe; the cops have their guns and the law on their side."

"Well, I know it's hard to understand," Dale said. "It's flabbergasting to me, too, but the gangs just keep going strong." Then he told me a story that could not be verified about Charlie Bowman and one of his gang members over in south Memphis approaching and somehow overcoming two young policemen; they beat up the cops with their own billies. I told Dale the story about being over near Forrest Park the night they found a fifteen-year-old boy dead. He had been attacked by the Charlie Bowman gang; someone had stuck an ice pick in his stomach. The poor boy was from east Arkansas, in Memphis visiting his sick uncle over at the Baptist Hospital, and was only looking for a restaurant to buy a hamburger; he was cutting across the park to Union Avenue. He didn't know people have to stay out of that park at night. Such were the conditions of the streets and neighborhoods of most of Memphis in those days. It made us forever cautious as we walked the neighborhoods.

For almost three years, up until I was about twelve years old, I made some good money helping Earlus Johnson find and sell baby squabs to downtown Hotel Peabody. Earlus had gotten into deep trouble with the law, so we had drifted apart. In the fall of 1938 I was thirteen years old and hoping to get a *Press Scimitar* paper route after my November 29 birthday. My main sources of spending money came from an old reliable pie-selling job and a new job I had as a daytime night watchman. Early on Saturday mornings, long before sunup, I would go down on Vance Street to Leonard's Bakery and check out two or three dozen hot pies that sold for five cents each. My best sellers were peach and apple fried pies and little round coconut pies. I'd learned that if I got to the feed mills and warehouses over on the Southern Railroad with the pies smelling fresh-out-of-the-oven, the workers often couldn't resist buying one if they had a nickel. I made a profit of twenty-five cents a dozen; if I sold all three dozen I would make seventy-five cents. I'd do my best to sell out by eleven o'clock, so I could make it on time to my next job that began at noon. I tried not to eat up all my profits by limiting myself to two pies each Saturday. This was a difficult task, but I managed very well with the exception of one cold October morning when I had very little breakfast. I sat down on a street corner, lost control and ate four pies in about fifteen minutes. I would make only a nickel profit on my first dozen pies. The situation created a strong conflict between my enterprising desire to earn money and the great feeling of having a full stomach. Without a doubt, that was the toughest part of that job: being with those delicious, tempting pies right there in a box under my nose and my stomach growling in hunger. It was especially difficult the first hour out when the pies were still hot and oozy and smelling so good. But I managed not to lose control again, and most of the time I was sold out by eleven o'clock. I would return to the bakery and pay my bill, then I would go straight to my other job.

I had acquired my daytime night watchman job at the Liberty Cash Grocery on Linden Circle Avenue quite by accident. The store had just finished some redecorating and new advertising when they put up a sign in the freshly-painted store window announcing they were going to hire three boys for extra work on Saturdays for a dollar a day. The sign read that the boys had to be at least sixteen years old. The day they took applications I was only thirteen, but I showed up anyway. I got in the line and when I came face to face with the manager I asked, "Do you have any kind of work for someone almost fourteen years old?"

"No," he said, his gruff tone reflecting his anger at being asked such a question when he was so busy. There were at least thirty boys there hoping for one of the jobs, and the manager and another man were looking over the applicants. They quickly reduced the number of boys to six; brawn was important I figured, because none of the scrawny boys were asked to stay. I hung around to see how they were going to pick the lucky three, but I stayed over to the side out of the way. The six remaining boys were asked lots of questions, and then the two men retired to a back office. They returned in about ten minutes and made their final selections. The three boys not selected drooped their heads and were slowly leaving the store with me trailing behind when the store manager stopped me and said, "You really wanna work, don't ya, boy?"

"Yes, sir," I replied.

"Come on back to my office," he said. I followed. He placed some papers on a desk, then he walked through a door that led to a back storage area. I followed him without saying anything.

"See that back door?" he asked as he pointed. "Many of our customers like to leave with their groceries through this back door to a parking lot out in the rear, so we can't lock it, and we also can't lock and unlock that storeroom all day long. We have been missing some cartons of canned goods and sacks of sugar in recent weeks and we think someone has been carrying them out during our busy hours on Saturday." He went on, "I'm going to give you the job of watching our storeroom from noon until midnight on Saturdays. You'll be a secret watchman, sort of a daytime night watchman," he said, and he laughed at his comment. "All you gotta do is hang around back here and watch; sit around like you're waiting on your parents and make sure no one leaves with anything from our stockroom." He paused a moment. "I'll pay you fifty cents a Saturday."

"I'll take the job," I eagerly replied.

Every Saturday in the fall of 1938, I worked in the morning selling pies and from noon until midnight as a daytime night watchman. At midnight every Saturday, if all had gone well, I would have earned a little more than a dollar. After work I had to negotiate the long eight-block walk home to avoid getting caught by one of the gangs. I did this successfully by never taking the same route twice, by keeping a keen eye open for suspicious cars and by avoiding places where I could get trapped.

My job as a daytime night watchman could have been terribly boring but it turned out to be full of excitement. Around eight o'clock my first night of work, a man leaving the back way put down a sack of groceries and came back into the stockroom. He was picking up a box of canned goods when he spotted me sitting in half-darkness over to the side. He dropped the box of canned goods, grabbed his sack of groceries and hurried out the back door. I ran and got the manager; he and another man rushed outside in time to see the man speeding away. They got his license number. They were proud of me and pleased with themselves for having the idea to hire me as a watchman. When things calmed down, the manager came back and said, "Good work, Alvin." He showed me the area where they kept all of the fruit. "In addition to the fifty cents a night, Alvin, you can have any of this fresh fruit you want to eat." A little later I helped myself to a big delicious apple, two bananas and several oranges. I almost made myself fruit sick every Saturday.

In late January of 1939, after turning fourteen the previous November, I got a *Press Scimitar* afternoon paper route that netted me over seven dollars a week. That much money meant I could do and have several things I could not previously afford. Of course, I gave up my pie selling and daytime night watchman jobs. After a few weeks I got far enough ahead with my money that I began acquiring certain items that I would never before have thought of buying. One week I got a ring for my keys and a billfold for my money. The following week I bought my first fountain pen. In early summer I went to the Memphis Fair Grounds and spent two dollars on rides and refreshments. One day, after looking over various articles at the dime store, I bought an Ace pocket comb that cost fifteen cents; it was the best comb one could buy in those days. I even bought a small shoe kit with polish and a brush and occasionally—not too often—I would polish and shine my shoes. Life became much better when I had some money to spend on ice cream, cold drinks and an occasional picture show with popcorn. One Saturday night I took a bath, put on a clean shirt, shined my shoes and decided I would walk down to the Linden Circle Drugstore and get a vanilla milk shake. I stood around afterwards and watched people play the pinball machines. Then I went outside and stood on the sidewalk, watching the cars go by. In about five minutes an old black Packard sedan slowly drove up. A fellow I knew named Billy Ennis opened the door, got out and passed by me as he went into the drugstore. Hurriedly, he said, "How are ya, Alvin?"

"Fine," I said. The motor of the car was still running and someone I didn't know was behind the wheel. I saw Naomi Bartlow all by herself in the back seat. Naomi was a very pretty girl, a year older than I, who attended Tech High; I had known her back in junior high school. She had long dark hair and was noted for bosom-filled sweaters.

As I stood there I could tell Naomi was looking at me; finally, she leaned over near the window and asked, "Alvin, do you have a comb that I could borrow?" I was startled that she knew my name, so I stood there in a state of discombobulation. She asked again, "Do you have a comb? I need to comb my hair."

"Sure," I said. I reached in my pocket and handed her my new Ace comb through the car window. When she took the comb she gave me a flirty look. She began combing her long dark hair, and I stood there mesmerized.

Suddenly, the car started easing away, so I jumped on the running board, stuck my head in the window and said, "You have my comb."

Naomi moved over to the far side of the back seat and said, "Come on in and get it" By then the car had gunned off fast and I couldn't jump off, so I climbed on in through the window into the back seat with her. The car quickly turned a corner and entangled me with the warm-bosomed Naomi; by the time I became un-tangled, the car had turned another corner and had come to a sudden stop. Nothing had been said the en-tire time, but it seemed as I was struggling to upright myself with Naomi in the back seat she was making moaning passionate sounds

As I opened the back door to get out, there was a large gang of thugs surrounding the car in a circle, waiting for me in the darkness. I had to think fast. I had heard that gangs would tease and tantalize their victims for a minute or two before they started beating on them. I had to think of something. I heard a voice say, "Well, we've got us a pretty boy tonight, and I recognized the voice as that of Charlie Bowman."

"We'll mess this pretty boy up real good," someone said. Over to my left were two boys in the circle who didn't seem to be all that big, so I walked over in their direction, bent over and made sounds like I was going to throw up. I diverted their attention just enough to shoot through them like a cannon ball. As I ran past them, someone's fist hit me on the back of my head, and one of them grabbed me but lost his grip. I tore up Dudley Street with the yelling maniacs right on my heels. As I approached Lamar Avenue, I knew I might have a chance to escape by running in and out of the busy traffic. I glanced back and saw that three of the gang members were only about ten yards behind. They were yelling and cursing like wild savages. When I got to Lamar Avenue, I ran out in the middle of the street with one of them so close behind me I could hear him sucking air. I was getting tired. I glanced over my right shoulder and saw that I had just enough time to cut in front of three cars coming from the west, so I did and my pursuers had to wait for the cars to pass.

The city was building a sewer system on the south side of Lamar Avenue that year, and there was an eight-foot deep ditch, at least ten feet across, that ran along that side for several blocks. I leaped across the ditch and landed on the other side with my arms and upper torso on top of the bank. I threw my left leg up, pushed up to my feet and took off running southward. I glanced back and saw the gang members standing on the other side of the ditch; some of them were climbing down into it, trying to get across. No one had tried my method. I zigzagged perhaps three blocks back into that neighborhood; I ran into a dark area between two houses and crawled far back underneath one of them. I could hear the gang calling out to one another as they searched up and down the streets.

I lay there frightened of my own breathing, it was so hard and heavy. My whole body was throbbing and I began checking out my body and physical condition. I could feel a large knot on the back of my neck and I had scratched and bruised my stomach as I slammed into the ditch bank. Also, my left knee was hurting. But I couldn't complain, because at that moment I still had my teeth and my head wasn't smashed. I heard several of the gang walk by on the sidewalk at least twice, and once I heard what I believed to be the old Packard cruising slowly down the street. I knew there could be spiders, rats and maybe even a snake under that old house, but I put it out of my mind quickly. I knew I had better wait a long time beyond when I thought the coast was clear, so I stayed under the house for about thirty minutes. Altogether I had been under there more than an hour. I eased out and went up the dark alleys, behind the hedgerows and down the Southern Railroad tracks to home. I could not help but think of how strange it was that my safest and most secure route home was down that dark Southern Railroad, considered by many as the most dangerous place in all of Memphis.

The next few days I made sure I stayed clear of places where I might get caught, even during the daylight hours. I ran into my friend Dale; he said he had talked to some people who had seen the gang chasing me down the middle of Lamar Avenue on Saturday night, and he wanted to be filled in with all the details. I started from the beginning and when I got to the part where I tumbled around in the back seat of Charlie Bowman's old Packard with Naomi Bartlow, Dale stopped me and asked, "You're telling me you were in the back seat with Naomi Bartlow and you're still alive?"

"Yeah," I replied, "but it was all an accident and you're right, I'm lucky to have survived that situation. The heavy Lamar Avenue traffic and the sewer ditch saved me." I went on, "You know, Dale, that back seat incident happened in three or four minutes, but I'll tell you the truth: when I was in that back seat all wrapped up with Naomi, it seemed to me that she was hugging and grabbing onto me like she was enjoying it. I'll tell you, I've never ever felt such a soft warm body." Dale wanted to hear more, but that's all there was to it. Then I told him about being under the house and how I got home down the Southern Railroad tracks.

"You had better not get caught now, Alvin," he warned. "They'll beat you for a week."

"I know," I said.

About two weeks later Dale and I went downtown to the Loews State Theater to a picture show called *Good-bye, Mr. Chips.* The ushers were holding back a large crowd of people out in the lobby until the main feature ended. I looked across to the other side of the lobby and saw Naomi waiting with another girl; just as I saw her, she saw me.

"Naomi Bartlow is over there," I whispered to Dale in a soft voice.

"Where?" he asked, and I sort of motioned to the left with my eyes.

"You want to go over there?" I asked.

"Not in a thousand years," Dale answered.

I looked over again; she was cutting her wicked eyes over toward us. I don't know what came over me, but I said, "Save my place in line; I'll be right back." I pushed myself through the crowd to the other side and approached Naomi and her girlfriend.

"I believe you have my pocket comb," I said in a friendly way to Naomi.

"Yes, I do; I'm keeping it for a souvenir," she said.

"Oh, you collect souvenirs?" I asked.

"Yes, things that come from special occasions, and I consider our recent adventure in the back seat of the car a very special occasion. Her eyes were enticing. Her girlfriend was looking at us in confusion. During the conversation I could not keep from glancing down at Naomi's white blouse that cut low across her well-formed bosom. She was wearing a bright flower-patterned skirt.

"Why don't you come over to my house sometime and I'll show you all of my souvenirs?" she said seductively.

"You're trying to get me killed," I said. "Do you know what would happen to me if Charlie Bowman caught me at your house?"

"Charlie doesn't own me and, besides, you seem to have lots of courage."

I concluded that she thought I knew I was in Charlie Bowman's black Packard when I climbed through the open car window that night.

About that time the feature ended and people started moving through the lobby, so I said, "Goodbye; good to see you," and I began pushing through the crowd back to Dale.

She called out across the crowd, "I live on Cossett Street," and as I looked back, she again had that look in her eyes.

Dale and I walked the three miles home after the picture show. We mainly talked about girls, and I told him what Naomi had said.

"Alvin," he said, "there are lots of girls. If I were you, I'd stay clear of Naomi."

I knew what he meant. "I'll tell you, Dale, Naomi has a way of making your blood boil," I replied.

"Your blood will be all over some street somewhere, he said." I knew he was right.

I found Naomi's address on Cossett from the phone book and during the next weeks I started walking down the street where she lived, even though it was out of my way. Twice the old black Packard was parked out front, but I never saw Charlie or any of the gang. One afternoon I walked down the alley behind her house, looked over the fence into her backyard and saw a flower garden and a yard swing. There was one small area planted with multi-colored zinnias. It smelled good back there, with lots of honeysuckle on the fences up and down the alley. For some reason I couldn't stop going by Naomi's house, but I never could get the courage to walk up to her front door. Maybe it was because I often had visions of Charlie Bowman answering the door and battering me on the spot.

Late one August day, after I had bought a new pair of brown and white saddle oxford shoes and after some deliberate thought, I decided I would go over to Naomi's, knock on the front door and tell her I wanted to see her souvenir collection. When I got there and started up the sidewalk, I suddenly noticed that the house was empty. I stood there maybe five minutes, wondering what had happened. A lady in the house next door came out and asked, "Are you looking for the Bartlows, young man?"

"Yes, ma'am," I replied. "I was going to visit with Naomi."

"Well, they have moved to Vicksburg, Mississippi," she said. "Moved last Monday. Mr. Bartlow works for the government fleet and he was suddenly transferred there." I thanked her for her help and walked down the street.

I had a strange feeling of relief, yet it was mixed with some genuine sorrow and disappointment. It had taken me so long to get the courage to take those steps up to Naomi's front door, and now it had no meaning at all. I still had problems. My paper route was giving me a steady income of seven dollars and fifty cents a week, so that was helping a lot with money problems. But I still had to watch out for gangs at all times. Now I also had become very aware of a new problem in my life that could come from full-bosomed, wicked-eyed girls. I had to face it; I wasn't going to get back my Ace pocket comb or get to see Naomi's souvenir collection. As I walked down Cossett Street, I noticed the sweet smell of honeysuckle in the warm August air. It was one of those late summer afternoons when everything had turned a blue-gray color. The whole world had succumbed to stillness. I decided I would go down to the Linden Circle Drugstore and get a vanilla milk shake.

The Henning Twins

JUST AFTER MY friend Harry Ashcraft turned sixteen early in 1942, he became increasingly interested in
double dating. By mid-spring he had acquired his
driver's license and his father was allowing him to have
the family car, a two-door 1936 Ford sedan, two nights
a week. Harry was eager to start dating, so almost every
time I saw him he would say with much fervor, "Let's
find some girls, Alvin, and double date." Harry was
from a well-to-do family that lived in a fine brick
house over on Hulbert Street, not far from the famous
E. H. "Boss" Crump home. He was very intelligent
and he often helped me with my lessons since I was
usually half asleep in classes after having thrown a
morning paper route.

I had told Harry about some of my erotic experiences with girls in the Bootheel of Missouri; therefore,
he had an overrated opinion of my ability to obtain
dates. There was a lot of difference between Memphis
girls and those in the Bootheel, and the truth was I
had not been all that successful at getting dates myself.
The girl I really liked and had dated some had moved
to Mississippi, so I couldn't ask for her help. Harry
made matters more difficult, because he didn't want to
date girls from our own school.

"Central High girls talk and gossip too much," he
said. At first I didn't understand his reasoning, but I fi-

nally decided Harry had so little experience dating that he believed the chances of having an embarrassing situation were great; if the girls were from other schools, there wouldn't be the problem of facing them in class. Such were the circumstances that led to some rather awkward experiences that year.

One day I was on East Street, trying to collect money owed me from people on my former afternoon paper route. I saw Sue Mae Blackstock sitting in her front porch swing, making a slight motion by gently pushing off with her left foot. I walked up, sat on her front steps and we had a conversation about our respective lives since completing junior high school the previous year. I learned she was attending Tech High School and liked it; I told her I was going to Central High and was also satisfied. After a while I said casually, "By the way, Sue Mae, I have a new friend at Central named Harry who has a Ford car, and if you have a friend maybe we could go driving and get something to eat some night on a double date." She looked a little startled because I had never shown any interest of that kind in her before, although I had known her for a long time. Sue Mae wasn't a beauty, but she wasn't bad looking, and she was well-known for her wit and cheerful personality.

"Well, Alvin, this is a surprise." Se paused. "If I find a friend and we go out with you, will you be my date?" she asked.

"Sure," I answered. "You'll be my date and you find a friend for Harry."

She got up, started for her front door, and said, "You wait here and I'll be right back. I'm going to make a phone call." After a while she returned and said, "My cousin Wilma and I will be glad to go riding with you and your friend."

"Great!" I replied. "We'll pick you up here about seven o'clock this coming Friday."

As I was leaving Sue Mae added, "Alvin, Wilma is not a very fast girl, and you tell your friend Harry that she doesn't talk very much."

"Sure," I said, "I'll tell him."

Monday at school I told Harry about finding two girls for our first double date; that's all we talked about during the week.

"Is Wilma pretty?" he asked.

"I don't know anything about her, Harry," I answered. "Sue Mae said she was not a very fast girl and that she doesn't talk very much. I'm guessing she may be a little shy."

Harry picked me up Friday at about six forty-five, and we arrived at Sue Mae's house right on time. The girls were sitting in the front porch swing. We walked up the steps and I awkwardly introduced the girls to Harry; Sue Mae introduced Wilma to us. Wilma just smiled. We got in the car and Harry said, "We'll go to get some barbecues at Pig 'N Whistle on Union Avenue if that's all right with everyone."

"That's great," I replied.

"That will be very nice," Sue Mae responded. Wilma just smiled. As Harry drove down Union Avenue I saw him taking sneaky glances at Wilma. While waiting for a red light to change, Harry looked back at me with a disconcerted expression. We parked on the dark side of Pig 'N Whistle, and the carhop was there almost immediately.

"What would you all like to have?" Harry asked.

Sue Mae said, "I'll take a brown pig sandwich and a Coke." There was a pause and Wilma just smiled.

"I'll take a white pig and a Coke," I said. There was a lull.

"Wilma will take the same thing I ordered," Sue Mae quickly asserted. Harry gave the order to the curb-hop. Sue Mae said, "My Aunt Thelma who lives in Illinois who was visiting here once thought that white pig and brown pig sandwich meat came from white and brown-colored pigs." Her comment wasn't all that funny, but Sue Mae and I started laughing.

I asked, "Is that really true?"

"Sure is," she replied. "The family took her over to Leonard's Barbecue Place on McLemore for sandwiches, and when we got home she asked how many different colored pigs were there."

"She thought there might even be purple pigs?" I questioned.

"I suppose so, she answered." The pig talk was not all that humorous, but Sue Mae and I caught contagious laughter, and laughter was causing more laughter.

Finally, Harry asked gruffly, "What's funny back there?"

The way he asked the question set off uncontrollable laughter. Wilma started laughing; when she in-
haled air after a long laughing spell she sucked it in
through her nostrils in a way that sounded like a pig
snorting. That made everything worse, and we were
laughing so hard the car was rocking. Harry looked
back at us and said, "Cut that out. Nothing is that
funny." With that I became hysterical with laughter
and was weeping. Sue Mae was in the same condition.
Just as there was a lull and we were about to stop,
Wilma snorted in air again, and we went at it some
more. Harry turned around and said, "Nothing is
funny," but then he started laughing a little. Wilma
was laughing so hard her gum flew out of her mouth
and landed on Harry's right pants leg. Wilma just
pointed at the gum, and we roared in laughter. She
picked the gum off his leg, put it back in her mouth,
and started chewing again. I glanced up and saw
people in the surrounding cars looking at us strangely.

The carhop brought our order and fastened a tray
on the slightly raised window of the driver's door.

"Two white pigs and two brown pigs and four
Cokes," the carhop announced. With that Sue Mae
and I went for another round of laughter. Harry paid
the bill; we ate our barbecue pig sandwiches and only
broke up twice. Afterwards Harry took us riding
around town. Then we all got quiet much earlier than
expected, so Harry drove back to Sue Mae's house; we
walked the girls to the front porch and said our polite
goodnights.

We were about two blocks away when Harry started cursing profusely and blaming me for getting him such a dreadful first date. He was angry.

"Harry, you can't blame me. That is what happens on blind dates. You never know what you will get," I said.

He cursed some more but calmed down a little. "There's got to be a better way of checking things out before blind dates," he said. It was quiet again, and Harry was under control.

"What was wrong with Wilma?" he asked with a tinge of compassion in his voice.

"I think she had some kind of speech problem," I answered.

About two weeks later Harry and I were eating pimento cheese sandwiches and drinking milk shakes at the counter of the Linden Circle Drugstore. Just before we finished I heard a voice behind me say, "Hi, Alvin Allen."

I turned on the counter stool. "Why, it's Betty Jane Spraggins! I haven't seen you since we were in Sophye Olive Fink's homeroom in the seventh grade."

"That's right," she responded. "We've lived in Nashville for the last three years and just moved back to Memphis."

I noticed that Betty Jane had filled out really well and was quite pretty. I introduced her to Harry who was staring at her. We talked about earlier times for a while, and then I said, "Say, Betty Jane, if you have a girlfriend Harry and I will gladly take you all out some night." She seemed hesitant, so I added, "Harry has a Ford sedan. Maybe we can go to a drive-in and get some food and then go play miniature golf or something like that." I had decided to put the first outing on an innocent basis. Harry was looking at me loathingly.

"Well, I live in a new neighborhood and haven't made many friends yet," she replied. "Give me your telephone number and I will call you."

As she was leaving Harry asked, "Where have you entered school?"

"Oh, I'm attending Saint Agnes School for Girls," she replied. Harry looked relieved.

As we left and were crossing the street Harry said, "If she gets a girl for a double date, I get Betty Jane. "

"Well, Harry, I think she might want to date me since she knows me."

"This blind stuff is risky," he said.

About a week passed; Betty Jane called to say she had a friend and we could pick them up at her house on Vance Street Saturday at seven o'clock. As we drove over that evening Harry said, "I want Betty Jane for my date tonight."

"Harry," I responded, "let's let things work themselves out." We knocked on her door and Betty Jane walked out followed by a very large girl. Betty Jane came over, took my arm, motioned toward Harry, and said, "Paulette, this is Harry and he is your date for the night." Agony and anger were written all over Harry's face. Paulette had a pretty face but was about a hundred pounds overweight. When we helped them into the car it appeared that the car sank down considerably. Harry gave me a disgusted look, but he never lost his gentleman's demeanor. We bought hamburgers at a drive-in on Parkway Avenue and never thought about a dimly lit barbecue place. We talked mostly about school, war and picture shows.

Afterwards we played miniature golf. The game went pretty well, but Palette had never played before and she wasn't very coordinated. Several times she swatted the ball like she was Byron Nelson on a driving range. Twice Paulette's balls zoomed across the playing course, causing people to jump out of the way. This embarrassed Harry; he was not rude, but he made no effort to help her. On some holes Paulette would take as many as ten or twelve strokes and she had trouble bending over to retrieve the ball from the holes.

We carried the girls home and said our polite goodnights. When we got a few blocks away I expected Harry to explode in anger, but he sank into a state of quiet depression. Finally, he said, "Let's go over to Jake's Pool Hall and shoot some snooker."

"Fine," I responded. We were quiet as we drove over to Madison Avenue. At last I broke the silence, "She was a little fleshy, wasn't she?" Harry looked at me with contempt and replied, "Huge, Alvin; she was huge." He felt better after beating me in three straight games of snooker.

As Harry drove me home I said, "If you ever learn to deal with girls like you shoot pool, you'll be a world-famous lover."

He laughed a little and said, "I'm certainly off to a good start as a lover."

Harry's experiences with Wilma and Paulette daunted his spirits considerably about dating, so in the next few weeks we did a lot of pool shooting, duck pin bowling and golfing.

In early September, just after entering the eleventh grade, Harry called early one evening and asked me to meet him over at Triangle Park to talk for a while.

"My mother belongs to a ladies' club," he said. "And one of the members has twin daughters about our age that she is anxious to introduce to two wholesome, respectable young men," he laughed as he told me. "This Mrs. Henning has talked to my mother on several occasions about me coming over to their home in Bartlett to meet them and to bring a friend," he went on. "That's it in a nutshell, Alvin. You want to go and meet the famous twins?"

"Do they look alike?" I asked.

"My mother says they look exactly the same and also act the same." He continued, "Two or three years ago they went to a twin convention up north and won some award for being so identical. According to my mother, Mrs. Henning always meets and gives approval of the boys the twins date, so we'll have to go over and sit in the living room and be scrutinized. I understand their father is sick, and has been for a long time, so Mrs. Henning does some things a father would normally do. Well, what do you say, Alvin? Are you game?"

"I suppose if they both look alike and both act alike that they would weigh about the same amount," I responded.

"That's not funny, Alvin," Harry shot back at me, but he was smiling as he said it.

"Sure, let's go see them," I said.

About a week later, on a rainy Thursday night, we drove to Bartlett and were greeted warmly at the front door by Mrs. Henning. It was an impressive two-story dark brick house. She told us the girls were still getting ready and would be down shortly. We sat in a large, softly lit living room and talked with Mrs. Henning. The conversation was designed to measure our characters. She was an attractive lady herself, perhaps in her mid-forties, and extremely serious and formal. She asked Harry several questions pertaining to morality, and Harry gave forthright and intelligent answers. I did not take inquisitional mothers so seriously as I should have in those days and responded with some answers that caused Harry to look at me with disapproval. Then she asked me about my religious background and I said, "Well, I have an aunt in the Bootheel of Missouri who has read the Bible twenty-seven times and is the county blood stopper" Harry froze and stared at his interlocked hands in his lap.

"That's interesting," Mrs. Henning responded. "I had a great aunt in Virginia who could stop bleeding with the use of faith and scripture. Tell me, is your aunt by chance of the Baptist faith?"

"Yes, ma'am," I answered. "All my mother's people were Methodists, but my Aunt Annie, the blood stopper, and all my father's brothers and sisters are Baptists." Harry looked relieved.

The twins came down the stairs and Harry and I were startled at the likeness of their appearance. Both were about five-nine and a shade on the thin side. They were wearing blue pique dresses with lace ruffles. Both had long, dark brown hair, hazel eyes, sharp features and were very pretty.

"Young men," Mrs. Henning spoke with pride, "I'm pleased to present to you my daughters, Doris and Donna." We were considerably awkward and they were timid as we made getting-to-know-you conversation. The twins sat together on a large sofa with their right legs crossing over their left legs; I noticed that the gentle, rhythmical kicking motion of their right feet was at the same tempo. I sat in a large chair on one side of the couch, and Harry sat in one on the other side. Mrs. Henning sat in a chair facing us but a distance away. She stayed out of the conversation as we discussed our scholastic objectives, ambitions and hopes for the future. One of the twins mentioned science, and Harry gave us a short but impressive lecture on Einstein, Copernicus and Sir Isaac Newton. Harry was one smart guy. Mrs. Henning excused herself and left the room. In a few minutes she returned with Mr. Henning. Harry and I shook hands with him and could tell he was not in good health. In a brief time Mr. Henning excused himself and left us to talk some more.

Around nine-thirty Harry said it was time for us to be leaving; he asked Mrs. Henning if we could carry the twins to a picture show sometime or maybe to the fairgrounds.

"I can tell you both are fine boys," she said. "Certainly; you may take them out any time you want."

On the way home all Harry and I talked about was how identical the twins were, even down to their body movements. I asked, "Do you think you can tell which one is which?"

"Well, I'm not sure," Harry replied, "but I think I can tell 'em apart. When we take them out I would like to date Donna."

"Which one was that?" I asked.

"She was the one sitting closest to me," he replied.

"Harry," I said, "I think the one closest to you was Doris."

"Well, then I'll take Doris if it was," he replied. "It will all work out," he added.

On Friday night of the following week we agreed that Harry could take his pick of the twins since he was the finder. As we drove to Bartlett he said, "I'll walk up to the one I think I like, and you can take the other one."

"And you're going to try to pick out Donna, right?" I asked.

"Yeah, the one that sat closest to me when we visited."

We arrived, talked in the living room about ten minutes and when we were ready to leave for the drive-in theater, Harry walked over to one of the twins and said, "If its all right with you, I would like to take you to the picture show." He was play-acting and being formal but he was smiling.

"And your name, Miss, is?" he was still acting formal. I thought it was his way of dealing with a clumsy situation.

"My name is Donna," she replied in an exaggerated manner.

Harry turned to me and said, "See? I was right."

Doris, also acting very sophisticated said, "I'm glad to have you as my date, Alvin." We were acting very silly.

"I'm very honored to have you as my date, Doris," I said with a continued British accent.

We had no plans to eat out on the first date, so we went straight to the Airways Drive-in Theater. It wasn't quite dark, and the picture show had not begun, so Harry volunteered to get some things from the refreshment stand. I talked with Doris about various topics as we sat in the back seat. Donna listened to music coming from an outside speaker. Just before Harry returned with cold drinks and popcorn I asked Doris, "The other night when we first visited you, did you sit on the couch near me or on the other side near Harry?"

"Why, I was on the other side near Harry," she answered.

I thought to myself, "This is going to get complicated."

We were still eating our refreshments when Harry put the sound box on the car window as the picture show began. The picture was *Brother Orchid* with Edward G. Robinson and Humphrey Bogart. From the beginning it looked like it would be a very exciting picture full of mystery, but it was hard to keep one's mind on the action. After about forty minutes Harry moved over and put his arm around Donna. Very carefully she removed his arm, never taking her eyes off the picture on the screen. I looked at Doris and we smiled at each other. Harry began taking sneaky looks back at us, and I could tell he was looking in the car mirror, trying to see what we were doing. I realized Doris knew what he was doing, so it made for a strange situation. After a while, in the darkness of the seat between us, Doris moved her hand on top of my hand. She started massaging my arm very slowly, all the way up to my elbow. I looked over at her and she had one of those Veronica Lake I'm-all-yours looks on her face. Harry and Donna were caught up in the picture show and he hadn't tried to place his arm around her again. Every so often they made comments to one another. Harry kept peeking back at us, so I thought I'd better go easy in the back seat and keep things as close as possible to the action in the front seat. It was Harry's car, and I didn't want to make him mad. Too, we needed to succeed on this first mission if possible. However, the hand and arm communication I was receiving was very intense, and Doris was still giving me an occasional seductive look. I began hoping the picture show would hurry up and end. Finally, it did, and we took the twins home and said our polite goodnights.

On the way home Harry said, "I think we did all right with the twins, Alvin. Don't you?"

"Yeah," I answered.

"I think we were wise in not trying to kiss and neck on the first date, don't you?"

"Yeah," I replied. I didn't tell him that Donna wasn't the one nearest him on that night of our first visit.

A few days later it was Mid-South Fair time in Memphis. Harry and I decided to take the twins to the fairgrounds. When we were at their house walking them out to the car, one twin drifted toward me and the other moved toward Harry, so we assumed we had the correct pairings. At the midway we rode various rides including the Pippen Roller Coaster, and viewed several side shows. We went into the house of mirrors and when we came out, Harry and I stood wondering which twin was which. They had fixed their hair for the night in a pompadour style and they looked more alike than ever; we just waited and finally one walked up to me and the other went to Harry. At that moment I decided I was going to look carefully for a mole or a scar or something else to help me with the twin identification problem. I didn't succeed right away, but I decided to persevere and try to find some identifying mark before the night was over.

Harry asked me to drive so he and Donna could have the back seat as we went over to Pig 'N Whistle for some barbecues. I drove in on the dark east side and gave the carhop our orders. As usual we talked about school, war and picture shows. After a while Doris and I got into a serious and lengthy conversation about a picture show called *Holiday Inn* starring Bing Crosby. I noticed that it was quiet in the back seat. I looked back there, and Harry and Donna were locked up in some serious smooching. Doris didn't look back, so I started talking louder and kept the conversation flowing. I put my hand down in the seat where it had been at the drive-in theater, but it rested there and was not touched. After a while, I eased my hand over on Doris hand, but she instantly pulled hers away and folded her hands together in her lap. I didn't get a Veronica Lake look all night. As I sat talking to her I saw a pearl ring on the third finger of her right hand. I didn't remember the ring from our arm and hand action that night at the drive-in theater. I decided I would check Donna for rings, and maybe it would help in keeping them identified. Doris said, "We have to be home at eleven, Alvin, and it is now ten-forty."

Without looking back I said, "Harry, the girls have to be home at eleven."

"We're ready," he said. "You keep on driving and take us to Bartlett."

When we got the girls home there was no kissing goodnight on the porch but just our normal polite goodnights. On the way home Harry was beside himself. "Boy, that Donna was one hot patutti," he said. "And does she know how to kiss." He went on and on about Donna. "You didn't kiss Doris, did you?" he asked in sort of a bragging tone.

"Nah, I'm not so sure she was ready for kissing," I replied. When we got to my house we sat and talked in the car for about an hour. I didn't mention the pearl ring that I had seen on Doris' finger.

During the following week Harry and I concluded that it would be shrewd of us to take the twins to church. They had mentioned their church activities in conversations. Too, we thought Mrs. Henning would be impressed and would continue to give her approval for us to date the twins. Harry made the phone call, and it was arranged to go to the evening service of the Bartlett Baptist Church on the following Sunday. The church was only three blocks from where they lived, so the four of us walked the distance. There was a modest gathering that night, and the singing of hymns was soft and drawn out. We sat on the back pew. The minister was a small man, about thirty-five years of age, and his sermon was soft and low-key, quite unusual for a Baptist preacher. His text was "I am the vine; ye are the branches," and his message was more like a lecture than a sermon. I was impressed with what he had to say, but I noticed that very few people seemed to be listening. At the end of the sermon we stood for prayer, and the preacher requested that everyone remain a short time for the baptism of two new members who had joined the church. During the final prayer, the hands of the twins were resting on the back of the pew in front of us, and I saw the pearl ring on Doris finger; I looked over and saw that Donna was not wearing a ring. I figured that ring was going to be helpful in telling the twins apart.

Soft organ music played as we waited for the baptismal service. The baptistery was a typical one with a river scene painted on the back wall behind the water, but it was different because it was situated on the side of the church building. The minister came out from a side entrance, stood in water chest deep and spoke briefly about the meaning of baptism. He went back to the entrance and brought out a young boy about twelve; the preacher said the appropriate biblical words and gently laid the boy backwards, immersing him in the water. Then he lifted the boy out of the water and said, "Raised in newness of life; and like Jesus he walks straight way out of the water." The young boy was assisted back out the door. Then this enormous lady came through the entrance assisted by the small minister. The visual impact of the immense lady and the much smaller minister instantly benumbed the congregation into a silent tenseness. I knew—everyone knew—that the laws of gravity and force would not allow the baptism to work. Harry and I exchanged glances. As the minister reached upward, put his left hand on the back of her head, and was reciting the biblical passages leading to immersion, I thought again, he cannot immerse that lady without a disaster. At the appropriate time she began leaning backwards. The preacher placed the small towel over her face but lost control of her and she went down like a giant oak. What stunned the congregation was the sound of the splashing water. Almost immediately our pew began shaking from body jerks born of restrained laughter. After the lady crashed into the water I looked downward and tried thinking of other things; I started biting my cheeks to keep from laughing. Then I looked up at the chaos in the baptistery; the little minister struggled to get her above water. The congregation had given a collective moan just as she had gone down and everyone watched in anguish. I felt Doris vibrating and dared not look at her. When I finally did, it was torturous not to laugh. Tears flowed down my cheeks as the pew shook. I looked over and saw Donna sitting stoically, the only person on the row not in pain from attempting to control laughter. In fact, Donna looked angry. I never knew how they got the large lady out of the water, because I refused to look over there again. Later on I was told that the minister completed the required biblical passages, but I heard none of it.

On the walk back to the twins home, Donna expressed anger at the three of us for laughing in church and, in particular, at something as holy as baptism. Near their home Doris, Harry and I sat down on the street curbing and went through a complete concert of wonderful laughter. Donna stood waiting in anger.

We stayed for a while at their home, but Donna continued to stew, so we left early.

Driving back to Memphis, Harry and I talked a long time about why people get spells of uncontrollable laughter at formal gatherings. We didn't solve the problem. Then Harry said, "Donna didn't find the big splash all that funny, did she?"

"No, she didn't," I replied. We didn't talk for while.

Finally, Harry said, "My daddy says that when there are identical twins, one of the twins usually is not as well-balanced mentally as the other. What do you think about that, Alvin?"

"Well, I'm not quite sure what I think," I answered. Again we drove along in silence. We each knew that the other one was wondering if what his daddy said was true, then which of the twins was the unstable one and which one was not. We didn't talk about the twins any more that night.

A few days later we arranged to take the twins on a double date to a regular theater to see a picture show. We sat in their living room as Harry read aloud from the newspaper the picture shows playing at various theaters around the city, allowing the girls to choose what they would like to see. Harry said, "*Ghost of Frankenstein* is showing at the Lamar, *Desperate Journey* is showing at the Madison, *Third Finger Left Hand* at the downtown Loews Palace."

"Who plays in *Third Finger Left Hand?*" Doris asked quickly.

"Myrna Loy and Melvyn Douglas," he answered.

It seemed to me that Doris looked over at me when she asked that question, but I didn't know why. We couldn't settle on a picture show, so Donna said, "I'll make the decision; it will be *Third Finger Left Hand* at the Loews Palace." So we went and afterwards everyone agreed that it was a very bad picture.

Harry offered, "To save the night well go get some barbecues at the Pig 'N Whistle."

We ordered a mixture of brown and white pigs and Cokes. I was in the back seat with Doris; I had checked the third finger on her right hand earlier and the pearl ring was there. After we ate the barbecues we talked about school, war and picture shows. I saw Harry place his arm around Donna and she removed it immediately. They got into a conversation about why Donna was not in a good mood that night. Suddenly, like a panther in the night, Doris leaped over, pushed me back in the corner of the back seat, and became a real live Veronica Lake, kissing me with passion. I surrendered to the situation but after about ten minutes wondered if there was ever going to be a rest period or any more conversation that night. Out of the corner of my eye I saw Harry look back at us twice. I heard Donna tell Harry that it was time to take them home. Harry didn't say anything but just cranked up the car, pulled out of the Pig 'N Whistle and headed toward Bartlett. On a dark stretch of road about two miles from their home, Doris gave me another passionate attack and again I surrendered. Just before arriving at their home we came up for oxygen and had some conversation for the first time since the first attack. On the front porch we did not kiss goodnight but just said our normal polite goodnights. While driving back to Memphis, Harry asked, "Man, what happened to Doris tonight? I saw you all back there smoochin' up a storm."

"It is hard to figure out, isn't it?" I replied.

"Yeah, Donna was as cold as an iceberg with me tonight," Harry said. We rode for a while.

"Harry, I've got a question for you," I said. "If your life depended on a correct choice, would you have any fear of having to correctly identify the twins? Could you really tell Donna from Doris?"

"No fear," he answered, "I know Donna; I have this special feeling for her, and her eyes are slightly different; besides, Doris wears a pearl ring on one of her right-hand fingers."

"You noticed that too, you rascal?" I responded. "How long ago did you notice that?"

"Several weeks back," he said laughingly.

"Well, they both sure do have severe mood switches," I replied.

"Everybody has mood switches, Alvin," he answered.

One Tuesday night in October, Harry phoned to tell me Mr. Henning had died in his sleep the previous night. Mrs. Henning had called Harry's mother and asked if Harry and I could carry the twins over to the funeral home for a brief visit on Wednesday night. Harry said, "I've already called Mrs. Henning and said that we would be there at seven o'clock. I've never been in a funeral parlor," he added.

We picked up the twins and they seemed more the same that night than ever before. They appeared to be handling their father's death well, and neither showed any signs of grief. We got in Harry's car and were heading toward Memphis when I noticed that Doris wasn't wearing her pearl ring. We parked out front of the funeral parlor and held the girls by the arms as we walked them up several steps to the entrance. We lingered behind as they walked down a quiet hallway. An attendant led the twins into a large, dimly lit blue room with an open casket. We were the only visitors present, and there was an aura of cold stillness in the room. The twins walked up to the casket and stood looking at their dead father. Harry and I held back a few feet, but we could see the body and it was the whitest corpse I had ever seen. We must have stood there in silence at least five minutes before one of the twins began sobbing in grief and the other one began to laugh. Harry looked at me in a state of disbelief. The more one twin sobbed, the louder the other one laughed. This went on for about ten minutes. Finally, they stopped crying and laughing and one of them said, "We can go home now." On the way back Harry and I made conversation as best we could. The twins were back to looking and acting exactly the same; there was no more crying or laughter. We took them to their front door and said our polite goodnights.

On the way back to Memphis, Harry asked, "That was Doris weeping so hard, wasn't it?"

"If it was," I replied, "that was Donna laughing, and I always thought Doris was the laugher."

"I noticed Doris didn't have her pearl ring on tonight," Harry said.

"Let's just say that no one had on the pearl ring tonight," I replied. He gave me a quizzical look. We rode in silence for a long time, each of us thinking our private thoughts. I was convinced both of us were thinking there might have been twin switching at times, but neither of us ever came out and said it.

About a week later Harry met a girl at school named Sarah and decided he would try a date with just the two of them. It worked out well, so we never again dated the Henning twins. Some time later Harry and I saw the Henning twins with two boys about our age, walking down Main Street in Memphis. We stopped and talked briefly. I noticed that one of the twins had a pearl ring on her finger.

As we walked on down the street Harry asked, "Do you think those fellows know which twin is which?"

"I don't know, I replied. "But I do know they had better not count on too much help from that pearl ring."

The Road Turned North

DURING THE FINAL weeks of my eleventh-grade school year, rumors were circulating about a football camp that was to be held in the Ozark Mountains during August, before the new school term started in September. The football coach had heard about a high school football team in Alabama that had won several state championships after having football camps in the Smokey Mountains, and he was making plans to try out this idea with our team in the Ozarks of Arkansas. In late May an article appeared in the school paper stating there was good reason to believe final approval would be given and the Memphis Central Warriors could begin their 1943 practice season in the beautiful Ozark Mountains.

I was approached by two of our better players, and they half-suggested that I go to the football camp if it came about, since I had shown good speed in running the hurdles during the recently completed spring track season.

"You might make a good end," one of them said. I did have better than average leg speed, and I dearly loved running; I got pleasure from playing allcomers tackle football on Sunday afternoons with no equipment, and I seldom missed going to the school's regular football games. But I was dubious of organized football. Besides, I was throwing the equivalent of three paper routes—over three hundred papers—and walking about ten miles every morning from two-thirty until I got through around six o'clock. This responsibility was enough to keep me from seriously considering the camp, so I put it out of my mind.

In early July I saw Donald Hemphill down at the Linden Circle Drugstore. He had obtained some recently printed information about the approved football camp and he was looking for someone to go with him.

"Look," Donald said, pointing to the sheet, "it only costs sixteen dollars for the complete week in the mountains, and it says clearly that newcomers are invited to try out." I took the sheet and read it carefully. "Sixteen dollars covers your train ticket there and all your meals for a complete week in the Ozarks," he repeated. "My family was over there several years ago, and they still talk about the beautiful scenery and the cool-running Spring River that has rapids and small waterfalls. You get someone to throw your paper routes for a week, Alvin, and let's go." I told him I would give it some serious thought. "August fifth is the last day to sign up," he said as he left.

Like other seventeen-year-old boys in 1943, I was aware that I would soon turn eighteen years of age and be off to a dreaded war. Many of us had learned to savor our remaining days and weeks before the uncertainty of the draft and the unknown. It was against my better judgment, but the idea of seeing the Ozark Mountains was the overwhelming factor that caused me to overcome many paper route problems and to make arrangements to go to the football camp with Donald Hemphill.

At midmorning on a Monday in late August, I found myself among eighty-six boys on a slow train easing its way northwest across Arkansas to the Ozark Mountains for a football camp. We did not have a special passenger car to ride in but were mixed with the regular riders in three different cars. Donald and I sat together and talked as we went through small farm towns and passed by many fields of hay, cotton and corn. At noon we ate the sack lunches that we had been advised to bring with us, since our only meal at the camp that day would be supper at six o'clock. There were few regular passengers traveling on that Monday, and the car we were riding in was quiet until several of the almost-sure first-string players started swaggering up and down the aisle being loud, singing and doing other things to break up the boredom of the five-hour ride. Nearly one-half of the boys on this trip were just trying out for the team and were green and easily intimidated by the returning senior lettermen and other proven players. Rollen Roper and John Trout, both hero players from the previous season at halfback and end, saw me sitting with Donald and came back to where we were.

"Hey, Alvin," Rollen asked, "are you sitting over here with all these meatballs?"

"Yeah," I answered. "Thought I'd give it a shot this fall; nothing much to lose. Might try out for end position."

The train jerked suddenly and was taking a sharp curve; this threw everyone standing in the aisle off balance, and they were grabbing for something to hold. The incident also set off a barrage of profanity and anger directed at the train, because it was upsetting their equilibrium. Someone said, "We are entering the mountainous area."

John Trout looked over at Donald and barked out in a tough voice, "What's your name, meatball?"

"Donald Hemphill," he answered softly. John Trout didn't say anything; he just continued to stare down at Donald like he couldn't wait to smash his tender body into the turf. Donald sat there like a cowed dog. The train jerked and swerved again, and John cursed the train. Then they sauntered back with some of the others to the passenger car ahead of us, and things got quiet. We sat and watched the scenery for a while.

Donald finally asked, "What is this meatball business?"

"All new players are called meatballs," I explained. "They like to be tough and scare the hell out of young players. Truth is, they are tough and there will be a lot of head-knocking this fall." Donald turned a little pale. He was a year younger than I and would be entering the eleventh grade. Like me, he was skinny, not quite weighing a hundred and fifty pounds, and had very little meat on his bones. However, he was a bit shorter than I and was a little more compact.

"Seems to me you should make the team, Alvin," Donald commented. "At allcomers games you're fast you block and tackle good, hit hard and always do good; everyone wants to be on your side when we choose up, I've noticed that."

"Well, I have a little speed, and I like to play down at the park, but I'll have problems with all the time it takes at practice. I'd have to give up my paper routes if I should make the team, and I need the money that I make," I replied. "We'll see how it goes up here this week." Actually, most of the star football players showed me some respect since I had lettered twice in track and in May had finished a close second to Clay Calhoun from Tech High School in the high hurdles at the regional track meet. Clay was considered one of the best athletes in all of Tennessee and was an all-state halfback in football.

Near the mountainous area we passed near small towns called Hoxie and Black Rock. The train was running along the Spring River, and we were beginning to see the small areas of rapids and clear water that we had heard about. The conductor announced that we would arrive soon at Hardy where our group would depart and hike to the campsite about a half-mile away from downtown. Hardy was no more than a train station, several small stores, a barber shop and a filling station. We walked perhaps four hundred yards west on a road that forked, and then we turned left toward the campsite. To the right, the road turned north into the mountains. We crossed the river on a very narrow, old rusty truss bridge and took a winding dirt road up a small mountain. We were pooped by the time we got to the top. The director of the campsite led us to four large cabins filled with army cots; the cabins would be our quarters for the week.

Our coach, named Spraggins, gave us a short talk and instructed us to be dressed without pads and ready to go to a practice field in one hour. At three o'clock we jogged as a group down the mountain; then we ran another half-mile down a gravel road to a small fenced-in green field that, until the day before, had been a cow pasture. The coach and his assistant lagged about a quarter of a mile behind. There on that hillside field slanting toward the river, the Central High Warriors began their football training camp. After entering the field through a cattle gap, several players eager to get at it started running out for passes. We had been there only a minute or so when a pass was thrown to a player and, long before the ball began to descend toward him, he tripped over a stone hidden in the deep grass, flipped and tumbled before coming to a stop. He got up with his jersey ripped and blood oozing from a badly scraped arm. Soon thereafter, another player running for a pass tripped and fell into a fresh pile of cow dung; it was all over the side of his face and the front of his jersey. I could hear the profane voices bouncing off the sides of a mountain across the river area. The coaches finally arrived; they had us leave the field and stand on the gravel road while they checked out everything. They tiptoed around the field, looking for rocks, stones and cow dung. Coach Spraggins called out for Rollen, who had been elected captain, to lead us in calisthenics out on the gravel road. The team, eager to put some life into a dismal beginning, did side-straddle hops in unison and the sound of rhythmical counting echoed through the valley: "One, two, three, four; one, two, three, four."

After thirty minutes of exercises, the coach picked twenty players to stay and hunt for stones and cow dung in the field. Two players were sent to borrow shovels from the campsite director to help remove cow dung. Rocks and stones were carried from the field and thrown into the roadside ditch. The remaining players were instructed to run back to the campsite for conditioning. That first day most of the players jogged until they were out of the coaches' sight, then walked up the dirt road that led to the mountain top. A little later we went swimming in the Spring River.

At six o'clock we walked as a group down the mountain, crossed the river bridge and went to a basement area below an old gray stucco building for the evening meal. They could only serve about thirty players at a time, so more than half of us waited outside for the first group to finish. I could tell as players left they were not overwhelmed with the food. That first meal was a plate of beef stew, two pieces of light bread, a very thin piece of apple pie and cool spring water. We ate by the light of three low-wattage light bulbs hanging from the ceiling. The basement smelled of mildew. There were no second helpings of food, but a lady who helped serve us kept saying we could have all the cool spring water we wanted. We immediately dubbed the dark and dreary eating place "the dungeon." After eating, players left the dungeon and started looking for a place to buy some food, but the only store there had closed at five o'clock. It was only the first day at camp and everyone was reluctant to complain. We walked back to the campsite disappointed and hungry. I remarked to Donald, "At least the blue of the evening is unique in this Ozark area." He appeared not to understand my statement. Even though it was August, soft gusts of cool air periodically rushed across the valley, and before we got to the top of the mountain it was almost cold. There were all kinds of restless activities in the cabins after dark. Some regular vacationers were in nearby cabins, and the sound of "Deep Purple" could be heard coming from a record player; it played over and over. In that same area someone was frying country ham. The air held an unusual mixture of sound and smell.

At breakfast the next morning we were served two thin pancakes with syrup, one small orange, one small glass of milk and all the cool spring water we wanted to drink. We reached the cow field for practice around nine-thirty. We took calisthenics for twenty minutes, and then the coach gave us a pep talk for another twenty minutes. Part of his spirited message was about watching out for rocks and cow dung in the high grass. Finally, we began scrimmage activities. After almost every play someone encountered another rock, picked it up, walked over to the fence and tossed it into the ditch. Within the first hour of practice every player had experienced cow dung in one way or another. We kept shifting around to different areas of the field, hoping to find a better place, but we didn't succeed.

At lunch we were served a cheese sandwich with a small portion of pork and beans, an apple and all the cool spring water we could drink. After lunch everyone rushed to the store down the street and began cleaning off the shelves of anything edible. I had brought only three dollars with me, so I limited myself to one candy bar, realizing the week was going to be a long one.

Afternoon practice at two-thirty consisted of one-on-one head-on tackling. We formed two lines of over forty players each. A player from the first line would run with the football as fast and as hard as he could, straight at a player from the second line whose objective it was to tackle the other player head-on. In a while we would alternate and the tackle side would become the runner side. This continued perhaps an hour; it was brutal and almost like roulette, because every so often some very large, two hundred and forty pound monster-type would be the runner, and he would have to be tackled by some skinny kid who weighed around a hundred and thirty pounds. The big guards and tackles would smash into the little guys with a mighty force, crushing them to the ground; they would lie there like they had been hit by a gravel truck. It was a strange and fierce activity to be taking place in the peaceful Ozarks on a meadow meant for bees, bugs and butterflies.

Just beyond midweek, the August heat became intense. The food got worse and the store down the road was running out of good things to sell. The cow dung was drying up some, but stones were still found at every practice. Players were sore, tired, grumpy, hungry and a few were secretly homesick; everyone was ready for the Ozark football camp to come to an end. Friday was especially miserable because the temperature had climbed to over a hundred degrees during the day. The one thing that had probably saved the football camp experience was the one hour of swimming in the river between the afternoon practice and the evening meal.

On Friday a young player named Logan, who was just entering Central High School from an out-of-state junior high school, made the fatal mistake of getting soap in his eyes while showering and was groping around to find his towel; when he couldn't find it he called out for someone to bring him one. The senior players were constantly on the alert for someone to do this, and one of them sloshed a big handful of red-hot rubdown liniment all over the poor boys scrotum while his eyes were still full of soap. This particular young player had no knowledge of this trick, and the shock and the pain caused him to believe that something had gone radically wrong with his vital area, so he fell down on the shower floor, screaming and hollering. Eventually, someone got through to him about what had happened, and he started washing himself with cold water and soap. Afterwards he went down to the Spring River and sat in the cool water for an hour. It was the highlight of the day for many, and laughter was plentiful. The event diverted minds from the evening meal. I walked down the mountain with Donald toward the town to eat. He thanked me for having warned him on the train about the red-hot liniment trick. "Boy, I bet that really hurts," he said.

"It does," I replied. "They did it to me in the tenth grade about the second week I was out for track. However, I had previously heard about the trick and washed myself off fast, but it was still a painful experience." We walked on quietly for a while.

"You know, Alvin," Donald talked softly so others would not hear, "I sort of felt bad by what they did to Logan; everyone seemed to be enjoying it, and they were laughing so much I didn't dare say anything."

I looked over my shoulder to see if anybody was near. "They really like playing tough tricks like that," I responded, "and that particular trick played on some people is just a little bit too much." Donald and I went on down into the dungeon to eat the evening meal: a rationed portion of spaghetti. Logan walked in looking sheepish. He was acting like he had done something wrong himself and still appeared embarrassed and wounded. When he got his spaghetti we called for him to come sit with us and it seemed to please him. He walked gingerly and sat down gently in his chair. We didn't talk about his experience but made conversation about going home on Monday morning.

We were finishing our meal, sitting and drinking cool spring water, when three of the senior star players came to our table. One of them said mockingly, "Say, red-hot Logan, I bet you'll run like a scalded dog in practice tomorrow." They roared in laughter; Logan looked humiliated. We didn't say anything.

That night around nine o'clock, everyone went to bed early; we were worn out from the week. It was so quiet I could hear the night birds calling in the forest. The record player in the nearby cabin was playing again, and the sound of "Deep Purple" wafted through the pine trees; I could no longer hear the birds calling. Someone started cooking and I smelled ham frying. I thought again how that was such an unusual mixture of sound and smell.

Saturday was much like the other days except that seven boys were on the injured list and half of the players at practice were hobbling around. There was a lot of griping about the supply truck that was to replenish the little store in downtown Hardy not making it for another week. I still had two dollars and sixty cents of my money and would have bought something that day, but the store was sold out of everything. Players were talking about food and how hungry we were all the time and this made it even worse. Late that night I heard "Deep Purple" again whiffling through the pine trees. I was grateful that no one cooked late that night, so I didn't have to suffer through the smell of ham frying.

On Sunday morning, the last day of football camp, I slept as late as I could and still make breakfast. There was to be no morning practice—just afternoon that day—and everyone was allowed to swim two hours that morning. When I got to the dungeon for breakfast, I was last in a line of five waiting for the cook to whip up a few more pancakes. I was the last person to get two pancakes and a small orange. I slowly ate the thin pancakes, since there was no rush to get anywhere. I realized I was the only one left in the dungeon, so I ate my small orange, peeling and all, and drank a lot of cool spring water. I left the dungeon and was walking back to the campsite when I came to the fork in the road; I saw a little old man sitting on a box by the closed filling station. About thirty yards beyond the station, the gravel road turned north into the mountains. I looked up that road for a while, then I walked over to the little old man and said, "Good morning."

"Howdy-do," he answered.

"Feels like it's going to be another hot day," I said.

"It's going to be a scorcher," he replied.

I looked down the empty road again for a minute and then asked him, "Where does that road go?"

"Mammoth Spring," he answered.

I thought a little more and then asked, "How far is Mammoth Spring?"

"Right at sixteen miles," he answered.

"Are there any stores or small towns or anything between here and Mammoth Spring?" I asked.

"Young man, there ain't nothin', I mean absolutely nothin', until you get to Mammoth Spring," he answered.

"Do any cars ever go up that road?" I asked.

"Very few on Sunday," he answered.

I made some quick calculations, looked down toward the camp area and didn't see anyone and then I turned and started walking north up the road. When I was up the road a piece I stopped and looked back, "By the way, is there a place to eat in Mammoth Spring?"

"Sure is," he said.

I hollered back, "Thanks for your help." He didn't reply.

In a matter of fifteen minutes I had walked over the top of two small mountains and was descending into a valley that looked to stretch at least a mile and a half across to the next mountain. Most of the mountains in that area were only three or four hundred feet high, but they were certainly too high and steep to be called hills. For over a year I had been walking about ten miles every morning, throwing papers in Memphis, and I thought I would have few problems getting to Mammoth Spring. After about two miles it seemed that every step I took was carrying me farther away from some kind of collective bondage. The stillness of the day was occasionally broken by the sound of a crow or a mourning dove. After a while I was so far out in the woods that when I rested a few minutes under the shade of a large tree, I could hear the soft wind whispering through the trees. I had walked at least six miles when I realized two things I had not planned on: one was that climbing steep mountains was tougher than the gentle inclines of Memphis streets; the other thing was I was getting thirsty and there seemed to be no solution in sight. I knew I had to think positively, so I spotted the top of a mountain that was some distance away and I told myself that when I got there I would be halfway to Mammoth Spring. It was hot but I could take the heat, however I was beginning to need a drink of water badly. I reached the top of the mountain that was my imagined halfway point and could see a broad valley ahead; I got to walk downhill for a long time. When I was beginning to climb up another mountain, still around six miles from my destination, I was sure I could smell something cooking somewhere. As I went farther down the road, the smell became stronger and I looked back through the woods and could see what seemed to be a small cabin. It was perhaps seventy-five yards back in the woods and barely visible; if it had not been for the smell of food cooking I never would have noticed it. I left the road and walked until I was maybe twenty yards from the small cabin and hollered out, "Hello!" I waited about thirty seconds and hollered again, "Hello! Anybody home?" Two weathered-looking middle-aged women in plain clothing came out on the porch and stood there, saying nothing. "Good morning," I said. "I'm walking over to Mammoth Spring from Hardy and have gotten hot and thirsty. Do you have a pump or a well so I could get a drink of water?" The women stood there like mummies with no expression and said nothing. An older man came out the door with a gun cradled in his arms.

"I sure do need a drink of water," I said, whining a little. They didn't move or speak. I walked backwards for maybe fifteen yards, turned and walked briskly out to the road; I walked even more briskly once I was on the gravel road. After about a mile I slowed down my pace, but I never once looked back.

I glanced at the sun and knew it had to be past eleven o'clock. I was too thirsty to be hungry. I realized that the next few miles would be the real test of my will and spirit. I wouldn't allow myself to regret my decision to walk to Mammoth Spring, but I was beginning to wear down. When I was perhaps four miles from my destination, I crossed a narrow road that connected from the east, and after I had walked about one-half mile beyond, I looked back and saw an old flat-bed truck turning off the road and heading my way. I half-heartedly thumbed for a ride; the truck stopped and the driver said he would carry me on to Mammoth Spring, about three miles away. There was another man up front with him, so I had a very bumpy but welcome ride on the back of the truck. They let me off close to the spring itself, and I spotted a drinking fountain where I drank some water. I had learned from earlier farm experiences in the Bootheel of Missouri never to drink much at first and to drink slowly when I had been without water for a long time. I walked over and looked at all the spring water coming out of the ground. A sign stated that two hundred million gallons came out of that one spring in a single day. A few people were standing around the Mammoth Spring, so I asked a man if he knew where a cafe was in town.

"Well, the cafe is about two blocks over, but I don't think they're open on Sunday," he said. I walked over there, and the man was right; a sign in the window read: CLOSED ON SUNDAY. This was a devastating blow to my vision of a delicious Sunday dinner. There were four old men sitting on a bench at the town square, so I approached them and asked where I could find a cafe to get some food.

"Everybody goes to Thayer to eat on Sunday," one of them said.

"Thayer?" I asked in a questioning tone.

"Yep, Thayer; it's only two miles away, across the state line into Missouri. Just follow Highway 19," he said.

I had walked only a short distance when a man gave me a ride. I told him my story of walking from Hardy to Mammoth Spring to get a good meal only to find the cafe closed, so I was on my way to Thayer. "You need to go to Martin's Cafe in Thayer," he said. "They have good plate lunches and always specials on Sunday. It is also the bus station, but they do have real good meals there." He let me out a block from the cafe.

In a short time a waitress at Martin's Cafe had served me a delicious dinner of fried chicken, cream potatoes, fresh string beans, sliced tomatoes and hot rolls. I checked my money carefully and added a piece of coconut cream pie for dessert. It took me a full hour to eat the meal and drink four glasses of iced tea. It was a welcomed eating experience after a week of eating in the dungeon. The fatigue from my long walk subsided and I knew the long walk had been worth it. The chicken dinner and pie cost a whopping eighty cents, which still left me with a dollar forty. When I paid my bill, I asked the man if buses ever ran to Hardy.

"Once a day on Sunday," he replied. "The bus will leave here at six-thirty tonight and will get you into Hardy about seven o'clock. A ticket to Hardy is thirty cents," he added. That was great news to me, because I didn't relish starting right back on that long trek to Hardy. It was right at two o'clock, so I decided to look over the little town. I walked all around downtown; after a while I noticed a two-story building that looked freshly painted in a dark rose-red color, and it had a large portico out front with rows of white columns and a drive underneath for cars to park and drop people off. Underneath were six long benches painted olive green. It was a lazy, hot August Sunday afternoon, and the downtown area seemed to be deserted. I sat on one of the benches in the shade and then realized how tired I was. I thought about how quiet and still everything was and lay down on the bench and fell into a restful sleep.

I had been sleeping about an hour when I heard the voices of women talking and giggling. When I opened my eyes one of them asked, "Are you waiting for someone, honey?"

I sat up in a stupor. "Ma'am?" I asked. They giggled some more. Standing there in front of me were three women dressed in satin dresses of orange, purple and yellow. Two were perhaps in their thirties, but one pretty black-haired girl with peach white skin looked about fifteen.

"Are you here to see someone special, honey?" the woman asked again.

"No ma'am," I answered. "I'm just taking a nap before I go back to Hardy on the six-thirty bus." The two older women laughed some more, but the younger black-haired girl didn't; I noticed that her face was without expression and she was looking off to the side.

"Well, honey, if you decide to come in we'll introduce you to someone," one of them said in an enticing manner as they walked into the building.

An old gray-haired man who looked to be seventy-five years of age was sitting on a nearby bench. He got up, sort of shifted over to my bench, and sat down beside me. "How did you like those gals?" he asked.

I hesitated a few seconds. "Well, they sure did have on pretty dresses," I answered.

"Hee, hee, hee," he laughingly responded, and he slapped his leg. "Boy, the real pretty is under those dresses. However, Margie, she was the one in purple, she's gotten a might fleshy in the last two years, but Bernice and Little Linda are two pretty women with pretty bodies." I didn't say anything, but I realized that something was unusual about everything, since I had awakened from my long nap. We sat for a while; the old man was looking straight at me. I think he sensed that I was muddled about the situation, so he asked unabashedly, "Young man, do you know you're sittin' in front of the finest whore house west of the Mississippi River?"

I was stunned for a moment and turned and looked back at the building, wondering how I could have known. "No, I didn't know that," I answered in surprise.

"The gals take Sundays off until about five o'clock; things will pick up around here in just a little while." About that time the small black-haired girl in the yellow satin dress came out of the building, letting the screen door slam behind her. She twisted over and sat on one of the green benches near us.

"That's Little Linda," the old man said. "She just started this year. She's Lora Mae's daughter. Lora Mae selects the men that get her." Little Linda crossed her legs and rhythmically kicked the top leg as she smoked a cigarette, blowing smoke straight forward. She never looked over at us.

"Little Linda likes you," the old man said. I can tell. You got any money?"

"Nah, I don't have any money," I answered.

"You mean you ain't got no money?" he asked.

"No money to speak of," I answered. He talked on, and in about ten minutes Little Linda got up, twisted back in the front door, again letting the screen door slam. During the next hour the old man told me the complete history of the whore house as well as many graphic tales of things that he had experienced, seen and otherwise knew about. The house was there because Thayer was a railroad hub; through the years, many railroad men had spent lonely nights in boarding houses in Thayer and the rose-red house of pleasure had just evolved. Toward the end some of his tales about what had happened there were beyond anything I had ever heard before. I asked him for the time, and he pulled a gold railroad pocket watch on a chain from his pants and said, "Young man, it is exactly eight minutes past five o'clock."

I said good-bye to the old man and started back toward the cafe and bus station. I went up a street with a rather steep incline for about a block and a half, and as I looked back the rose-red whore house was glowing in the late afternoon sun, contrasted against the dark gray background of other downtown structures. While looking at the whore house, I saw two black cars drive up in front and park; men crossed the street to enter. The old man was right; things were picking up after five o'clock.

For my evening meal at Martin's Cafe, I had two hamburgers and another piece of pie. After paying thirty cents for my ticket back to Hardy, I still had enough left to buy eight bars of candy to take back to the camp. I knew the other players were starved, and I had a feeling that the candy might come in handy in some way. I had a mixed bag of Baby Ruth, Power

House and Mr. Goodbar. A snub-nosed bus arrived twenty minutes late, but by seven o'clock we were bumping back down the lonely road that had brought me to good food and new experiences. I watched the day ease into deep purple and wondered if I would hear music again that night. The mountain valley had turned a deep blue color, and it was almost dark when we arrived at Hardy.

I departed the bus and walked toward the campsite. Three of the players were standing on the bridge talking. When I got close one of them asked, "Is that you, Alvin?"

"Yeah, it's me," I answered.

"Where have you been? Everyone had concluded that you had drowned in the river," he spoke with alarm. "They have been searching everywhere all afternoon for you." Then he hollered out loudly, "Alvin is here! Alvin is here!" I could hear his voice echoing up the mountain. We walked down the road and started up the mountain; three or four others joined our group.

"Where have you been?" I was asked again with impatience.

"Well, I've been to Mammoth Spring and Thayer, Missouri," I said.

"How did you get there?" someone asked.

"Walked there and rode the bus back," I said.

One of them said, "Boy, a lot of people are gonna be mad at you. They went downstream all afternoon looking in the river for you. When you were not at practice, two players said that they had seen you swimming this morning."

"Well, I wasn't swimming this morning, so they were wrong," I said.

When we reached the top of the mountain, Rollen, John, and Slick were standing there in the dim light. They cursed me severely and were quite upset because they had been put on a special search team and had wasted a lot of their free time looking for me. They acted like they wanted to rough me up for disappearing. Just as they edged in closer I said, "I'm sorry I caused trouble," and I reached in my sack and started handing each of them a candy bar. They hesitated a moment, then each took a candy bar and started gobbling it down. Rollen still looked mad so I gave him an extra Baby Ruth, just as one would try to appease an angry dog with a bone.

The coaches came by and reprimanded me, but I could tell they were relieved that I was alive and hadn't drowned. In a few minutes I was in my cabin, where Donald and a half-dozen others gathered around my cot, wanting to know about my adventure. "Tell us what you did," Donald asked.

I didn't respond immediately, so they kept insisting. Finally, I talked about the long walk, the heat, the thirst, the strange people in the cabin, the Mammoth Spring, and then I spent at least twenty minutes describing in great detail the delicious chicken dinner. They were in agony after that, so I pulled out the remaining candy bars and broke them up into several pieces; I gave out the pieces as fairly as I could. They devoured the candy quickly and then we sat quietly for a few minutes. I didn't tell them anything about the whore house. A little later I told Donald that I would tell him some more on the way home on the train. We went to bed. "Deep Purple" was not played that night. I heard the night birds calling and some dogs barking at a distance.

On the way home the next day, I was still getting a mixture of attitudes from the other players toward me. I could tell a few were still angry, but I didn't have any more candy bars. Some just laughed it off. I also could tell that a few of them secretly viewed me as a minor hero. Donald reminded me that I was to tell him something else on the way home, so we went to the back of the train and I told him the entire story of the rose-red whore house that was supposed to be the finest house of pleasure west of the Mississippi River. Donald gave me his complete attention; he had lots of questions, and I gave him lots of questionable answers. Then we rode a while without talking. We had passed the town of Marked Tree, which meant we would be home in about an hour.

Later as we crossed the bridge going into Memphis, Donald asked, "Alvin, what made you go off like that yesterday?"

I thought about it a moment, then answered, "Well, Donald, my pancakes were very thin yesterday morning. When I was on the way back to camp and I got to where the road turned north, it just seemed to be the right thing to do."

On Tuesday I turned in my football uniform after deciding to keep my paper routes and concentrate on track my final year. Donald made the football team and in time became a star player. Central High School had one of the finest football records ever that year, losing only one game in the season and that, ironically, was by one point to a team over in Arkansas. The coach must have been right: having a football camp in the mountains led to a championship team. Perhaps the success of the team had something to do with all those hot practice sessions on fields of stone and cow dung. Or maybe it was from drinking so much cool spring water.

The Wild Blue Yonder

ON A HOT, mid-July summer night in 1941, I was returning home from collecting money on my afternoon paper route when I saw what looked to be a gang of white boys fighting in front of the Linden Circle Theater. I had learned long before to skirt around and try to avoid such gang wars, so I quickly turned into the high-hedged, heavily-bushed front yard of an old house to watch the action from a half-block's distance. About that time two squad cars arrived and boys began to scatter. I heard a movement over in the bushes a few yards away, and it was there that I first saw William Wharton. He came crawling across the yard, bent over so as not to be seen; he told me who he was and said he was new in the neighborhood, having just moved there earlier in the week. I told him who I was and thought immediately that he had to be smart to know instinctively how to avoid the gang fights and to know how to hide and watch from the bushes.

"Do they have many gang fights like this?" he asked with an air of excitement in his voice as we watched a few remaining boys exchange blows.

"Almost every night during the summer," I replied. We were talking softly so we wouldn't be heard. "If you're new to Memphis you had better learn the neighborhoods, and learn how to stay clear of these gangs. I tell you, they beat the hell out of people just for the fun of it," I said.

In a few minutes, after it looked safe, we eased up the street to where William lived, sat on the steps of his front porch and talked for a while. He told me his mother, stepfather, older sister and he had moved from West Memphis, across the river, so he could attend better schools in Memphis. During our conversation we discovered we were both 15 years old and would be entering the tenth grade at Central High School in just a few weeks. I told him a few things about myself; I told him where I lived and offered to show him around the neighborhood. I left his house an hour later, taking a circuitous but safer route to my house about four blocks away.

As I walked along in the warm darkness of the night, I remember thinking that I had never met anyone in my life who had as much enthusiasm as William.

The next night, just after Mother and I were finishing supper, there was a knock at the front door. I opened it and there stood William. I introduced him to my mother and noticed that he was so well-mannered and he was somewhat smaller than I had remembered from the night before. He was about five-six or maybe five-seven, and looked to weigh about one hundred twenty pounds; he had black curly hair and black beady eyes. I could tell my mother was impressed with him.

"I came over to tell you, Alvin, that my stepfather works for a company that owns several theaters in

Memphis, and he can get us in free. So if you want to go with me sometime, just let me know." He spoke rapidly but clearly.

"Sure, I'd like to go," I replied.

"Well, how 'bout tomorrow night?" he asked. "The Rosemary Theater over on Jackson Avenue has a double feature and one of the pictures is *Dive Bomber,* a real good airplane picture show with Errol Flynn." He was getting excited. "I love airplane pictures," he added.

"Okay," I said. He turned to leave, and I offered to walk part of the way back to his house with him.

When I returned, my mother said, "Your new friend William is such a nice, well-mannered young man. And isn't he full of life?"

"He sure is," I answered.

The next night William and I walked halfway across Memphis to see the double feature. He depended on me to take us up alleys, down back streets and across certain railroad tracks in order to avoid gangs that roamed the city. While walking back home that night, he talked mainly about airplanes and how he wanted to be a pilot. He had an uncle over in Jonesboro, Arkansas, who had taken him up in a private plane on several occasions, and William was so thrilled and stimulated by those flights that he had made being a pilot his life's dream.

I suppose William and I went to a dozen picture shows before school started that September. One night late in August, while walking home after seeing *Honky Tonk,* a very good picture show full of love and passion,

William suddenly asked me, "Alvin, have you ever kissed a girl?" He asked this with almost the same zeal he had when he talked about airplanes.

"Yeah, I've kissed a girl," I replied.

"I don't just mean friendly kissin'," he asserted. "I mean real kissing as they did in that picture tonight."

"Yeah," I said.

Then he stopped walking, grabbed me by my arm, and asked, "You mean you've kissed a girl on the mouth the real way, you know what I mean?"

I could tell William was in the mood for talking about girls and related things, so I spent the next thirty minutes talking about my experiences with older farm girls in the Bootheel of Missouri. Step by step and story by story, I told William about Missouri Bootheel girls in haylofts, on pallets in storm houses on thundering nights and about picking wild dewberries one summer with an older girl who took off her clothes to spread chigger salve all over her body.

I could tell William was having the finest time of his life; his eyes reflected the same wild wonder that was there when he talked about airplanes. "You're a lucky guy, Alvin," he said. "You're a lucky guy," he repeated. "You're the luckiest guy I've ever known."

"Aw, I don't know about that," I said in a modest way.

We walked along and said nothing for a while; he broke the silence. "I wouldn't want you to ever tell anybody, Alvin, but I've never kissed a girl." He spoke with a tone of disillusionment that I had rarely detected from William. Again there was silence.

"Alvin," he finally said, "I'm gonna tell you one other thing that you must never tell anyone."

I promised.

"Two years back we visited my stepfather's sister in Paducah, Kentucky. I was thirteen then, and they had a daughter who was also about thirteen. Well, me and their daughter Melinda had been in their sun room on a Sunday afternoon, playing games and listening to the radio. She had a sun-suit outfit on with short shorts. I had noticed all day long how smooth her legs looked, especially just above her knees. I'd never seen skin so smooth, so I ran my hand across her legs to see if it felt like it looked. Well, Alvin," he went on, "she jumped up and started screaming and kept screaming like she'd been scalded by hot water. Anyway, all the grown folks who were up in the living room came running in and she just stood there still screaming. 'What's wrong, darling? What's wrong, Melinda?' her mother asked."

" 'He touched me,' she finally blurted out, and then she started bawling. All those relatives were standing there staring at me with hate and anger. My mother asked with irritation, 'What have you done, William? What have you done to Melinda?' "

"I didn't do anything," I said, "I was only seeing if her skin felt as soft and smooth as it looked." No sooner than I said that, my stepfather grabbed me, dragged me out to the back and whipped me with a board for about ten minutes. They sent me to my room and treated me like a criminal the rest of the visit."

"That's terrible," I said.

"I didn't do anything, Alvin. I really didn't." He sounded a little choked up. "You know what bothers me even today, Alvin?" He was very solemn. "I stayed completely away from Melinda for the remaining days we stayed there; she never looked at me again until the day we left. While we were driving away, I looked out the car window at Melinda and I swear she was smiling and had this wicked look on her face like she knew exactly what she had done."

We walked along in silence for a while. "Now you must not tell anyone what I just told you, Alvin." I promised that I wouldn't.

William and I became good friends that August and September. After entering high school we had different agendas and schedules, so we didn't see each other as often. By November everyone at school knew William Wharton was Mr. Enthusiasm: he became a model ROTC cadet with impeccable dress and behavior; he got a small part in the fall school play; he became a reporter for the school paper; and he sang tenor in the male glee club. The word also got around that he was very smart and was excelling in math and science. There were few things that William didn't have an interest in, and he would try anything.

In the fall for many years, on Sunday afternoons at 2:00, there was an allcomers tackle-football game in a large field west of Bellevue Junior High School. There were no officials of any kind, no helmets, no gear or equipment. Someone would show up with a football; we'd set the boundaries, choose up sides and play until dark. If thirty players showed up, we'd play fifteen on each side. We'd make up the plays in lengthy huddles; it was rough and serious stuff.

One day in late October, William showed up to play. He was on my side that day in the huddle, and he kept asking if he could run out for a pass or carry the ball. Finally, Monty, who was considered one of the best players and by far the best leader, said to William, "You go block Elmo on this play. Go over there and wipe him out." Elmo was an Italian boy who weighed about two hundred ten pounds and was slow but solid as a rock. He always played linebacker, and everyone knew to run around Elmo and never attempt to block him.

I watched William as he zoomed across the field, left the ground at full-speed and threw his entire body onto Elmo. William bounced off him like he had hit a fully-grown oak tree. I watched William wobble back to the huddle; he was pale and his eyes were glazed. Again, Monty made up a play and said, "You did a great job on Elmo, William. You go block Elmo again." William, only half-speed now, ran and threw his body onto Elmo. He succeeded only in crushing his own body.

Back in the huddle I spoke to William softly, "Just brush him, William; don't block him." He was so groggy by then that he didn't know what I meant.

Monty called on William to block Elmo all afternoon. Finally, when darkness came and we stopped playing, I saw William wobbling slowly toward his house. I was so tired and beat up myself I could not help him home. But William didn't give up; he kept coming on Sundays just to be a part of the group. It appeared to me, in time, William learned to take better care of himself.

It was on that field on December 7 of that year, a latecomer joined the game about 2:30 p.m.; he said that Japan had bombed our ships in Pearl Harbor. Most of us didn't know where Pearl Harbor was, and a few playing that day had never even heard of Japan. We talked about the bombing for about ten minutes; then we continued to play ball until dark. It wasn't until the following summer of 1942 that we fully realized the meaning of America being in World War II.

During the year of the tenth grade, William had met a friend named Richard, and I had made a new friend named Harry. In the summer of 1942, before entering the eleventh grade, the four of us began doing things together. We shot pool and snooker at a pool hall on Madison Avenue. We bowled duck pins, went swimming or often sat in a park talking about life and our futures. Since we were all rapidly approaching the age of seventeen, every so often we would get serious about whether or not we would have to go to war. William was the only one of us who was eager for time to fly; he was ready to go. Harry and I had talked on occasion and had a secret understanding between the two of us that we were not so eager to take up arms; we agreed we would never express this to anyone for fear of being ostracized.

Among the four of us I was a minor hero. The first year in high school, I had gone out for track late in the spring and managed to finish third in the high hurdles in the big regional track meet held at Crump Stadium. I received a small bronze medal which I wore on a chain that draped from my belt to my pants' pocket. Every time William saw the medal he would ask if I thought he could run a track event and win a medal. "Maybe you could run the mile or eight-eighty," I suggested. He said we'd talk about it later.

The eleventh grade was a little difficult for me, because I had taken a *Commercial Appeal* paper route and delivered papers from two-thirty to five-thirty every morning. I could hardly stay awake in classes at school. I delivered papers on the dreaded Elmwood route, which was famous for its spooky dark passages and dead-end streets with no lights. I made one throw in Elmwood Cemetery itself and another at a notorious morphodite's house, where the morphodite supposedly had grabbed paperboys in the past. On several occasions William volunteered to go with me and help, just for the sheer pleasure of experiencing fear. His family didn't approve and forbade his going, so we rigged up a system where I pulled a string hanging out of his bedroom window that was tied to his big toe. This would wake him up; he would dress in the darkness, crawl out

of the window and off we would go. He would always
be back in bed before his family got up for breakfast.

It wasn't too long before I realized that one reason
William was going with me to throw papers was so he
could talk. One morning as we walked along in the
darkness William said, "Alvin, I still haven't kissed a
girl."

"Well, I haven't in some time myself," I replied.

"Well, but you have before, and it's beginning to
bother me."

A little time passed; I didn't say anything.

"I had this date last month," he said. "I guess it was
a date. I took Anna Mary Weeks, who lives across the
street from me, to a picture show and then we returned
to her house. We sat on her front porch swing and
talked. Then I gave her my Ronald Coleman routine
for about ten minutes and then tried to kiss her, but
she just turned her head and laughed," he said.

"What's the Ronald Coleman routine?" I asked.

"Well, I learned it from the Ronald Coleman picture show I saw about a month ago. I saw the picture
three times. I've memorized his lines; I've even practiced sounding like him." He demonstrated his Ronald
Coleman routine for me at four-thirty in the morning,
there in the spookiest part of Memphis. It was weird.
"William, you don't do that," I said.

"Don't what?"

"Well, you don't practice how to be romantic," I
said.

"Well, how do you do it? I don't seem to know what to say or do." He said this with a desperate tone of voice.

"I don't know, William," I said. "Let me think about it a few days and I'll try to decide what you should do." This seemed to put his mind at ease.

We threw the last papers on East Street, turned, and walked down the Southern Railroad in pitch darkness, still an hour before sunup. William started singing the Army Air Corps song in full-voice.

"Up we go into the wild blue yonder, climbing high into the sky." His tenor voice bounced off the dark brick buildings. "The Glee Club is learning all these songs for a special program next week in assembly. Did you know that, Alvin?" he asked.

"No, I didn't know that, William," I answered curtly. Sometimes I got a little put out with William early in the morning.

"I really do love the Air Corps song best of all," he said. He sang it off and on all the way home. It was times like these that made it difficult to understand William.

In late February, William decided he wanted to try some event in track. In March, during the early days of practice, the coach had all the new runners who had no idea about the various events to run a mile. There were about ten runners in the test race, and William stayed in the pack, unsure about pacing or anything else; to my surprise, he finished fourth. Several runners never finished the race. I hugged William and said,

"Say, you may be a distance runner. You did great."
Actually, the times were slow, but Central did not have
any distance runners left from the previous year, and
the coach was searching for anyone to help in the mile
and eight-eighty. This fourth-place finish led to a new
William. It seemed everywhere I saw him from then
on he was running.

We went downtown one Saturday morning to the
Cossett Library and checked out the only two books on
track and field. We read them and shared a secret; both
of us felt we had the upper hand because we had running knowledge the other runners didn't. I ran the
high and low hurdles and William ran the mile. At
dual meets we both did well. We practiced and worked
hard for the West Tennessee Regional meet at Crump
Stadium. We talked and dreamed of medals hanging
from chains. I knew that William had no chance for a
first or second place, but with a smart race he had a
good chance for third. The night of the big meet our
coach had told William to stay right behind the guy
running third in the race and to out-sprint him to the
finish line.

"Run for third," the coach had said.

And twice, before William walked over to the
starting line, I told him, "Run for third."

As they shot the gun, something came over
William; he took off very fast, got a big lead, and was
about twenty yards ahead of the field. At the end of
the first lap there was a look on William's face that I
had never seen before. I knew he was setting too fast a

pace. He stayed out front, and people in the stands were screaming, "Come on, William! You can do it, William!"

When William finished the third lap his face was white, and I could tell that he was just about dead. As he entered the first turn of the last lap, runners began passing him like he was standing still. Every runner in the race passed William on the back stretch, and he finished dead last, coming across the finish line almost in a walk. I grabbed him to keep him from falling. Gasping for breath, he couldn't talk. Harry and Richard helped me pull William over to a bench, and we got a cold cloth for his head. I ran my events and got a second and a third. William was the last person from the field when the meet was over. We helped him dress after his shower and I walked him home. Just before we got to his house, he said, "I think I set too fast a pace, didn't I, Alvin?"

"You sure did, William."

"I wanted to win, Alvin. I don't know what came over me. I wanted to win so bad." William suffered great humiliation for a few days, but school was out for summer a week later.

The summer of 1943 was a time of concern for all boys age seventeen. On our next birthdays we would all have to register for the draft. In those days patriotism was so strong a boy couldn't even say he dreaded registering for the draft. Blue and gold stars were hanging in the windows of almost every home. Every family had fathers, sons, brothers or other relatives away in the conflict. Relatives and friends gave much advice to seventeen-year-old boys, some suggesting that we quit school and join up early to get the branch of service we preferred. A few boys did.

One night in August, William called and asked me to meet him in the park to talk about how he could make sure that he got into the Air Force instead of the regular Army. President Roosevelt had approved a new name for the Air Corps; it would now be called the Air Force. William was always hinting around for someone to volunteer early with him for the Air Force.

Harry and I sat on the same park bench a few nights later; we vowed to continue our secret plan to wait for the draft to get us rather than volunteer for anything. We decided to tell no one, not even our parents, of this plan. Even though we had feelings of guilt over these secret talks, we still had grave concerns about being turned down once we were inducted and becoming a 4F. Death was better than being a 4F.

William telephoned again and asked me to meet him at the park late in August. He had dated a new girl in the neighborhood the week before but never got the courage to try to kiss her goodnight.

"It seems, Alvin," he was serious again, "when I get a girl on her front porch to say goodnight that I sort of choke up. I still don't know what to say or do." There was a long pause. "You said once a long time ago that you'd help me figure this out, Alvin," he said in a whining way.

"I know, William, but things like this are hard to work out." I could see he was suffering, so I said, "I have a cousin who lives over in north Memphis and he is very smooth with the girls. The next time I see him, I'll discuss this with him." I didn't tell him my cousin was only sixteen years old; I had to say something. It seemed to brighten him up.

That year the falling leaves of autumn seemed to bring a new restlessness. Strange feelings surfaced about not being ready for coming of age. We were brave, strong and ready for adventure, but there was always a deep down feeling of not quite being prepared for the horrors of war. Of course, William spoke almost daily of finding wings to fly in the sky.

Winter came early in 1943. The first week of December, only a week after I had registered for the draft, the school principal announced that all boys in the eleventh and twelfth grades were to report to the auditorium at two o'clock that afternoon. About one forty-five, we heard the sound of a military band. The music was wafting through the halls and stairwells of the school. We recognized the Air Force song; it was repeated over and over. Shortly before two o'clock, Harry, Richard, William and I converged outside the auditorium as the band continued to play. The band began to march in two lines down the aisles of the auditorium that led to the stage. William was beside himself, almost turning flips. The rest of us walked slowly into the auditorium, and Harry and I hid out in some back row seats. William insisted we go closer to the stage. Harry and I refused, so Richard went to the front with William. The band continued to play. In twenty minutes a Tyrone Power-looking lieutenant in a crisp uniform covered with medals, ribbons and shiny brass walked up to the microphone and addressed us in a sincere, professional tone. The essence of his message was that the Air Force had just approved some openings for pilots and it was a day of opportunity for us all.

"Sign up with us now. You can finish your high school diploma, and you will be one of the fortunate ones who will have a reserved place for two years of special pilot training." He went on, "After the war this training will convert into college credits, and you will have experience that will help you in becoming a commercial pilot."

He gave many grand reasons for joining up that day. Tables with other officers were set up on the front of the stage for those interested. When the program was over, William was waving his arms for us to come on down front; we didn't. Twenty-five or thirty of our classmates did. Harry and I walked out to the school steps. In a few minutes William rushed outside, holding papers he had to carry home for signatures and bring back the next morning. We watched him run full-speed toward home. His mother signed the papers that night; at last, William was going to be an airplane pilot.

The Christmas season wasn't quite the same that year. Almost all of us were registered now, and we could be called for military duty at any time. Draft boards were unpredictable in those days, sometimes calling boys before graduation and sometimes allowing them to finish school. It was a young age to live day by day, secretly dreading the mail. In early January, William called me early one night, very excited. "I got my call today, Alvin! I leave in two days for flight school."

Even though he was excited, he didn't sound as exuberant as I thought he would. A few days later Harry and I rode the streetcar downtown to see William off on a night train to an Air Force training camp in Texas. He was all smiles; his mother cried.

I gave up my paper route, deciding I would spend my final school days getting some much-needed sleep. I also planned to train extra hard that spring in order to be a winner in the hurdles my final year. I found a way to get into Crump Stadium and set up three hurdles on a dirt runway under the north stadium where I could practice in the cold weather and on rainy days. We got word from Texas in late February that William had washed out in pilot training and had been placed into gunnery school. Winter went fast and time was racing. By mid-March I was already in good shape for track; everyone else was just beginning to train. In late April I was resting on the north stadium seats, after running some conditioning wind-sprints, when I saw Harry coming across the football field. I could tell by the way he was walking that something was wrong; I had a strange feeling.

"William is missing in action, Alvin," Harry said. "He's probably been killed," he continued, choking a little.

I knew he wasn't joking. "What happened?" I asked.

"All I know is that he is missing from a bombing mission over Germany. It happened three or four days ago. I have no details except that it was William's first mission. Richard's father called my dad at work about it today. He's getting information from a pilot in William's outfit." Harry waited as I showered and dressed. We went down to the park, sat on a bench and talked until way after dark.

One night about a week later, Harry called me to meet him at the park again; he said he had some more news.

"William's body is missing, Alvin," he told me. "The War Department has informed William's family that he probably fell out of his rib-gun turret somewhere over Germany during an air battle. They have no report on his body. My dad says the German pilots have found a blind spot on the B-17 bombers, and that a German fighter plane can concentrate heavy machine-gun fire on the rib-gunners till there's absolutely nothing left of the turret."

"What?!" I exclaimed in shock.

"It's very reliable information, Alvin. My Dad says sometimes the bombers that make it back have rib-gun turrets that are just bloody, stained areas. They just wash them out with hoses and re-equip them."

"That's sickening," I replied.

"It's terrible," Harry said.

We sat and talked late into the night.

I went undefeated in the high and low hurdles and won two gold medals in the big regional meet. The time in the mile run was very slow, and William, if he had been there, could have easily won a medal. Harry, Richard and I graduated in May, and Richard joined the Marines in June. Harry and I, for various reasons, were not drafted until August; we were fortunate enough to be placed in the Navy. All three of us survived the war.

In 1946, when the war was over, I returned to Memphis from the Pacific. I found out from friends that William's body had never made it back from Europe. Our friend William Wharton, who got to live a little bit more than eighteen years, never got to win his medal in track and never got to kiss a girl. William had faced life with spirit and enthusiasm, and on a day in April, 1944, he left this world, somewhere over Germany, up in the wild blue yonder.

Smoke, Tears and Cinders

EARLY ONE NIGHT in late May of 1944, two days after we had graduated from high school, Harry called me to meet him at Triangle Park to talk about our status with the draft board. We were eighteen years old and had registered for the draft months earlier; both of us had been classified 1-A but were given student deferments until we graduated. Now we were trying to decide how many official days we had left to inform the draft board that we had received our diplomas. Harry and I shared the same philosophy about the war: we considered ourselves patriotic and willing to go to war, and we were grateful we weren't classified 4-F and therefore ostracized by others. Yet we were not gung ho to take up arms as some of our friends. We wanted to delay our contribution to the war as long as possible. We had to keep our feelings to ourselves, however, since nearly everyone in our families, as well as friends and neighbors, believed that just thinking about not going to war was wrong and indicated a lack of courage.

Harry and I lived with our feelings of guilt and from time to time had serious talks about how to survive the war. Our attitudes were partly shaped by the fact that several servicemen from our extended families had been killed or wounded or were missing in action. Too, our close friend William Wharton had been called to duty from his senior year of high school by the Air Corps and had already been killed in action. We were hanging on to our freedom as long as we could.

I arrived at the park early; Harry arrived in about ten minutes with one of his father's old business satchels, crushed full of news articles and other documents regarding the law and the selective service. We sat on a park bench near a street light so Harry could show me printed materials that he had collected to help support some of his theories and ideas. He was not only smart but downright shrewd in many areas.

"The way I see it, Alvin," Harry said, "we are supposed to report to the draft board within five days of our graduation. But its not clear what constitutes graduation. Now, we went through commencement exercises last Monday, but we won't pick up our final report cards at school until this coming Friday, June the second. So we'll count that as our official graduation day. Now, five days from Friday ends on Wednesday, June the seventh, so let's plan to go on that day and let them know we have graduated."

"Harry, are you sure we can wait that long and not get into trouble?" I asked.

"Sure, I'm sure," he replied. "Or I'm at least confident that it fits within the parameters of another selective service document that states that one should notify the draft board of any major change in one's status within ten days." So we agreed on that plan. We sat and talked late into the night about other major decisions we would have to make as time came nearer to our being drafted. Our spirits were low about it and we dreaded the coming days, but we agreed we'd better not let our friends and families know how we felt.

Tuesday, June 6, 1944, was the long-awaited D-day, and the newspapers and radios brought the news about the Allied forces landing on the northern coast of France. The next day, June 7, Harry picked me up in his father's 1936 Ford, and we drove down to the draft board to inform them that we had graduated from high school. To our surprise, the people in the office paid little attention to our reporting in on the fifth and last day; they informed us that we would be notified approximately two weeks before we would leave for an induction center. Harry politely asked a middle-aged lady who seemed to be an important clerk or secretary, "Ma'am, is there any way of getting a rough idea of how long it might be before—."

The lady interrupted Harry and said firmly, "Young man, there is no way whatsoever in knowing how long it will be before you get your notice for induction. But as we stated, you will be notified at least two weeks before leaving." She wasn't mean, but there was no compassion or warmth in her voice. We left the draft board and drove across town to see a new picture show called *Casablanca* that everyone had been raving about. Afterwards we agreed that it was a good picture.

Life became an anxious waiting game. After a week had passed we expected the mail delivery to bring our draft notices any day. The mailman in my neighborhood arrived around noon each day; often I would be home for lunch and standing out on the porch waiting for him. I would quickly look through the letters, experiencing a sense of relief when there was nothing for me. Then I would call Harry—if he had not already called me—to see if he had received his notice. After a while we realized that watching for the mailman was causing added anxiety and frustration, so we attempted to live as if the draft notices might never arrive, although we knew they would.

We continued to meet at the park. One night in late June, Harry said, "We had better start thinking about ways of staying out of the Army, Alvin." He pulled an article he had found in some magazine out of his satchel. We walked over and sat on the curbing directly under the street light. The article contained a chart showing the different branches of the service with information about each, including the length of basic training.

"Look," Harry pointed out, "the regular Army has just started a new procedure requiring only six weeks of basic training. The Navy has boot camp training for twelve to fourteen weeks, the Marines fourteen to sixteen weeks, the Air Corps pilots get thirty to sixty weeks training, the paratroopers get eighteen weeks of basic training before combat and assignment to action."

"Why is basic training in the Army so short?" I asked.

"My dad knows this man who is an expert on military and war matters, and he says the Army is now only teaching the new recruits how to shoot a rifle, how to dig a foxhole and then they give them all of their shots and send them straight to Europe where they learn how to be a soldier on the front. My dad says we had better start thinking of how to get into another branch of service rather than the regular Army."

"How do you do that?" I asked.

"My dad is checking into that today. I'll call you about it tomorrow when I find out," he said. We talked a while and then there was a lull.

"Harry," I asked, "does your mother cry much?"

He looked at me strangely and replied, "Why do you ask that?"

"Well," I went on, "my mother asked me a few days ago about how long I thought it would be before I had to go into the service and I said, 'Not long, Mama,' and she started bawling and went out on the back porch for a long time. Too, she's been fixing all my favorite meals and keeps banana pudding in the refrigerator all the time. The other night while eating supper I looked over at her and tears were flowing down her cheeks and I had not said a thing." I paused for a moment. "I just wondered about your mother."

"She cried the other night," Harry said, but he didn't elaborate. We sat quietly for a while.

"Harry," I asked, "have you ever seen your father cry?"

"What's all this sudden talk about crying?" he blurted.

"Don't get so riled up," I responded. "I've just been thinking about it lately since my mother cries all the time."

Harry said, "I've never seen my father cry; I don't know if he's ever cried."

"I've never seen my father cry either," I said. "You know, Harry," I went on, "one summer when I was fourteen years old, staying with my Aunt Annie and Uncle Will up in the Bootheel of Missouri, there was a death in the family, and at the funeral all of the women cried and most of the men didn't. One night later on, I asked my Uncle Will, who was known for his knowledge of the earth and many other things, 'Why don't men cry like women, Uncle Will?' Uncle Will never answered anything in a hurry, but he finally said, 'Men cry backwards, Alvin Junior. The tears flow back inside,' and the large fingers on his hand were gesturing toward his eyes. I didn't know if he was kidding or serious, so I asked him, 'Is this something men learn to do?' He waited before saying, 'Everybody cries; most men simply learn to cry back inside.' "

Harry didn't say anything. "And you know, Harry," I continued, "a few days ago I made a short trip up to the Bootheel to tell everybody good-bye, and when I got ready to leave Uncle Will stood there with real tears flowing from his eyes. That's the only time I ever saw him cry; ever." I could tell Harry didn't want to talk about crying anymore, so we left the park and headed our separate ways.

Early the next morning Harry called and said excitedly, "Alvin, I'll pick you up in about twenty minutes and explain some things to you as we drive downtown to the draft board." As we rode along, Harry explained that there was a little-known draftees' right and privilege that allowed a man to sign a form for a particular branch of the service; when he was inducted, and if they needed recruits for that branch of the service, then he could get into the requested branch. "My dad says the best bet for us is to sign up for the Navy, so let's go do it," he said."

"That's all right with me," I replied. We went to the draft board that last day of June, told them what we had heard, and signed the form requesting the Navy.

A gorgeous girl named Jaunita had returned to Memphis from Mississippi during the twelfth-grade school year, and I was spending many nights in east Memphis on her front porch swing, heavily involved in summer love. She had me starry-eyed and this helped in taking my mind off of the draft and the war.

Sears and Roebuck and a local drugstore were giving me part-time work that kept me from being broke. I had bought no clothes in months; I had gone to the cobbler twice to have soles and heels put on my only pair of shoes, because I was determined to wear them until I was drafted. My mother still cried a lot, and one day I discovered the blue star she was planning to hang in the window once I was gone.

In the middle of July, Harry and I were beginning to hear sarcastic remarks from people about why we were still in Memphis and not in the war. There were rumors that we were in some way dodging the draft. Harry's mother had received a phone call from someone asking if he had been declared 4-F.

The Allied forces were moving fast across Normandy, but we knew that it would be a long time before Germany would surrender. And then there was Japan to be dealt with. Hitler had access to a new miracle weapon, the V-1, a flying bomb that was jet propelled without a pilot, and London was being devastated by it.

Finally, on August 9, 1944, we received our draft notices. The letters from the government said we would be leaving from the Memphis Union Train Station on August 23, at nine in the morning. On that day, almost three months since high school graduation, Harry and I were among twenty-six eighteen-year-old boys waiting to board the last coach of a steam locomotive that would take us to Oglethorpe, Georgia, for induction. The last ten minutes before boarding was filled with agony as mothers, sisters and other female relatives of the young draftees were sobbing forward tears and hugging and kissing their boys good-bye. Fathers, brothers and other male relatives were stoically extending their hands for good luck and probably crying backwards. Some of the fathers hugged their sons good-bye.

In a matter of minutes we were rolling across north
Mississippi with all of the coach windows raised as
high as possible so the hot, humid air would reduce the
sweltering summer heat. It was one of those late summer days when breezes were few and the temperature
reached the upper nineties. Our coach was old with
worn, hard seats. It had been added to the end of the
regular train for the draftees. Harry and I sat together
quietly. One of the recruits, attempting to break the
tension, said jokingly, "This damn coach was probably
used in the Civil War." No one laughed. Many of the
boys stared out the windows at the passing scenery. A
few were pacing restlessly up and down the aisle like
boxers before a bout. One or two braggadocio types
were loudly talking about how they couldn't wait for
some real war action. Most of the boys, however, were
sitting in silent anguish, concerned about their unknown futures. Everyone was acting brave, and if there
were any tears they were flowing backwards.

About eleven thirty, a soldier put in charge of our
group for the trip came in with boxes of sack lunches.
He went up and down the aisle, pitching the sacks to
the recruits like a zoo keeper feeding his animals.
Lunch was one dry ham sandwich and one orange.
Harry said, "Good god, what a beginning!"

About one o'clock we entered the northern part of
Alabama, and even with the coach windows open, the
heat was torrid. The two noisy boys had settled down,
worn out from bragging about their toughness and ea-
gerness for battle. We rolled along with just the clack-

ing sound of the rail tracks below. I was near an open window on the sunny south side of the coach, viewing the area's late summer crops, back roads, gullies and farm buildings.

Earlier I had gone up to the front of the coach for a drink of warm water from a paper cup; as I returned to my seat I could tell from facial expressions that everyone was experiencing some degree of agony as they rode along in silence. There wasn't a cloud to be seen that day. The black smoke from the steam engine locomotive hugged the ground and left a trail, stretching out at an angle a long distance behind the train. Once, the train had turned northeast and for a brief moment the black smoke swept in through the windows, causing some coughing and cursing, but it cleared up quickly. I watched the long trail of smoke several hundred yards out from the train and thought that if that smoke hugging the ground ever paralleled the path of the train for any length of time, we would be in for a good smoking.

There were few people in the fields that day, and only a small amount of traffic traveled on the roads and highways. Northern Alabama was in the grip of late August stillness. I watched the trail of smoke; it seemed to be darker than ever. I noticed that it was slowly edging closer toward the path of the train. Harry was half-asleep, so I didn't say anything to him. I saw the trail of smoke edging closer and closer; suddenly, the coach was engulfed with choking black smoke so thick that it blurred our vision and burned our lungs. The train path and smoke trail ran parallel for at least two full minutes, causing much yelling, coughing and cursing. There were a few attempts to lower windows, but it was too late. Our eyes burned as we gasped for clean air. The train jerked, turned, and as quickly as we had been engulfed, a breeze came through the north windows and cleared the coach of smoke. Through tears and burning eyes we saw that everyone and everything was covered with a myriad of tiny black cinders. Nature and spirit had worked together for a brief time, allowing a group of boys destined for war to tear-away the smoke and cinders, helping to lighten heavy hearts. One skinny pale boy from Arkansas, who had been sitting alone all the way from Memphis, was still tearing away the smoke and cinders thirty minutes later. No one said anything to him. After all, it was our first day on the way to war.

It seemed to me that the experience of smoke, tears and cinders changed the mood of the young draftees to one of resignation. Just before dark there was even a little singing and laughter. We arrived at Chattanooga, Tennessee, after dark; we were whisked into two army trucks and rushed to Fort Oglethorpe, Georgia. Each of us was given a single blanket, and we spent the night on army cots in screened-in barracks.

The following day we were hurried through several mental and physical examinations. Two recruits from the Appalachian hills of east Tennessee fainted while having blood drawn for tests. We were told they had never had a shot of any kind before and didn't know about having blood drawn. At three o'clock the several hundred new recruits who had passed all the tests stood in a large field, waiting for their specific assignments. Harry and I learned that once they gave a welcoming speech and released us for assignment designation areas, we should make a mad dash for Building 278, where the Navy assignments were made. The first recruits there would have a better chance of getting into that branch of the service. Harry and I took short cuts that didn't work out; I was ninth in line and Harry was eleventh. The assignment officer said some fast words that no one could understand, but at the end he said, "Now, what branch of service do you want? Army or Navy?" Everyone in front of me selected the Navy; their papers were stamped and they were sent out an east door.

Every single recruit had chosen the Navy, and when it was my turn I said, "Navy."

The assignment officer stamped some papers, then pointed and said, "Out that door."

The recruit between Harry and me was probably mixed up or in the wrong building. When he was asked, "What branch of the service do you request?" he answered with confusion, "You mean I can choose? I hadn't planned on that."

The assignment officer became irritated and said, "Make up your mind, fellow, there is only one place left for the Navy today, and if you want it, you can have it; but hurry it up. Do you want the Army or the Navy?"

"Well, I didn't know I could choose," the recruit replied."

Harry had overheard the assignment officer say that there was only one more Navy slot left, so he jumped into the conversation, "Say, friend, if you're undecided, let me go with my buddy over there into the Navy." I was waiting at the door.

The recruit was still confused and asked Harry, "What is it you want me to do?"

Harry repeated his request and his eyes became moist. The officer yelled, "Make up your mind! Army or Navy?"

"Aw, hell, give me the Army," he said, "and let this fellow go with his buddy." They stamped him army, and Harry was the tenth and last Navy recruit that day. There were about eighty people left in the line. It was such a close call, Harry could hardly talk for a while.

The ten of us were sworn in the next morning at the Chattanooga Navy Recruiting Station; they hastened us to a train that took us to the Great Lakes Naval Training Center in Illinois. One of the first things we did after arriving was take off our clothes and put them in a cardboard box to be shipped back home. I thought it was foolish to send home my old, worn-out shoes, but they required us to ship everything. The next two days we were rushed around—naked most of the time—for various tests and finally given our dog tags, service numbers, identification materials, a mattress and a sea bag full of navy clothing. On the third day, from an outside platform in an open field, one hundred and twelve names were called out to form Company 1731; Harry and I were still together.

We alternately ran and walked about four miles to the back side of the Green Bay area of the camp to the barracks that would be our quarters for the next twelve weeks. In three days we became known as the poorest company of the entire Great Lakes area. Almost everyone on our roster was from Tennessee, Arkansas, or Kentucky, and there were many uncoordinated and very slow learners in our group. One day Harry remarked, "It looks like we've been caught up in a company of lame brains, Alvin." We drilled more, ran more, walked more and exercised more from sunup until late at night. The harder they pushed us, the worse we seemed to get. At the end of three weeks we were officially classified as the worst-performing company ever in the Green Bay area. Our company captain banned us from the PX, so we couldn't even get a Co' Cola. It didn't matter all that much because we were drilling on the grinder late every night and couldn't have gone anyway. Our company scores were the lowest in all areas of achievement with the exception of our rifle range records. It turned out that the six or seven southern boys who could never keep in step, make up their beds right, or tie a square knot could shoot straight. However, the scores weren't high enough to move us from our low rating, so we were always on report and suffered much scorn and ridicule.

One day they marched our company with our gas masks already in place over our heads into a large tear gas chamber for a training activity. A voice from a loud speaker gave us orders on how to take off our masks. Place the mask over the right arm. Place your left hand on the shoulder of the man in front of you. Now, file out slowly, the voice instructed. We had been informed to keep our eyes closed once in the chamber after removing the masks. Some boy from eastern Kentucky screamed and began wildly charging about, causing our entire company to panic and stampede for the only exit. Of course we opened our eyes to a scene of complete madness with people falling over one another. We were hollering and yelling, our eyes severely burning and stinging beyond belief. It took ten minutes to get all of us out. The captain of our company shouted profanities at us for a good half-hour. As we sat and teared the gas from our eyes—and probably teared a little for our battered spirits—a medic arrived and put drop in our eyes, explaining to the captain that we had been overexposed to the gas. Trucks carried us to Lake Michigan, where we sat on the shore and held our eyelids apart with our fingers, so that the wind from the lake could cool our swollen eyes.

While sitting there I said to Harry, "This has been hell!"

"Well, look at it this way, Alvin, if we had gone into the Army, by now wed be learning how to stop bullets in Europe." Harry and I always took turns cheering each other up. We stayed there until dark. It was the first time we had not rushed since arriving at the Green Bay area.

They trucked us back to our camp. Since it was so late the company had to have what was called late chow: fried Spam, pork and beans and corn bread. Almost everyone griped, but I liked late chow. Our eyes remained badly swollen for about two days. Company 1731 never got any better at anything. In fact, the company captain gave up on us and even stopped cursing us for a while.

One morning I overslept and was late for the 0450 early muster. For punishment I automatically drew the "clothesline watch" that night. I had to stand at attention outside the barracks with a wooden dummy gun and guard a clothesline. The watch was from midnight until 0400 in the morning; the irony of it all was that there were never any clothes hanging on the clothesline. It was October, the nights were cold and I was feeling low. Guarding an empty clothesline was humiliating, but it gave me a lot of time to think about how tough boot camp had been and how much I wanted to be free of it, especially the regimentation. In the service I could never be by myself. Suddenly I realized that guarding that clothesline was the first chance I'd had to be alone in months. But I wanted to be free to walk across a wide hay field, or down a seldom traveled country road on a warm summer afternoon.

About 0200 that morning, it seemed to get darker and colder. I realized that my thoughts had made me homesick, and that I had been crying backwards for ten or fifteen minutes. Then something happened and tears came forward for just a while. I knew no one would ever know. I felt much better the next day.

Getting Me and Paloff Home

ON THE FOURTH day of August, 1945, from the top of Mount Tantalus on the island of Oahu, Paloff and I watched as airplanes soared over Pali Pass and on through the Nuuanu Valley below us toward the airport at Honolulu. We had climbed several mountains on the island, but we returned often to the Tantulus peak to experience being in and out of the clouds that hovered around the top of the Koolau range. Climbing mountains was one way of dealing with the war; it helped take our minds off of being away from home for so long.

Paloff and I were the youngest of two hundred men in a high-security unit that made terrain model relief maps to aid in the invasions during the war. We were nineteen years old in a unit composed mostly of men in their twenties and thirties; however, there were some in their early forties and a few older officers. Paloff and I had friends in the unit, but being the youngest brought us much kidding and resulted in a particular comradeship. Our work area was located in a well-guarded building in the Aiea area of Pearl Harbor, where almost weekly we would see battered, crippled warships return to the harbor for repairs.

"What did you make of Captain Bailey's speech Thursday morning?" Paloff asked as he gazed across the valley.

"It beats me," I replied. "It sure doesn't make any sense if they keep the same deadline for the completion of Sweet Potato." Sweet Potato was the code name given to the terrain models for the next Pacific invasion that we were currently working on, night and day. We were not supposed to use the actual names of invasion sites if we knew them. We had learned early that the next invasion was to be on the southern end of the island of Kyushu, Japan. Captain Bailey had called a muster of the entire unit the previous Thursday morning to tell us that we were going to slow down in our work. At the end of his talk he had given everyone a three-day pass for rest and recuperation. This had come as a big surprise to us.

"I believe they're going to scrap Sweet Potato and invade one of the other islands of Japan and just start over," Paloff said. "At least that seems to be the thinking of almost everyone in the unit; nothing else makes much sense." About that time it became overcast as the clouds rolled in around us, and we could no longer see the valley. When we were engulfed in the clouds, the air became heavy with the fragrant aromas of the tropical world. The flowers and flora reminded me of home in a mysterious way. Perhaps I was reminded of the sweet smell of honeysuckle after a rain on a humid summer afternoon in the Missouri Bootheel. We sat quietly for a long time.

"Alvin," Paloff asked despondently, "do you think we will ever get home again? Seems to me this war could go on for years."

"Yeah, I know it could," I answered, "but we'll have to get home someday because all wars eventually end. At least that's what R. O. says."

R. O. was one of the older men in our unit and was respected for his wisdom. He was our secret mentor. I had been in a downcast mood one day, and R. O. had said, "You must remember, Tennessee," he called me Tennessee, "every war in all of history has ended." He was always being philosophical. When I questioned the meaning of things he would respond by saying, "You will get it in time."

Paloff and I sat there a little dispirited and quiet for a while. The misty clouds moved on, and in a matter of minutes we could see the valley and out across the broad blue Pacific. Realizing we were very homesick, we didn't say anything more about home that day.

On Monday morning, only the eight to four work crew was scheduled to continue work on Sweet Potato; the other two shifts, the four to midnight and the midnight to eight, were informed not to report to work. I had been working the four to midnight shift, so I took a long afternoon nap. Later, I left the barracks and walked over to the work building where I saw some of the men from our unit standing out front, in a state of turbulence. When I inquired about their excitement one of them said, "Haven't you heard, Alvin? They've dropped an atomic bomb on Japan!"

"What does that mean?" I asked.

"Here," he tossed me the Honolulu paper, "read about it."

The headline on the paper read: "ATOM BOMB DROPPED ON JAPAN." The news article continued: "The atomic bomb, a new weapon of unprecedented destruction, was dropped on Hiroshima, Japan, at 9:15 a.m. today. The atomic bomb is more than one thousand times greater than the most powerful conventional bomb." I ran into the work building, looking for someone who knew about atomic bombs. I couldn't find R. O., but I did find Penz checking his mailbox. Penz was from Philadelphia; one of the older, intellectual types in our unit, he was known for his broad knowledge. "Tell me about atomic bombs, Penz," I asked excitedly.

He was unusually calm. "I know very little about atomic bombs, Alvin, but I do know enough to say that atomic bombs could end the war."

"You mean that, Penz?" I asked.

"Read your newspaper, Alvin," he responded, "The atomic bomb appears to be a weapon of awesome power." Penz walked off toward the barracks.

I ran out of the building, through the guard gate and all the way to a different barracks where Paloff slept, but I couldn't find him. There was talk about the bomb late into the night in our barracks.

Four days later U. S. planes dropped a second atomic bomb, equal to twenty thousand tons of TNT, on Nagasaki. The newspaper said a blinding flash occurred when the bomb was dropped; a minute later a pitch black boiling cloud of dust and churning debris was one thousand feet off the ground, and above it white smoke climbed like an expanded mushroom to twenty thousand feet. Paloff found me in my barracks that night, and we went outside and sat in the wind and talked. "Everyone thinks the war will end, Alvin," Paloff commented.

"It sure looks like it," I responded. "But you can never tell about the Japanese; they may hang on forever and ever."

The next day the paper read: "President Truman Warns Japan to Surrender or Be Completely Destroyed." Japan began to talk of surrender, but they did not surrender officially until Wednesday, August 15. This was the long-awaited V-J day. Only eleven days had passed since Paloff and I had sat atop Mount Tantalus, believing it would be years before the war would end and we would get to go home.

That night Oahu became an island of mass hysterical celebration. Hundreds of glaring searchlights from ships at Pearl Harbor, land bases and secret locations in the mountains cast their beams back and forth across the dark sky. Large and small guns fired from everywhere. Screeching sirens and loud horns blew, and frenzied servicemen yelled in the streets. The celebration continued; by midnight I knew it wasn't going to stop any time soon. The noise became disconcerting, so I returned to the barracks to go to bed, but found everyone there in a state of drunken revelry. I used my keys to the barracks laundry room, went in, made a pallet out of some laundry sacks, stuffed my ears with cotton and tried to sleep. As I lay there the building rattled occasionally from large guns firing. Every time the building shook, I wondered why noise was so much a part of victory celebrations.

I slept for a while; about 0500 my hard pallet felt even harder. I removed the cotton from my ears and noticed things had calmed outside. I walked out into the darkness and over to the work building, where I got a can of pineapple juice from the cold-drink box. It was still dark as I walked up to nearby Mona Loa Ridge, which had a view across the harbor; I sat down and waited for daybreak. In a while the sky turned a warm gray, then a rich lilac, and then a deep orange. The sun rose quietly. There was an unusual stillness over Pearl Harbor. It was August 16, 1945: the first day after the war.

Three days later Captain Bailey mustered the unit for a speech and some special announcements. He informed us that everyone in the unit had been approved for a naval unit commendation because of our quality work; the commendation would be recorded in our service records. He announced he was leaving immediately by plane for Washington, D. C., to make arrangements for those of us who did not have enough points to be discharged, so we could be transferred there as soon as possible to work on a special project. He praised our work for another thirty minutes even though everyone was getting restless.

Within three days the captain and two other officers left for stateside. Our unit was put on a one-day-on, one-day-off work schedule with no duty on week-ends. We began the long wait for orders to go home. The first three weeks were not too bad; we were elated that the war was over. But we watched daily as more and more ships loaded with servicemen headed for home without us.

By mid-September there was a lot of restlessness, anger and agitation in the unit, because we had no idea when we would get our orders. The war had been over a month when our unit was called together and informed that we had been placed on a three-day alert program: one day we would be told we were to depart for home, and we would leave within three days.

"So," the officer in charge said, "you're in paradise, men; take advantage of it. You may have a few days before you depart, but it could be a matter of months."

That afternoon Paloff and I walked down, sat on a rocky bank and watched the ships coming in and going out of Pearl Harbor.

"Alvin," Paloff said, "maybe that officer was right. We may never get back here again, and were all going crazy waiting for our orders. Why don't we continue climbing the mountains on this island?"

"Sounds good to me," I replied. So every other day, when we were free, we would follow trickling streams and narrow trails and scale another mountain. Paloff had a large geographical map that showed all of the roads, back roads, streams, trails and paths on the entire island. We had already reached the summits of most of the northern Koolau mountain range, so we decided to concentrate on the southern Waianae range. On our climbing days we would leave the base with sack lunches at sunup, hitchhike to the area closest to the mountain and try to reach the summit by early afternoon. By the end of September we had reached many mountain tops.

One day in early October, just after dark, we returned from climbing to discover everyone going berserk and packing their sea bags. "We're going home, Alvin!" someone yelled to me as I walked into the barracks. "We leave the day after tomorrow. Orders came through at noon today. Rumor has it were going home on the battleship *Missouri*." Everyone was shouting, singing and celebrating. We packed that night and all the next day. On the third day we mustered at 0800 at our work building and marched with all our gear down to the embarkation area off of Pearl Harbor. We were told to stand at ease on an open area of asphalt out from a dock. At noon we marched back to a chow hall about a mile away for our meal. Afterwards we returned again to the designated area and waited. Some men napped on their sea bags and gear, some played cards, some like R. O. and Penz were reading, some just talked. Several restless men walked back and forth like lions in a cage. We could see the bow of the battleship *Missouri* in the harbor, but most of the ship was obscured by other ships and Navy buildings. Late that afternoon the officer in charge of our unit called us to attention and informed us that someone had overestimated the number of returnees that could fit on the *Missouri*; there was no room for us, so we had to return to our barracks.

That long, difficult walk back up the slopes to the barracks had the visual impact of a death march. We walked slowly, and everyone was silent. When we went to late chow, we had fried Spam, pork and beans and cornbread. Everyone was griping about the food when I said, "I don't know why everyone complains so much about this food; I like beans and cornbread. It reminds me of the meals I had back in the Bootheel of Missouri." Everyone at my table got quiet and stared at me with disgust. I didn't say another word about the food; I just quickly ate my beans and cornbread. Our terrain model workshop was already closed, and the major equipment had been packed and crated for shipment back to the states. We had no work to do, so we were released for daily liberty and told to check in once a day for possible orders to ship out.

One day Paloff and I climbed Mount Palikea. There were no major mountains left except Kaala, which was supposed to be off-limits to climbers because tunnels had been dug into it where tons of ammunition had been stored for the war. We visited with an old native Hawaiian at Makaha who drew us a map of trails, showing us how to scale Kaala from the western side. He said that no one would ever know about us because the trail was uncharted. The next day we started up the mountain at daybreak, and in the early afternoon we reached the flat area at its summit; it was lush, undefaced and beautiful. We sat surrounded by exotic flowers as we ate our sack lunches. Clouds bringing rain would come and go rapidly; the wild flower fragrance was unbelievable. Several times the sky cleared enough so we could see ships heading north, out from the western shore. Paloff said, "We'll soon be on one of those ships going home, Alvin."

"Yep, can't be too soon for me," I responded.

Two days later we were alerted to be ready to leave the barracks the following day at noon. Everyone was skeptical that we were really leaving, but at mid-afternoon the next day several trucks arrived and carried us to the far side of Pearl Harbor where an LST (landing ship tank) had docked briefly to take on food and passengers. We carried our gear aboard and returned to the trucks to ride up to our last late chow at Pearl Harbor. We thought it was odd that we did not eat on board the ship.

We returned to the dock and boarded the vessel. Just before darkness, the LST eased slowly through the narrow opening of Pearl Harbor, then turned up the western shore of Oahu. Paloff and I saw the Waianae mountain range where we had recently climbed silhouetted against the sky. We had conflicting feelings of exuberance about finally heading home, and an unexpected tinge of sadness about leaving. By sundown we could see the island faintly, from a distance. We were on our way home.

It was time to assess our transportation. Things had happened suddenly; after the dismay of not getting to leave on the *Missouri*, no one really believed we were out in the ocean on an LST loaded to the brim with returning servicemen. LSTs were not built to be ocean-going vessels. They were small, flat-bottomed invasion boats that could run onto Pacific beaches; most navy men referred to the vessels as boats rather than ships because of their small size. Once someone said that the designer of the LST got the idea from a shoe box. Large hinged doors on the bow of the hollow boat would open, allowing tanks, trucks and other vehicles to drive ashore.

When we boarded, each man was handed a small card with a number corresponding to a number on a cot where he would sleep during the long voyage. When we climbed down the ladder into the tunnel-like hold, we saw hundreds of cots covering the tank deck surface. Two narrow passages ran the length of the ship and several narrower passages led outward to cots set up end to end and side by side. For the one hundred and eighty of us looking for our numbered cots, the search took almost an hour. My cot was located two rows from where the doors opened, up in the uppermost bow of the tank deck area. About forty men from our unit were in that zone up front, and all of our cots were on the slightly inclining ramp leading up to the bow doors.

We could tell that our coming aboard at Pearl Harbor was a major aggravation to everyone already on the LST. Before our arrival, there were perhaps two hundred passengers coming from the Philippines with little space for breathing; crushing in another one hundred and eighty bodies made things wretched. Because there were so many on board, we were by necessity put on a two-meals-a-day chow schedule for the entire voyage: one in the morning and one in late afternoon.

That first night I realized the flat bottomed LST did not split the water but took it head-on. As we hit shallow waves the front end of the boat would rise up and settle down in a series of jerks, so those of us up front on the ramp were shaken mightily all night. Every so often a large wave would hit the bow doors like a canon blast, startling most of us into sitting positions. We got little rest the first night out and those of us up front knew it was going to be a long and arduous voyage. We stood in line the next morning for over an hour, dead-tired from the jolting and no sleep. Eventually, we entered the small superstructure at the rear of the boat and exited with a tin tray of powdered scrambled eggs, two pieces of toast, a small amount of jelly and one orange. Eating was done out in the open, standing up, squatting down or sitting on the deck. There were so many passengers on board, it took nearly two hours to send everyone through the line. I seldom complained about food, but I found green lumps in the powdered eggs. We were told the powdered eggs were real eggs that had been dehydrated, but no one could ever explain what those green lumps were. Thus, no one ever ventured to eat them.

I spotted Penz as he was finishing his morning chow; he was one of the unlucky ones like me who slept up in the bow. I walked over to him and said, "Penz, I had a hard time sleeping up there with the jerking and slamming of waves on the bow door. Did it bother you?"

"The worst night of sleep I've ever had in my life," he answered. "What worries me," he continued, "is that the sea was relatively calm last night." He looked out across the wide water. "What will it be like when the swells get ten or twelve feet high or even higher? What will it be like if we hit a bad storm? These boats are not made for the outer ocean, Alvin. I've heard that some of these boats have been lost in storms." Penz excused himself and went down below.

The next three days were about the same with a lot of standing in line. Between meals, one could find a few men playing cards, a few shooting craps, some talking, a few gazing out across the water, a few reading, some pacing back and forth and a few lying around in shorts, hoping to keep their dark tans for home. We learned early that we had only salt water for showers, so everyone ruled out showers. Since there were so many passengers, we began to think there might be a food shortage on board because food lockers on LSTs were not very large. Because the portions being dished out at chow were small, many men were complaining of hunger, including me.

The fourth day of our voyage I became concerned about two things: one, it seemed the boat was moving unusually slow; two, we had been traveling due north since leaving Pearl Harbor. Paloff had a compass, and we had checked the ship's direction several times each day; the direction was north on every occasion. I looked around about twenty minutes before I found Penz reading in an unarmed gun turret up on the bow deck. "Penz," I asked, "why are we going due north? The United States is east. Too, it seems to me we sure are moving slow."

"You are observant, aren't you?" he replied. "Well, Alvin, I talked with one of the Lieutenant JGs who happens to be from Pennsylvania and who's been on this ship for several years. He gave me a little scoop. First, we are heading due north, hoping to reach the North Pacific Drift. Up there the ocean currents flow toward Canada and the sea is often less turbulent."

"But isn't that out of the way?" I asked.

"Our mission on this voyage, Alvin, is to arrive, to get there. You know we are going into Seattle, don't you?"

"No," I answered. "I thought we were headed for San Francisco."

"Hopefully, we will end up at Seattle," he replied.

"How long will it take?" I asked.

Penz seldom smiled, but he did in response to that question. "It will be longer than you might think," he answered. "Sit down for a minute." He looked around to make sure no one was close enough to hear, then he said firmly, "Keep this to yourself, Alvin, and I mean it. There's no need alarming anyone."

I knew he was going to tell me something important. "I won't talk," I promised.

"I had concerns about this boat when we first got on it. I knew we were going slow on the first day. So I asked my friend from Pennsylvania to level with me about our voyage. An LST has two diesel engines; this boat was built early in 1942, and both of the engines have had it. It took them ten days longer than expected to get to Pearl Harbor from the Philippines. This is one of the first LSTs built, and they're going to scuttle it once we get to Seattle. The boat is seldom at full power; most of the time we are going at one-half speed, maybe five or six knots at the most. What they hope to do is reach the North Pacific Drift—sometimes called the Japan Current—and that will help push the boat on in to Canada somewhere up above Seattle. But you be sure to keep your life jacket on at all times, because these boats don't take well to sea storms." I sat quietly. Penz must have noticed the look of concern on my face.

"Now don't worry, Alvin, this old boat will make it. It's just gonna take a few days longer than expected."

I sat with him for a while, and then I left to take a turn around top deck. Almost everyone was up there, standing in the sun. About ten minutes later Paloff found me, pulled me over to the side, and said he had some scuttlebutt, "We're not going to San Francisco, Alvin, we're heading for Seattle," he announced softly.

"Really?" I responded.

"Too, we've been going north all this time to reach some ocean currents because the engines are giving a lot of trouble." He was almost whispering.

"Is that so?" I replied, acting surprised. "Who gave you all this information?"

"A very reliable source," he answered, "and I promised not to tell who it was. Keep it under your hat. They don't want to get everyone unduly alarmed."

I wondered if there was anyone on the boat who didn't know the so-called secret of why we were going north and where we were headed.

We were lucky that the sea was moderate to calm the first week. Most of us up by the bow doors were getting used to the waves crashing against the doors and the boat's jerking. We were beginning to sleep better. However, with all those unshowerd men crammed together so closely, the odor in the tank deck area was becoming rank.

On the fifth day, Paloff and I got the night watch guard to wake us thirty minutes before sunrise. With several others, we watched the coming of a new day at sea. The experience was so exhilarating, we decided to do it again. The next morning, just as the sun broke the horizon line, the sea was so calm and still that it seemed as if the boat were cruising on a massive sheet of gold. There wasn't the slightest ripple anywhere on the ocean with the exception of the outgoing wake left behind our flat-bottomed boat. The absolute calm lasted about two minutes; in five minutes the waves returned with the glistening of zillions of small diamonds of light, playing in the water. Paloff and I tried to tell the others in our unit what we had seen that morning, but we had a difficult time describing the utter stillness and the sheet of gold. Some of the men didn't believe any of our story.

Later that day Paloff and I talked with one of the old salts who had been in the Navy and at sea for fifteen years. He told us that a sea area of absolute tranquillity like that was a rather rare phenomenon, and it was even rarer to see one with a sunrise or sunset. He had seen a few in his navy career. Paloff and I talked about our experience until darkness.

We had been at sea ten days, slowly easing northward across the Pacific toward the Japan Current, when things gradually turned worse. We were awakened early one morning to a rough sea. Large waves were crashing into the bow doors so loudly that no one could sleep, so most of us went top deck early. The day was overcast and the wind seemed to blow from all directions. We were taking on the large waves at an angle, causing the craft to rock up and down and back and forth. Five or six men suffered from extreme seasickness. The turbulence lasted all day.

That night the sea calmed down as we ate our late meal. I was going through the chow line with Paloff. Four dead-faced, always unpleasant mess-hall assistants were dishing food into our tin trays. We were given two pieces of dry toast, one slice of bologna, a medium portion of spinach, one small boiled potato and a scoop of sliced peaches. When I saw the large vat of sliced peaches, I felt an overwhelming warm sensation rush through my body: I loved peaches. The mess-hall assistant, half-looking, dipped into the vat and placed into a section of my tray three very small peach pieces and a little syrup. I knew better and I knew it wouldn't work, but I shoved my tray forward slightly and gave him a begging look for a little more. He cursed me and yelled, "Move it on, Mack!"

I went out on the deck where the sun had come out and the wind was much colder. I sat on the deck with Paloff and ate. Paloff found some ice in his spinach and said, "What the hell is this? This spinach is cold and has ice slivers in it!"

"This is bad," I responded.

Sid, a man in our unit who heard us complaining, said, "I don't want to make you fellows any more up-tight than you are, but if you really want to know how bad your food is, then hold up your toast to the sun and look at it."

"What for?" I asked.

"Don't ask, Alvin, just do it," Sid responded.

Paloff and I held our bread up towards the sun and looked. Dozens of tiny dark specks could be seen in the bread. "What are all those specks?" Paloff asked.

"Weevils," Sid answered. "Well-baked weevils. That's why we always have toasted bread; the weevils get double-cooked that way," he added, laughing.

Paloff and I just sat there. We each had one piece of bread left. "How long have you known this?" Paloff asked.

"About a week," Sid replied. "Weevils won't hurt you. In fact, they are a good source of protein." Sid laughed again.

It took a while, but we ended up eating the bread. Paloff excused himself and went down below. I saved my three small peach slices for last and slowly ate them. Sid was still amused at the situation. He was another of those intelligent, mature men in the unit; he seemed to roll with the punches of life. I told him how I had forgotten my pride for a moment and begged for more peaches in the chow line. "Got cursed out badly, I explained." I sensed he understood that I was upset.

"If that incident bothers you, and you want to learn a lesson about man's concern for his fellow man, Alvin, you meet me right here at sunset and I'll show you something really interesting."

"What kind of lesson?" I asked.

"There you go again; you're so apprehensive," he replied. "Don't ask so many questions; just be here at sunset."

I went down to the tank deck for a while to check on Paloff. Just before sunset I returned to find Sid waiting. "Follow me," he said. I followed him back aft along a narrow passage that led to the rear of the boat. The wind had picked up, and it was getting colder. He climbed up on a large metal box and said quietly, "You get up here, too." It was becoming dusky dark. We were sitting on the east side of the boat, back in the dark shadows, and could see everything in the rear. "Sit still, don't talk, and just watch," Sid instructed. In a few minutes a door opened from the rear of the galley. Two cooks carrying a large vat of leftover food, poured the contents overboard into the ocean. They went back inside and returned with another vat filled with food and also poured its contents into the ocean. That vat had held the leftover boiled potatoes from late chow. Then the cooks came out with a third vat and again poured the food into the ocean: several gallons of sliced peaches. Sid held his finger up to his lips for me to remain quiet. He knew I was ready for mutiny. The cooks went back into the galley and closed the door. Sid said, "Let's go down below in the hold and I will try to explain things to you."

Sitting down there on the cots Sid took time to explain the system of rationing for meals in our situation. "Those dishing out the food have only orders from higher authorities to not run out of certain foods. So those on the food line give out small portions to everyone to make sure that they don't run out," Sid said. "Now, if their work assignment had been to have no peaches left after serving the last man, it would have been almost impossible. And if they ran out of peaches before serving the last man they would be found incompetent and be in trouble. So, they purposefully give out small portions to fulfill their orders and have some left over. Then they pour what's left into the ocean."

"That's absolutely insane," I angrily said. "I'm starving right now along with all the others. There's got to be a better way. They just poured all that good food out into the ocean, Sid," I said, "and they have no concern that people are hungry."

"You had better learn, Alvin, that in the collective life there are many flaws with systems, and you are experiencing what might be called a navy system flaw."

"I don't understand," I replied. "Surely they could find a way to get the food to all these hungry men if they wanted to."

Sid smiled and said, "It's not that easy, Alvin, but I assure you, you won't starve." I went to bed that night hungry and confused. For a long time I thought about why Sid had taken me to see the cooks throw away all of that good food.

The next day the sea was tumultuous, and for the first time we encountered larger swells of water, one after another. The sea was so rough we were constantly trying to maintain our balance, and several men became seasick again. When we were top deck that day we held on to anything fastened down for security and looked out through the mist and spray at the enraged ocean. The overwhelming sense of how small our vessel was, tossed about in that massive body of water, caused more awe than fear. Down below, the noise was greater than ever from waves crashing against the hull and from the increased shifting of equipment and strain on the boat's structure. The ship's crew was constantly inspecting a section of the boat near the middle that was welded and bolted together; the section was groaning as if it might break apart. That particular area of the boat screeched even on calmer days. The sea remained rough and uneven for two full days.

After two weeks had passed, one morning we awakened to a more placid sea. We got to top deck and realized that we were just floating. The scuttlebutt was out that we were in the Japan Current now, slowly moving eastward toward Canada, and that both engines had quit and were being repaired. Fortunately, the sea was tranquil. At early chow we were given even smaller portions of food, but everyone had acquiesced to the situation and sat around on top deck, eating quietly without complaint. That first day of floating directly toward home was decidedly different from the others. Few men displayed negative emotions; almost everyone stayed on top deck all day, standing or sitting in the sun with a crisp, cool wind blowing across the boat.

That afternoon Paloff and I and three other sailors settled in a sunny place out of the wind and talked about our respective homes and food. When it came my turn, I told them many things about eating country food in the Bootheel of Missouri. Some of the things I discussed were poke salad, side meat, turnip greens and collards, chitlins, and chocolate and meat-grease gravy. We began telling stories related to food, and I told about the time during the thirties at an Arkansas coon hunt when they killed so many they had enough livers for a coon liver dinner. After a while several other men joined in our story-telling group. I told them about how my Grandmother Bradie would fry all of a chicken except the entrails, so that at her house one would find not only the good parts on a platter of fried chicken but also the neck, the head and the feet.

"Feet?" one of the men from Boston questioned.

"Yep, my grandmother clipped off the toenails with some big scissors, battered the feet well, and cooked them longer in deep hot grease. She also insisted on getting to eat the chicken heads by a special way of sucking out the brains." I noticed that one fellow from the east stood up and left in a hurry like he was sick and couldn't listen anymore. The rest of us talked till late chow.

As usual, we had paltry servings. That night some of us stayed top deck for a long time to experience the silent drifting of our vessel on the ocean. It was different from the quietness of places at home; on the ocean there were no night sounds from birds and animals and insects. Some of us stayed up even later; we walked up to the bow, listened and were overwhelmed by the awesome composure of the ocean. We slept well that night, and awakened the next day to find the engines still not working and the boat still just floating.

During early chow Penz explained to some of us that it might not appear that we were moving at all, but we were in the Japan Current, and even though the speed of the current varied from place to place, we were drifting slowly toward Canada. Someone asked what would happen if we hit bad weather without working engines.

"We would need a lot a luck not to capsize," Penz replied. "All vessels need power to take swells head-on so you can ride them like hills." The weather was calm and sunny, and that day was as pleasant as it could be except for our anxieties about not moving any faster and our hunger. Someone mentioned we had traveled so far north that we were not too far from Alaska. Penz commented that where we were located on the Pacific was one of the deepest parts of the entire ocean and that was why the color was such a deep dark blue, almost black. We had seen two ships at a distance that morning; this made us feel better, since it seemed to indicate that we were closer to normal shipping lanes.

At midmorning a group gathered and began to talk about unusual life experiences. I told about when I was five years old and my father took me to see a man hanging from a tree in a place called Braggadocio in the Bootheel of Missouri. This inspired a few questions about that area of the country, and I ended up talking about my Aunt Annie who had the ability to stop bleeding by reading scripture, my Uncle Estes who had the power to break up storms with an ax and my Uncle Will who could read the signs of nature and predict the coming of cyclones. As I finished talking about Uncle Will, I glanced to the left and noticed my friend R. O. had joined the group. He stood there with his arms crossed, looking amused. R. O., a man who had helped me adjust to the unit when I first arrived, was intelligent and seemed to be reading all the time. He listened as the talkers revealed their unusual experiences in their respective home places. We talked and listened until time for late chow.

The story telling had made the two days of drifting go by faster. Later that night, down below, R. O. came over to the bow area where several of us were sitting on our cots talking about the strangeness of the two days of floating in the Pacific. Almost immediately someone asked, "Are we ever going to get to Seattle, R. O.? Is this damn boat going to make it?"

R. O. hesitated a moment, smiled like he knew, and said, "We are almost there, mates. Be of good cheer, we are almost there." With those words he turned and left for the area where he slept. I wondered why when R. O. said those things they always sounded so true. I could tell everyone felt better after his short visit. We slept well for a second night.

The following morning the moaning from the center of the boat and the sound of large waves smacking against the bow doors awakened us. When we went top deck, we could tell at least one engine was working because we were taking the waves head-on. Food was meager at early chow, and we knew it was not going to be a good day. But with an engine running we had to be going somewhat faster, and this was getting us closer to home.

The next three days were monotonous, with the sea just rough enough to make it uncomfortable; everyone became grouchy and dejected. Someone said we had already been at sea three weeks, and I had lost count. It seemed to be a never-ending voyage.

Paloff mentioned that there was a sailor who was selling small bottles of whiskey and K-rations up front near the ladder area.

"Have you ever eaten K-rations, Alvin?" Paloff asked.

"No, I haven't; have you?"

"No, but I'm not going to pay a dollar for a can of something out of a lifeboat that he paid nothing for," he replied.

Early that night, after another day of rationed food, I ambled up the narrow passage to the area by the ladder and asked who sold K-rations. A sleazy-looking sailor asked, "You have a dollar, Mac?"

"I've got one," I said and held it out in my hand.

"You wait here." He went back through a door in the engine room and returned. He took my dollar and handed me a can, which was about the size of a sardine container. I went to my cot, opened the can and began eating. It tasted like salty potted meat. I was so hungry I ate the whole can. Someone mentioned that I was supposed to drink a lot of water with it, so I went up front and drank some. In about thirty minutes my stomach became bloated as if I had eaten a whole turkey, but I was full and felt good.

The sea got violent again that night and the ship began to strain and groan. I could tell by the pounding on the bow doors that the waves were massive. Before I went to bed, a man near my cot said, "You know, if this damn boat should break in half I sure would want to be on the other end because that part would float."

I thought he might know what he was talking about. The slamming of waves and the jerking motions were severe, and my stomach hurt, but I finally fell asleep. In the middle of the night I dreamt that the ship suddenly broke in half. According to several witnesses, I leaped straight up and yelled out, "It's sinking, it's sinking, it's sinking!" and in a matter of seconds I had negotiated the distance from my cot in the bow to the back ladder by running straight across—and on top of—many sleeping sailors. The night guard caught me at the ladder, shook me and told me that I was running in my sleep. In the meantime about half of the passengers thought the ship was sinking, and there was a big jam of humans trying to get up the ladder all at one time. The lights were turned up and everyone was assured that the ship wasn't sinking; we struggled back to our cots. During the six or seven minutes it took to stagger back to my cot, I received a considerable amount of verbal abuse.

The next morning I caught a lot of flack from many sailors about my sleep running. Fortunately for me, about midday the sea became so angry that it took their minds off of the nighttime disturbance. That evening the ocean was at its worst. The ship's groaning was louder than ever, and the tossing became relentless. There was little sleep.

At chow the next day someone mentioned that they believed we were only about two days out from Seattle; that news lifted our spirits. The sea was calm and we were beginning to see other ships. Most of us

stayed top deck all day and looked eastward with scanning eyes.

The next day it was rumored that we could possibly
sight land before dark, so many of us continued to
search the horizon. Late that afternoon something
dark appeared far away, above the horizon and
someone said it might be a mountain peak on
Vancouver Island. We entered fog suddenly and
darkness came. That night on top deck it was cold; the
fog became dense, and visibility was down to a few
feet. We began to hear the foghorns of ships around
us. Paloff said he had heard that we had entered a
straight between Vancouver, Canada, and the state of
Washington. If he was correct, we were about seventy
or eighty miles from the Puget Sound area and Seattle.
But I could tell we were hardly moving. Finally, we
went below, crawled under blankets and listened to
foghorns all night.

The next day it was as if nothing had changed except the fog which was white instead of dark, and was
so heavy it was dangerous walking about the ship. We
waited for it to lift. Sometimes it seemed to get thin-
ner, and the boat would move along slowly; then the
fog would thicken and the boat would slow to a stop.
This went on all day. Foghorns never ceased blowing.
Paloff and I were standing top deck, peering out
through the fog, when we realized R. O. was standing
right behind us. It was as if he had just appeared, but
we hadn't heard him walk up. "What are you boys
searching for in this fog?" he asked, smiling.

"Land, Seattle, a wharf, anything," Paloff answered.

"R. O., have you ever seen such heavy fog?" I asked, and before he could answer I asked, "When do you think it will lift?"

As usual R. O. was slow to respond. "Yes to your first question, Alvin, and in time to the second."

It took me a few seconds to mentally digest what he had answered. R. O. was amused at us as usual. He turned to leave, and I called out to him, "R. O.!" He turned and looked back, "Fog always lifts, right?"

He gave a broad smile and said, "You are beginning to get it, Tennessee; you're finally beginning to get it."

Paloff commented, "R. O. really is a great guy, isn't he!"

"He sure is," I replied.

That was one long foggy day for us. Everyone was shocked at late chow, because we were given large servings of some pretty good food. Afterwards we stood outside and searched through the fog for any visual signs of land. Darkness came, and with foghorns still sounding in all directions, I went down to my cot to sleep. I knew by the slapping of water against the bow doors that the boat was creeping along slowly in the night.

About an hour before daybreak Paloff shook me from my sleep and said, "Come on up top deck. There's something strange going on." I put on my clothes and found him on the starboard side with five or six others, looking out across the fog. Paloff pointed and said,

"Look over there, Alvin, and watch what happens."
First, there was darkness. In a few seconds there was a
faint reddish glow, then the glow got redder, and then
it became even redder. Then there was darkness again.
In about five seconds the sequence repeated itself.
"What do you think that is, Alvin?" Paloff asked with
excitement.

"Aw, some kind of a fog signal, I suppose," I
replied.

"We've watched it for an hour now," he said.
"There's been no sign of anything; just the coming and
going of that red glow." I watched with them for
maybe twenty minutes; there were many wild guesses
as to what it was. By that time there were fifteen or
twenty men top deck, and everyone was watching the
red glow. Suddenly, just as if some omnipotent con-
troller of a fog curtain pulled a lever, we saw in big red
letters: DRINK. Then, directly underneath, COCA-
COLA. And below that, a third line: IN BOTTLES.
Nothing else could be seen anywhere. The large sign
read: DRINK COCA-COLA IN BOTTLES. It was
our first indication of landfall.

The mist and fog began to lift, and we could see
the silhouette of Seattle against a deep dark-blue background. In just moments the sunlight broke through,
and we saw the city ahead of us with a streak of clear
blue sky above it. Paloff looked at me with a big smile
and said, "Well, Alvin, we made it home!"

"Yep, we made it home!" I responded. We watched the shore line for a while and then went for our last early chow.

As we walked along Paloff asked me, "Alvin, do you know what?"

"What?" I asked.

"All voyages come to an end."

I laughed with him, "corked" him gently on his arm and said, "You're getting it, my friend; you're getting it."

Epilogue

AFTER RETURNING from overseas, I was stationed at the Anacostia Naval Center in Washington, D. C., where those of us left from the unit made a large terrain model for the Bikini Atoll atomic bomb tests in the North Pacific.

I was informed on Christmas eve, 1945, that my mother had been fatally injured in an automobile accident in Memphis while coming home from work. I returned for the funeral and we buried her in Elmwood Cemetery near the Southern Railroad. When I was discharged from the Navy in the early summer of 1946, I returned home to Memphis and went by my old house; I noticed zinnias and other flowers blooming in the neighbors' yards but ours was barren. I realized then that flowers mostly come from those who put seed in the ground.

I decided to go to college and spent most of the summer of 1946 hitchhiking around the country, looking at possible schools and universities. I decided to attend Louisiana State at Baton Rouge and purchased a well-kept 1929 Model A Ford to assist me on my journey there.

Early one July morning before I left, I crossed over the Mississippi River on the Harahan Bridge from Memphis to the Arkansas side and made a pilgrimage northward on Highway 61, to the Bootheel of Missouri. Times were better than in my boyhood days; I saw no beggarmen on the way. All day long I traveled up and down dirt and gravel roads that seldom curved, visiting relatives at their homes and farms. Some were prospering and some were struggling, but they all had flower gardens. Late that afternoon, I drove out on the road to Cottonwood Point and sat with Uncle Winston and Aunt Myrna and reminisced. Aunt Myrna recalled that as a small boy I had confused growing-up with blowing-up and was found lying in a flower bed, watching zinnias blow-up as workers blasted tree stumps in a nearby field. Suddenly, I was visually captivated by their yard full of brilliant zinnias in tones of red, yellow, scarlet, crimson, salmon, pink and even bronze. As sundown and darkness approached, I left the Bootheel for Memphis, comforted to know that zinnias continue to grow on either side of the river.